Strike Force Delta

I0570288

The

Hunt

For

The

Scorpion

G W Grant

ISBN   978-1-936062-28-7

Published by:
Desert Wind Books
www.desertwindbooks.com

Visit G W Grant on the web at www.gwgrant.us

Comments are welcome

In memory of those that have perished while fighting to preserve our way of life. Your sacrifice will not be forgotten.

CAUTION

This novel is of a graphic nature and contains profanity which may offend some readers.

NOT SUITABLE FOR YOUNG CHILDREN

Chapter 1

The White House
Washington, D.C.

With the Presidential election only a few months away, President Ike Matthews sat at his desk in the Oval Office going over his speech that he was to present that evening at a campaign fundraiser. Satisfied that his speech covered the key points that he wanted to make, he opened the middle drawer of his desk and placed his speech into the drawer. The intercom on his telephone beeped just as he was closing the drawer. He pushed the intercom button on the telephone. "Yes Mrs. Clark," he said in a normal tone of voice.

"Mr. President, the committee members you wanted to meet with are waiting for you in the conference room," Mrs. Clark informed the president.

"Tell them I'll be there in a few minutes," President Matthews instructed Mrs. Clark, and then he pushed the intercom button on the telephone to cancel the intercom call. He got up from his seat and walked to the door, and opened it. He stepped out into the reception area and closed the door. "You know where I'll be if anyone should need me," he said to Mrs. Clark and began to walk toward the conference room.

When President Matthews arrived at the entrance to the conference room, the Secret Service agent who stood by the door opened it, and the president entered. Everyone in the room immediately jumped to their feet while the Secret Service agent closed the door.

"Have a seat, gentlemen," President Matthews said as he walked over to the table and sat down. "I know you're wondering why I asked you here, so I'll get right to the point." He waited until everyone returned to their seats before he continued. "I called you all here to inform you that as of now; Strike Force Delta, known to some as Strike Force, is one-hundred percent operational."

"Mr. President, I'm still not sure that we need this new Delta unit," the Chairman of the Senate Intelligence Committee was quick to point out.

"I agree," the Chairman of the House Appropriations Committee jumped in.

"Mr. President, what can Strike Force do that Delta Force or the Seals can't?" The Chairman of the Senate Armed Forces Committee asked.

"We've been over this from top to bottom months ago," President Matthews fired back. "Strike Force is ready. Give them a chance to prove themselves."

"Has General Richwood decided on who he thinks should run Strike Force?" The Chairman of the Senate Intelligence Committee inquired.

"General Richwood is meeting with a Colonel John Wilson today; he's a former Delta Force commander. General Richwood told me that in his opinion, Colonel Wilson is the right choice to command Strike Force."

"I'm still skeptical about starting this new unit. Especially during an election year," the Chairman of the Senate Armed Forces Committee was quick to point out. "If Strike Force becomes an embarrassment, it could cost some of us the election in November."

"I'm not worried about the election in November," President Matthews snapped.

"Maybe you're not worried, but we are," the Chairman of the Senate Armed Forces Committee jumped in. "We're not as confident about this as you are."

"I, assume complete responsibility for Strike Force," President Matthews assured everyone. "I will deal with any blowback from this."

"Then I say give this a chance, and see what comes out all of this," the Chairman of the House Appropriations Committee said. "The

President has more to lose if this fails than any of us do.

"Okay, let's see how this plays out," the Chairman of the Senate Armed Forces Committee reluctantly said.

"Even though I think this is a bad idea, I guess I'll play along with this for now," the Chairman of the Senate Intelligence Committee added. "I..." The Chairman of the Senate Intelligence Committee stopped talking when the door to the conference room suddenly opened.

The Secret Service agent who stood outside entered. "Mr. President, I'm sorry for the intrusion sir, but you're needed in the Situation Room."

"Gentlemen, I'm sure you can find your way out," President Matthews said as he got up from his seat.

President Matthews followed the Secret Service agent out of the room and closed the door. He walked to the Situation Room where a Marine, who was dressed in his dress uniform and armed with a nine-millimeter Beretta M9-A1 sidearm, snapped to attention and saluted President Matthews.

President Matthews smiled and entered the Situation Room. Everyone sitting at the conference table in the room jumped to their feet. The Marine closed the double-doors and returned to his post. President Matthews walked over to the conference table, located in the middle of the room and sat down in the seat at the head of the table.

∗ ∗ ∗ ∗ ∗

The Pentagon
Arlington County, Virginia

Colonel John Wilson entered the reception area to the Chairman of the Joint Chiefs of Staff, General Thomas Richwood's Office, and closed the door. "Hello Emily, you're looking lovely today." He commented. "I believe the general is expecting me?" He said as he headed for the door to the general's office.

"Yes, he is," thirty-three-year-old, Major Emily Harris answered as she jumped to her feet. "If I were you, I wouldn't keep the general waiting too long," she continued while she returned to her seat behind her desk.

Smart-ass, Colonel Wilson thought as he opened the door to the general's office, and then entered.

"Jesus Christ Wilson don't you believe in fuckin' knocking first," General Richwood snapped.

"Sorry sir, it won't happen again."

"Just close the damn door and take a seat. I have something that might interest you."

"I'm all ears, sir," Colonel Wilson said while he closed the door. He walked over to the chair in front of General Richwood's desk and sat down.

"A few months ago, the president instructed me to put together a special unit to combat the growing terrorist threat," General Richwood began. "John, I want you to command this unit."

"I'm honored sir, but what makes this unit any different than the other units we have that can go after terrorist?"

"The difference is that you pick your missions and that you control your missions from your own base of operations without any interference from anyone. You report directly to the president and myself, and no one else."

"What about the personnel?"

"I have hand-picked each one of them myself. Every one of them has volunteered for this unit. So John, can I count on you to take this assignment?"

"Yes, sir. I'm your man, sir."

"Good. This new unit is called Strike Force Delta, but mostly referred to as Strike Force. The facility is located on a secluded part of Tinker Air Force Base located just outside of Oklahoma City," General Richwood began. "The entire facility is surrounded by a fifteen-foot chain link electrified fence; with razor ribbon wire coiled at the top. Outside the fence, there are microwave transmitters at each corner that beams a signal down the fence line that will detect any motion near it." The general paused for a moment before he continued. "Armed guards, dressed in full combat dress and armed with the M-4 carbine rifle, patrol the inside fence perimeter and provides security for the main entrance to the compound. A special identification card is needed to gain access to the Strike Force compound."

"Does the security personnel know what the facility is used for?"

"No, they do not, and it needs to stay that way."

"Security sounds tight, sir, but what's to keep someone from dropping in from the air?"

"The airspace around the facility is restricted. A threat from the air is not a problem. The facility has eight stationary medium-range surface-to-air batteries. Each battery is equipped with six of the latest MIM-104A Patriot launchers. There is also six M61 Vulcan twenty-millimeter guns strategically placed around the perimeter."

"That's a lot of fire power, sir."

"Yes, it is, but I felt it to be necessary. The defense systems have been tested, and they do work."

"Roger that, sir."

"Everyone assigned to the Strike Force facility dresses in civilian clothing, giving the illusion to the base personnel or anyone who might be watching that they are civilian contractors," General Richwood continued. "The living quarters for Strike Force personnel is separated from the base personnel living quarters. It can only be accessed by a special key-card."

"I see," Colonel Wilson commented.

"The main building is the brains of the Strike Force operation. It is equipped with a fully operational Communication Center, an Operation Center, and administrative offices. Each room in the building is partitioned off with a sound-proof see through material. The Communication Center has unlimited access to communication satellites, giving Strike Force, the ability to communicate with Strike Force units wherever they are deployed. The Operation Center is equipped with state-of-the-art electronics that will be needed to monitor and run Strike Force operations. From this control center, you will have surveillance satellites at your disposal; so you can monitor terrorist activity around the world."

"What about training?"

"Training facilities are located on the south end of the compound. It is equipped with everything your team members will need to train for their upcoming missions."

"Who's my second?"

"Captain Nathan Hale will be your second. I believe you and Captain Hale have served together?"

"Yes, sir, we have. I look forward to working with Captain Hale."

"One last thing; there are four hangars that were specially built to house the aircraft that Strike Force will have at its disposal. These hangars contain two C-130-J aircraft specially modified for Strike Force use, six Black Hawk helicopters, and a Gulfstream G550 jet aircraft. General Richwood opened the right-side bottom drawer and removed a large brown envelope, and closed the drawer. "The material in this envelope will explain the procedures you must follow; as well as the inner workings of Strike Force," the general said while he handed Colonel Wilson the envelope. "Your Strike Force identification card is in the envelope. You'll need that to gain access to the facility. Do you have any questions?"

"No, sir."

"There's a car waiting to take you to Andrews where a Gulfstream G550 aircraft is waiting, with Captain Hale on-board."

"Sir, I haven't packed any of my gear."

"Your gear is already on board the aircraft," General Richwood said as he got up from his seat. "

With the large brown envelope in hand, Colonel Wilson jumped to his feet and saluted General Richwood. "I understand, sir."

General Richwood returned Colonel Wilson's salute and returned to his seat while Colonel Wilson left the general's office and closed the door. General Richwood pushed the intercom button on the telephone on his desk and waited for Major Harris to answer his call.

"Yes, general."

"Get me President Matthews on a secure line a-sap."

"Yes, sir," Major Harris acknowledged and canceled the intercom call.

It wasn't long before the intercom on General Richwood's telephone beeped. "Yes."

"Sir, the president, is on line two," Major Harris reported.

"Very well," General Richwood acknowledged and pushed the intercom button on his telephone to cancel the intercom call. He removed the telephone receiver from the telephone and put it to his ear while he pushed the button that was flashing on the telephone. "Mr. President, sir."

"General what do you have for me today?"

"Sir, I just got done talking with Colonel Wilson. He has accepted the job of Strike Force Commander."

"Very well general; keep me informed of any new developments."

"Yes, Mr. President," General Richwood acknowledged. "I'll let you know the minute I hear something from Wilson."

"Good day general," President Matthews remarked, and the line went dead.

General Richwood no sooner returned the telephone receiver to the telephone on his desk when there was a knock on his door. The door opened and Major General Larry McCoy, commanding general of the Joint Special Operations Command (JSOC) entered, and closed the door. He walked up to General Richwood's desk and snapped to attention. "Permission to speak freely with the general?" General McCoy asked as he saluted General Richwood.

"Of course, you may," General Richwood answered while he returned General McCoy's salute. "What's on your mind today Larry?"

"A few minutes ago I got a call from the Chairman of the Senate Intelligence Committee," General McCoy began as he sat down in the chair in front of General Richwood's desk. "The Chairman told me that the president has activated a Spec-ops unit called Strike Force Delta. Is this true?"

"It could be."

"I understand that this unit is not under the control of JSOC?"

"That's correct," General Richwood fired back. "If you have a problem with it, I suggest you take it up with the president. I'm like you Larry; I'm a soldier. I take the orders handed to me by my commander-in-chief without questions. I suggest you drop your opposition to Strike Force and let it go. The president has made up his mind about this."

"I still think this Strike Force Delta unit is unnecessary," General McCoy pointed out. "I guess only time will tell who's right about this."

"You have nothing to worry about Larry," General Richwood assured General McCoy. "Strike Force could turn out to be an asset to everyone. Besides, if they should flop on their ass it will be on the president, not us."

"I see your point, sir, but I still don't like this one bit."

"Times are changing," General Richwood pointed out. "The world is changing. We need to change with it and find new ways to combat the growing terrorist threat. I think Strike Force could help us do just that."

General McCoy glanced at his watch. "If you would excuse me, sir, I have a staff meeting to attend," he said as he got up from his seat. "With your permission, sir," he concluded as he saluted General Richwood.

"Stop by anytime," General Richwood said as he returned General McCoy's salute. "My door is always open."

"Good day, sir." General McCoy walked over to the office door and opened it. *What a crock of fuckin' shit,* he thought as he exited General Richwood's office. *And a waste of my time,* he continued to think while he closed the door.

General Richwood got up from his seat and grabbed his uniform jacket. He put on his jacket while he walked to the office door. He opened the door and stepped into the reception area. Major Harris jumped to her feet and snapped to attention. "I'll be gone for the rest of the day," he said as he walked to the exit door. "You can reach me on my cell if you need me."

"Yes, sir," Major Harris acknowledged as she saluted General Richwood.

General Richwood returned Major Harris' salute and opened the door. He exited the reception area and closed the door.

I wonder what bug bit him on the ass. Major Harris thought while she returned to her seat.

Chapter 2

Two Months Later

The Pentagon
Arlington County, Virginia

General Richwood sat at his desk going over the latest intelligence reports when the door to his office suddenly opened, and President Matthews entered. General Richwood jumped to his feet and saluted the president. "Mr. President, what an unexpected surprise sir."

"Have a seat general," President Matthews suggested while one of the Secret Service agents that accompanied him closed the door. President Matthews walked over to the chair that was in front of General Richwood's desk and sat down. "General, we might have a situation brewing in Afghanistan that might require the services of Strike Force."

"How bad is it?" General Richwood inquired.

"No one is sure of anything yet," President Matthews answered. "The CIA and NSA have reason to believe that A'zam al Shammari might be in Afghanistan. If he is in Afghanistan, we need to find him and stop whatever he is planning before it's too late."

"I agree Mr. President. If A'zam al Shammari, a known al-Qaeda terrorist, has popped up on our intelligence sweeps you can bet that whatever he is planning it can't be good."

"There's one more thing. It was brought to my attention a few hours ago that Shammari might have the formula for manufacturing VX nerve gas."

"That's not good," General Richwood remarked. "If that psycho has the means to make the VX nerve gas, he won't hesitate to use it."

"That's what has me worried," President Matthews said as he got up from his seat. "We need to stop him before he can do any harm to others."

"I agree Mr. President," General Richwood said as he jumped to his feet. "I'll get Wilson on this a-sap," he continued as he saluted President Matthews.

President Matthews snapped General Richwood a salute back. "Let me know the minute you come up with something," President Matthews said while he walked to the office door. "We need to move fast on this one," he continued as he opened the office door. He exited General Richwood's office and closed the door.

General Richwood picked up the telephone receiver from the telephone on his desk. He dialed the direct number for Colonel Wilson at Strike Force Delta command and put the telephone receiver to his ear.

"Wilson," Colonel Wilson said when he answered.

"Wilson, I just got done talking with the president, and he needs for you to look into something for him. The president wants you to look in the area of Feyzabad, Afghanistan and let him know if you see something that looks out-of-place. It is believed that A'zam al Shammari may be in the area."

"General, If he is anywhere in Afghanistan, I'll find that slime-ball."

"Wilson, this could turn out to be nothing, but the president wants to be certain that nothing has been overlooked."

"I understand, sir; I..." Colonel Wilson stopped talking when he heard a dial tone. He shook his head and returned the telephone receiver to the telephone on his desk. *So, Shammari is in Afghanistan,* he thought as he looked at the crisis board on the wall that was used to track terrorist activity, and to identify hot spots worldwide. *Shammari, I don't know what you're up to but whatever it is, it can't be good;* he continued to think while he picked up the controller for the pointer from his desk and pointed it to Afghanistan on the world map. He clicked the controller, and the screen displayed a full-size detailed map of Afghanistan.

Without warning, the door to Colonel Wilson's office opened and Captain Nathan Hale, nicknamed Bulldog, who was second in command of Strike Force Delta, entered. "You look as though you've seen a ghost," Captain Hale commented while he closed the door.

"I just got off the phone with General Richwood."

"Oh, what's up?"

"A'zam al Shammari," Colonel Wilson answered. "The president believes that Shammari is in the vicinity of Feyzabad, Afghanistan."

Captain Hale walked over to the chair that was in front of Colonel Wilson's desk. "Any idea what he's doing there?" He asked as he sat down.

"The general didn't say. He just said that he wanted us to look at the area and see what we find."

"That's odd."

"Yes, it is, I get the feeling that the general isn't telling us everything he knows."

"What makes you say that?"

"Just a hunch," Colonel Wilson answered as he got up from his seat.

"So, what are we going to do?" Captain Hale inquired as he got up from his seat.

""We do what we were asked to do," Colonel Wilson answered as he walked to the office door. "Let's just hope that we find Shammari, and put an end to his terror once and for all," he continued while he opened the office door.

Colonel Wilson exited his office with Captain Hale not far behind. They walked to the Operation Center and entered. Colonel Wilson walked over to the control panel where the person who was responsible for monitoring the satellites was sitting. "I need to see what's going on in sector eleven in Afghanistan," Colonel Wilson instructed the satellite technician. "Especially around Feyzabad."

"That might be a problem," the satellite technician pointed out. "Every time our birds (satellites) pass over the area we can't see what's going on in the town. Something there is blocking out our Looking-glass (satellite)."

"There's only one thing that can do that," Captain Hale began.

"Yeah, I know," Colonel Wilson said before Captain Hale could finish. "They must have satellite jammers around the town; but how did they get such high-value hardware?"

"My best guess would be that they stole it somewhere," Captain Hale was quick to point out. "I'll look into that and see if someone is missing any satellite jammers."

"Good luck with that," Colonel Wilson remarked. "I doubt if anyone reported something like that stolen."

"It's still worth a try," Captain Hale pressed. "Doing something is better than doing nothing."

"I see your point," Colonel Wilson gave in. "See what you can find out." Colonel Wilson turned his attention to the satellite technician. "I want our Looking-glass' (satellites) re-tasked, so we have an uninterrupted feed of the area around Feyzabad, Afghanistan," he ordered. "I want to know what goes in and out of there."

"No problem," the satellite technician acknowledged. "We should have a live feed in a few mikes (minutes). I can send it to your plasma screen in your office if you want me to."

"That'll work for me," Colonel Wilson commented. "Bulldog, stay on top of this and keep me informed of any new developments," he continued as he walked to the exit door. He opened the door and stepped into the hallway, and closed the door.

Three Days Later

Colonel Wilson arrived at his office early and found Captain Hale sitting in the chair in front of his desk drinking a cup of coffee. "You're here awfully early," Colonel Wilson commented as he entered his office and closed the door. He walked over to the coffee pot and poured himself a cup of coffee. He took a sip from his cup and then walked over to his desk. He sat his coffee cup down on the desk and sat down in the chair behind his desk. "You got something for me?" Colonel Wilson asked when he saw that Captain Hale had a folder in his hand.

"The Brits sent us this," Captain Hale said, referring to the folder he had with him. "I think you'll find this to be very interesting," he continued as he handed Colonel Wilson the folder.

Colonel Wilson opened the folder and scanned through its

contents. When he got to the pictures, he studied each one of them carefully; he didn't want to overlook anything. When he finished, he picked up his coffee cup and took a sip of coffee, and then returned the cup to his desk. "Did you look at any of this?"

"Yes, I took the liberty of going through it before I brought it here for you to look at. My contact at MI-5 said that he passed this same information on to the CIA, and they told him to drop this matter."

"You're shitting me?"

"No, I'm not. That's what I was told."

"Did your MI-5 contact say how he got this information?"

"He said that he had the SAS send in a surveillance team to look around the area."

"So, they gave this information to the CIA, and the CIA just as much told them to fuck off?"

"It appears that way."

"I wonder what else the CIA is hiding," Colonel Wilson remarked.

"I'm sure the CIA has told the president about this," Captain Hale was quick to point out. "Maybe he wanted us to verify this before he took any action."

"I want you to put Popeye and Hammer's assault teams on standby. Tell no one about this new information. For now, I want to keep this between us."

"Roger that," Captain Hale acknowledged as he got up from his seat. "I'll get right on it," he continued while he picked up his coffee cup from Colonel Wilson's desk. He hurried over to the coffee pot and sat his cup down next to it, and then he walked over to the door. He opened the door and exited Colonel Wilson's office, and closed the door.

Colonel Wilson picked up the telephone receiver from the telephone on his desk. He put the telephone receiver to his ear while he dialed the number for General Richwood's office at the Pentagon. After a couple of rings, Major Harris answered. "Emily, this is Wilson. I need to talk to the General."

"One moment please," Major Harris said.

"Wilson, what you got for me?"

"General, I have indisputable proof that A'zam al Shammari is indeed in Feyzabad, Afghanistan."

"You're certain about this?"

"Yes, sir, I am. I also have indisputable evidence that Shammari is manufacturing VX nerve gas in Feyzabad."

"Let me brief the president and I'll get back to you. In the meantime, be ready to move on this in case the president decides to okay an op."

"We're ready general."

"Good," General Richwood commented, and the line went dead.

Colonel Wilson waited for a dial tone, and then he dialed the phone number for the Strike Force maintenance office at the hangars where the Strike Force aircrafts were housed.

"Chief, this is Wilson," he said when the maintenance chief answered. "I want a C-130J aircraft fueled for maximum range and have the pilot and his crew standby and be ready to go on a moment's notice."

"We'll have it ready within the hour. I'll notify the pilot and crew to stand by."

Colonel Wilson returned the telephone receiver to the telephone on his desk. He put the report and the photographs that Captain Hale had brought to him back into the folder. He picked up the remote to the plasma screen and swiveled his chair around to face the plasma screen. *Let's see what's going on at Feyzabad,* he thought while he pushed the power button on the remote. The screen came to life, and he watched the live satellite feed of the Feyzabad area.

He watched the live satellite feed for hours until the telephone on his desk began to ring. He switched off the plasma screen and swiveled his chair around, and placed the remote down on his desk. He removed the telephone receiver from the telephone and put it to his ear. "Wilson."

"Wilson, the president, has authorized you to plan and execute an assault on Feyzabad," General Richwood said. "Your mission is to capture A'zam al Shammari and the VX nerve gas. Afterwards, you are to destroy the lab used to manufacture this gas. Leave nothing behind. Do you understand?"

"I understand general. The assault teams will leave nothing behind that would indicate that the VX nerve gas was ever there."

"Good luck to you and your people. Make us proud Wilson," General Richwood said, and then the line went dead.

"Fuckin' dickhead," Colonel Wilson mumbled while he returned the telephone receiver to the telephone on his desk.

"You shouldn't talk to yourself like that Wolverine," Colonel Wilson's personal assistant, Second Lieutenant Samantha Cooltrain, nicknamed Giggles, who was standing in the doorway to the office, pointed out. "People might get the wrong idea."

Colonel Wilson looked at Lieutenant Cooltrain and smiled. "Yeah, I see your point. Is there something you wanted?"

"The aircraft maintenance chief called. He said to tell you that the aircraft you requested is in hangar nine. It is fueled, and the pilot and his crew are standing by for further instructions."

"Anything else?"

"No, that's all. I'll be at my desk if you should need me," Lieutenant Cooltrain said and then walked back to her desk, and sat down.

Colonel Wilson picked up the telephone receiver from the telephone on his desk. He put the telephone receiver to his ear while he dialed the number for Captain Hale. After a couple of rings, Captain Hale answered. "Bulldog, I want you, Popeye, and Hammer to meet me in the conference room in ten minutes."

"I'll get right on it," Captain Hale acknowledged.

Colonel Wilson returned the telephone receiver to the telephone on his desk to cancel the call. He got up from his seat and picked up the folder that contained the information that Captain Hale had gotten from MI-5, and walked out of his office. "I'll be in the conference room if you should need me," he informed Lieutenant Cooltrain as he walked by her desk.

He walked to the conference room and could see through the transparent wall that everyone he wanted to talk to was in the room. Colonel Wilson entered the conference room, and everyone jumped to their feet. "Take your seats," He said while he closed the door. "We have a lot to go over and not much time," he continued to say while he walked over to the conference table. He sat down in the chair across from them and laid the folder down on the table in front of him. "Gentlemen, this is the first tactical operation that this unit has executed since Strike Force was formed, so keep in mind that we can't afford any fuckups on this one."

"We won't let you down Wolverine," Lieutenant McDonald assured Colonel Wilson. "We'll get the job done."

Cocky little fucker, Colonel Wilson thought before he continued. "Popeye, since you're senior in rank you will be in tactical command of both assault teams."

"Roger that," Lieutenant McDonald acknowledged.

"Hammer you will assist Popeye."

"I understand, Wolverine," Lieutenant Shea acknowledged.

"Gentlemen, you're about to embark on a mission of the highest priority." Colonel Wilson began. "Thanks to the help we have received from MI-5 and the British SAS, we know that A'zam al Shammari is in the town of Feyzabad in Afghanistan. We also know that he is manufacturing VX nerve gas there."

"That's some wicked shit," Lieutenant McDonald commented. "VX kills fast, within a few seconds I'm told."

"That's correct," Colonel Wilson said. "VX kills everything it comes into contact with in only a few seconds. You're dead before you realize that you've been gassed. No one is safe as long as this idiot has the VX in his possession. That's why we need to destroy this laboratory and capture Shammari, and seize the VX gas."

"What if Shammari isn't there?" Lieutenant Shea asked. "Any idea what his target might be?"

"Not a clue, so let's hope the dickhead is still there when you get there. There is enough information in this folder to assist you in planning your operation," Colonel Wilson said while he tapped on the folder on the table in front of him. "Popeye, at the end of this briefing I will give you this folder; you and Hammer can plan your assault on the target while en-route. You know what you're up against so make sure you take the equipment you'll need with you. "Questions?" Colonel Wilson waited a few seconds before he continued. "I want you and your assault teams in the air within the hour. There's a C-130J waiting in hangar nine. Watch your six over there gentlemen."

"Always," Lieutenant McDonald remarked as he and Lieutenant Shea got up from their seats at the conference table.

Colonel Wilson handed the folder to Lieutenant McDonald. He and Captain Hale remained seated at the conference table while Lieutenant McDonald and Lieutenant Shea exited the conference room and closed the door.

Thirty Minutes Later
Hangar Nine

Colonel Wilson pulled up in his Humvee just as the ground crew was pulling the C-130J 'Super' Hercules aircraft from the hangar. He got out of his Humvee and walked over to where Lieutenant McDonald was standing. "Hang on to this," he said as he handed him a smoke canister. "You're going to need this to identify yourself to the extraction helicopter."

"Anything else?" Lieutenant McDonald asked.

Colonel Wilson pulled out a piece of paper from his shirt pocket and handed it to Lieutenant McDonald. "I wrote down your call sign as well as the call signs for your air support and the extraction helicopter. I'll see you when you get back."

Lieutenant McDonald ran back to join the others while Colonel Wilson got back into the Humvee and drove off.

"Our equipment is on board, and the men are secured in their seats," Lieutenant Shea reported.

"Good, let's get this show on the road," Lieutenant McDonald commented as he walked up the back cargo ramp, with Lieutenant Shea not far behind.

Lieutenant McDonald and Lieutenant Shea walked to the empty seats, and they each sat down in one and strapped themselves in. Seconds later, the C-130J 'Super' Hercules aircraft began to move and gain speed, and then leave the ground.

Chapter 3

Five Kilometers North Of Feyzabad, Afghanistan
0235 Hours Local Time

It was a moonless night, providing excellent cover for the Strike Force team as they parachuted to the ground undetected. Everyone quickly checked their weapons and equipment to make sure they were in working order. They put on their M-42 gas mask over their headset and attached their night-vision equipment to their battle helmet. They positioned their night-vision equipment into place and then activated it.

First Lieutenant McDonald looked at his watch. "We have plenty of time to get in and out before the sun comes up," he pointed out to Second Lieutenant Shea. Lieutenant Shea nodded his head, indicating that he understood. "Okay people, let's move out," Lieutenant McDonald said over the radio headset.

The Strike Force team moved toward their objective, with Lieutenant McDonald and Lieutenant Shea leading the way. They stopped and took up a defensive position on a hill overlooking the town. Lieutenant McDonald took out his night-vision binoculars and scanned the area around their target and the town.

"How's it look?" Lieutenant Shea asked.

"I see two tangos on the east side and two on the west side of the town guarding the street, Also, there are two tangos guarding the entrance of the target," Lieutenant McDonald answered while he put the night-vision binoculars back into its carrying case.

"Roger that," Lieutenant Shea acknowledged.

"Hollywood, Sambo, I want you two to take out the tangos on the east side of town," Lieutenant McDonald said over the radio headset. "Preacher, Smoke, I want you two to take down the tangos on the west side. Afterwards, I want you to secure your positions in case more of their friends decide to show up. Tank, I want you and Bull to take down the two tangos at the target entrance and secure the area. The rest of us will enter the building and carry out the mission."

With Lieutenant McDonald and Lieutenant Shea leading the way, the Strike Force team moved closer to the town. Hollywood and Sambo made their way to the east side of the town. Preacher and Smoke proceeded to the west side of the town while Tank and Bull moved in on the target building.

The rest of the Strike Force team, along with Lieutenant McDonald and Lieutenant Shea took up positions across the street from the target building and waited.

"Eastside tangos neutralized," Sambo reported over the radio headset. "Area secured."

"Roger that," Lieutenant McDonald acknowledged.

"Westside tangos neutralized," Preacher reported over the radio headset. "Area secured."

"Roger that," Lieutenant McDonald acknowledged. "Keep a sharp lookout and let me know of any changes," he waited a few seconds before he continued. "From this moment on we go silent; no broadcasting over the headset unless it's absolutely necessary." He touched the earpiece to his radio headset and deactivated its microphone and listened while each member of the Strike Force team acknowledged his order and deactivated the microphone to their radio headset.

Tank and Bull proceeded to the entrance to the target building and then neutralized the two guards. With the defenders at the entrance to the target building neutralized, Lieutenant McDonald and the rest of the Strike Force team quickly joined Tank and Bull. They readied their HK-416N assault rifles with their silencers attached and entered the building.

"Remember there could be some nasty shit in here so be careful," Lieutenant McDonald warned. "No shooting unless absolutely necessary and keep your gas masks on at all times; any questions?" He waited a few seconds before he concluded. "Let's move out."

With the aid of their night-vision, they navigated down the

darkened hallway in a single line. Lieutenant McDonald led the way, with Lieutenant Shea following close behind. A few yards down the hallway, it dead-ended into another hallway.

"Hammer, take Boomer and After Shock and go right," Lieutenant McDonald whispered to Lieutenant Shea. "I'll go left with Playboy and Terminator."

Lieutenant Shea nodded his head, indicating that he understood. "Boomer, After Shock, with me," he ordered in a whisper.

Boomer and After Shock both nodded in acknowledgment and followed Lieutenant Shea. Playboy and Terminator followed Lieutenant McDonald down the hallway in the opposite direction. The hallway dead-ended in front of a door, with a door on each side of the hall.

Lieutenant McDonald noticed that the lights were on in the rooms. He hand signaled Playboy and Terminator his intentions. Seconds later, they kicked in the doors and entered the rooms at the same time. Their night-vision quickly adjusted to the light. After a quick inspection, they discovered that the rooms were empty except for some metal tables that were lined up along one wall.

The air quality in each room was checked using the biological, chemical, and poisonous gas detection meter; that each of them carried with them. Afterwards, they turned off the light in the rooms and assembled back in the hallway.

"This doesn't make any sense," Terminator commented. "It appears that the rooms were cleaned out recently. I can't help but wonder if they knew that we were coming."

"I agree," Playboy added.

"Let's move out," Lieutenant McDonald ordered.

Playboy and Terminator followed Lieutenant McDonald back down the hallway the way they came. They had only gone a few feet when Lieutenant McDonald heard a noise behind them. He quickly turned around with his HK-416N assault rifle ready for action. He saw several armed terrorists emerging from one of the rooms that they had just checked.

Without delay, Lieutenant McDonald opened fire with several single-shot bursts. Playboy and Terminator were quick to react and joined in. In a matter of seconds, the terrorists were neutralized.

Playboy and Terminator checked the fallen terrorists to make certain that they were no longer a threat while Lieutenant McDonald hurried to the room where he suspected the terrorists had emerged from. He looked around the room and saw nothing out of the ordinary until a trapdoor in the floor opened, and two more terrorists entered the room.

Lieutenant McDonald did not hesitate; he opened fire, killing the two terrorists. He ran over to the opened trapdoor in the floor and fired a few shots down the hole. He then removed one of his AN-M18 smoke grenades from his Combat Tactical Vest, pulled the pin, and dropped it down the hole. He slammed the trapdoor shut, placed the two dead terrorists on top of the trapdoor, and hurried back out to the hallway where Playboy and Terminator were waiting.

"I want the two of you to booby-trap each doorway," Lieutenant McDonald ordered. "I'm sure these assholes weren't alone."

Playboy and Terminator each took out two M18-A1 Claymore mines and a roll of tripwire from their backpacks and booby-trapped each doorway while Lieutenant McDonald booby-trapped the other.

With their task completed, Playboy and Terminator followed Lieutenant McDonald back down the hallway in the direction where Lieutenant Shea and his team had gone earlier. They went a few yards down the hallway when Lieutenant McDonald stopped.

"What's up?" Playboy asked.

"Terminator, do you have any Claymores left?" Lieutenant McDonald inquired.

"Yes, I do," Terminator answered.

"Good," Lieutenant McDonald commented. "I want you to leave a surprise behind in case any terrorists get past our other safety measures and try to come up behind us again."

"No problem," Terminator acknowledged.

Without saying another word, Lieutenant McDonald continued up the hallway with Playboy following close behind. Terminator removed the last two Claymore mines and the remaining tripwire from his backpack. He booby-trapped the hallway to prevent more terrorists from sneaking up on them again, and then he hurried up the hallway to catch up with Playboy and Lieutenant McDonald.

* * * * *

Lieutenant Shea and his team came to a door at the end of the hallway. He noticed that the lights were on in the room. He hand signaled Boomer and After Shock his intentions. Lieutenant Shea kicked in the door and entered, with Boomer and After Shock following close behind him. Their night-vision quickly adjusted to the light. The room was filled with all kinds of research and laboratory equipment.

The occupants of the room opened fire with their AK-47 assault rifles. Lieutenant Shea was knocked off his feet when two rounds struck his body armor in the chest. However, a round hit him in his right leg as he fell to the floor.

Boomer and After Shock opened fire with several three-round bursts from their HK-416N assault rifles and the four men in the room dropped to the floor. The room looked like a bomb had gone off inside of it. There was little left of the laboratory that was once there.

Boomer rushed over to check on Lieutenant Shea while After Shock searched the room to make sure there were no more occupants and that the terrorists on the floor were no longer a threat. He then walked back over to Boomer, who was tending to Lieutenant Shea's wounded leg. "How is he?" He asked.

"His body armor stopped the rounds from entering his chest," Boomer replied.

"The fuckers got lucky and put one in my leg," Lieutenant Shea commented.

"Don't worry Hammer, you'll survive," Boomer pointed out. "The bullet went straight through without hitting anything vital." He continued as he tightly wrapped Lieutenant Shea's wounded leg with a bandage to stop the bleeding. "You'll be back up on your feet before you know it."

Boomer finished bandaging Lieutenant Shea's leg wound and stood up. He took out his biological, chemical and poisonous gas detection meter and checked the air quality in the room. Meanwhile, After Shock searched the dead terrorist for any documents that they might be carrying.

Hearing the sound of AK-47 assault rifles, Lieutenant McDonald, and his team hurried down the corridor. By the time they got to the end of the hallway, the fighting was over. Lieutenant McDonald stood in the doorway to the room and quickly assessed the room's condition. "What a mess," he commented.

"Hammer took a through shot in the leg," Boomer was quick to point out.

Lieutenant McDonald looked at his friend sitting on the floor. "You just wanted a reason to sit on your ass," he jokingly said.

"Fuck off," Lieutenant Shea shot back.

"Sit-rep," Lieutenant McDonald ordered, ignoring Lieutenant Shea's comment.

"We put down four tangos, and the room is secure," After Shock reported. "I also found a backpack on one of them that has a lot of papers in it; they look important."

"Popeye, I have something that you need to see," Boomer pointed out while he walked over to Lieutenant McDonald. He showed him the reading on his biological, chemical and poisonous gas detection meter.

Lieutenant McDonald looked at the reading on Boomer's meter. He touched the earpiece to his radio headset that activated the microphone. "Listen up," he said over the radio headset, "The presence of VX nerve gas has been detected so keep your gas masks on; Popeye out." He touched the earpiece to his radio headset again to deactivate its microphone. He turned to Playboy and Terminator, who was standing behind him. "I want the two of you to take care of Hammer." He then turned back to Boomer and After Shock. "Let's wrap it up here. Grab what papers you can find, and get the fuck out of here."

Playboy and Terminator helped Lieutenant Shea up from the floor and left the room with Lieutenant McDonald following close behind them. When they reached the entrance, the sound of AK-47, automatic weapons fire filled the night. Boomer and After Shock arrived at the building's entrance a few seconds later.

"Where the fuck did they come from?" Lieutenant McDonald asked.

"They must have been laying in wait; waiting for us to exit the building," Tank pointed out.

"If that's so, then they knew we were coming," Playboy added.

"Knock it the fuck off," Lieutenant McDonald snapped. "We need to find a way around those assholes."

"I got something that will shut those little fuckers up," After Shock said and readied the M-32 MGL multiple-shot grenade launcher that he had with him. He aimed it at the terrorists who were firing at them from across the street, and pulled the trigger three times. The forty-millimeter grenades shot out the tube one after the other and hit their intended target with devastating effect, killing the terrorists who were firing at them.

"So much for minimizing collateral damage," Lieutenant McDonald chuckled. He touched the earpiece to his radio headset to activate its microphone. "Sambo, I want you and Hollywood to go to the extraction point," He ordered. "Preacher, I want you and Smoke to head to the extraction point too. We'll meet you there shortly."

"Roger that," Sambo acknowledged over the radio headset.

"On our way," Preacher said over the radio headset.

Lieutenant McDonald touched the earpiece to his radio headset and deactivated its microphone. "Let's get the fuck out of here before we run into any more surprises. Tank, take point; After Shock, you bring up the rear."

The Strike Force team started to follow Tank out of the building when the Claymore mines that Terminator had placed in the hallway exploded.

"Keep moving," Lieutenant McDonald shouted. "We need to get the fuck out of here."

The Strike Force team did as Lieutenant McDonald ordered and followed Tank out of the building and down the alley between the buildings. Once they were clear of the town, they proceeded to the extraction point where the rest of the Strike Force team was waiting.

Daybreak was approaching, and Lieutenant McDonald knew they were running out of time. "Terminator, I need the satellite radio."

Terminator wasted no time; he set up the satellite radio, and then he handed the satellite radiotelephone receiver to Lieutenant McDonald.

Lieutenant McDonald put the satellite radiotelephone receiver to his ear. "Red-fox this is Sundance, do you copy."

"Sundance, this is Red-fox."

"Red-fox, the target is hot. You are authorized to neutralize the target to cover our extraction; do you copy?"

"Roger Sundance, I copy."

Lieutenant McDonald held the satellite radiotelephone receiver to his ear and watched as an F/A-18F Super Hornet aircraft descended on the town and fired an AGM-65L Maverick air-to-surface missile. The missile hit its intended target, and the building exploded, killing the terrorists who were inside. "Great shot Red-fox," Lieutenant McDonald said over the satellite radio. "You're clear to return to your patrol area. Thanks for the assistance."

"Roger Sundance, Red-fox out."

"Terminator, tune the sat-com to one-seven-five-two," Lieutenant McDonald ordered.

"Sat-com set," Terminator reported.

"Raptor two-five this is Sundance, over.

"Sundance, this is Raptor two-five; we're coming up on your position. Pop the color of the day (smoke) to authenticate, over.

Lieutenant McDonald removed the smoke canister that Colonel Wilson had given him from his combat vest. He pulled the pin and tossed it on the ground. The canister ignited, and purple colored smoke rushed out of the canister. "Raptor two-five I authenticate, over,"

"Roger Sundance, we're two mikes (minutes) out. Get your people ready; Raptor two-five out."

"Roger that, Sundance out." Lieutenant McDonald handed Terminator the satellite radiotelephone receiver. "Secure the radio."

"Roger that," Terminator acknowledged and packed up the satellite radio.

"Let's get ready people; the extraction helicopter will be here in two mikes (minutes)."

The Sikorsky CH-53 Sea Stallion helicopter landed not far from where the Strike Force teams were waiting. Everyone quickly climbed on board the helicopter, and then it took off. Thirty minutes later the Sikorsky CH-53 Sea Stallion helicopter landed next to the Strike Force C-130J 'Super' Hercules aircraft that was waiting for them.

The Strike Force team disembarked from the helicopter and boarded the C-130J aircraft, and the helicopter took off and headed back to its base. The pilot powered up the C-130J aircraft jet engines and soon afterwards, the aircraft began to move and pick up speed. Seconds later, the aircraft lifted off the ground and proceeded to its cruising altitude. Once the C-130J leveled off at its cruising altitude, the pilot gave the okay for the Strike Force assault team to move about the aircraft.

The medical team that was on board the aircraft moved Lieutenant Shea from his seat to a table that was set up behind a curtained off area, and the doctor began to attend to his wounded leg.

"Terminator; have the pilot send Strike Force Command the all clear signal," Lieutenant McDonald ordered. "Inform them that the primary packages were not at home. Also, let them know that Hammer is wounded in the leg and that the doc here is attending to his wound."

"Roger that," Terminator acknowledged.

"Boomer, any luck translating the papers you found back there?" Lieutenant McDonald inquired.

"Working on it Popeye. I should be done by the time we land."

"Good, let me know what you find," Lieutenant McDonald commented. "Maybe we can figure out where Shammari and the VX gas went off to." *Someone really screwed-the-pooch on this one;* he thought as he got comfortable in his seat. He closed his eyes and drifted to sleep.

Chapter 4

Strike Force Delta Command
Tinker Air Force Base
Oklahoma City, Oklahoma

Colonel Wilson returned to his office from lunch and sat down in the chair behind his desk. He picked up the folder that was lying on his desk and opened it. *That was quick,* he thought when he noticed that the folder contained the after-action report from Lieutenant McDonald about the Strike Force operation in Afghanistan. He carefully read the report; paying close attention to every detail, and when he finished he closed the folder. *We're going to get hit again,* he thought as he stared at the picture of his dearly departed wife that he kept on his desk. He couldn't help but remember the nine-eleven attack on the Pentagon where she was killed. It felt as though it happened just yesterday. "God, I miss you," he mumbled while fighting back his tears. He was startled when the telephone on his desk began to ring. He pushed the speakerphone button on the telephone in front of him. "Yes."

"Wolverine, Popeye would like to see us in the conference room," Captain Hale said.

"I'm on my way," Colonel Wilson said, and then he pushed the speakerphone button on the telephone to end the call. He pulled himself together before he got up from his seat and left his office.

He walked to the conference room and entered. Captain Hale and Lieutenant McDonald immediately jumped to their feet. "As you were,"

Colonel Wilson said and took a seat next to Captain Hale at the table in the middle of the room. He waited until Lieutenant McDonald and Captain Hale returned to their seats before he continued. "Popeye, I've read your after-action report, and I must say I found it interesting. I haven't had time to talk to General Richmond about any of it, so I have no idea what Washington's reaction is going to be on this. Are you sure A'zam al Shammari is in Pakistan?"

"Yes, I am," Lieutenant McDonald quickly answered. "I have the translation of the documents we retrieved from our raid on that laboratory," he continued, referring to the folder that was lying on the table in front of him. "I know for a fact that A'zam al Shammari is in Pakistan; and that he's planning his next move. It's no secret that he has the VX nerve gas at his disposal, and we all know that he has the balls to use it. We need to go into Pakistan and put Shammari down before he has the chance to use the VX."

"Sending a team into Pakistan is going to be hard to sell to the president," Colonel Wilson was quick to point out. "Especially since the Pakistani government is still pissed about the Bin Laden raid."

"Pakistan is harboring a known terrorist, a very dangerous one at that," Lieutenant McDonald commented. "There's got to be something we can do about this."

"All we can do for now is track Shammari's movements, and wait for the president to decide how he wants to handle this," Colonel Wilson said in a calm voice.

"So you're saying that we need to wait for Shammari to use the VX before we hunt this asshole down," Lieutenant McDonald pointed out.

"No, that's not what I'm saying," Colonel Wilson shot back. "Our hands are tied on this matter. We can't go after Shammari until the president gives us the go ahead, so for now, we keep an eye on this idiot and wait." Colonel Wilson paused for a few seconds to let what he had just said sink in before he continued. "Is there anything else you wish to discuss?"

"I think you should read the translation of the papers that we found in that lab," Lieutenant McDonald answered, and then offered Colonel Wilson the folder that was in front of him. "I'm sure you'll find its contents interesting," he continued while Colonel Wilson took the folder and sat it down on the table in front of him.

Colonel Wilson opened the folder and quickly scanned through the papers. When he was finished, he closed the folder. "Who else knows about this?"

"Just me and my team," Lieutenant McDonald replied. "Playboy translated it on the way back from Afghanistan."

"Good, let's keep it that way," Colonel Wilson commented. "Is there anything else?"

"I think that covers it," Lieutenant McDonald answered.

"I'll pass this information on to General Richwood," Colonel Wilson assured Lieutenant McDonald. "I'm sure he'll brief the president on this. What the president does about it is his call. If you don't have any more questions, I suggest you get back to your people and see to it that they keep a lid on this."

"I'll get on it," Lieutenant McDonald assured Colonel Wilson. He got up from his seat and left the conference room.

"What's going on?" Captain Hale asked after Lieutenant McDonald closed the conference room door.

Colonel Wilson slid the folder in front of Captain Hale. "Take a look for yourself."

Captain Hale opened the folder and examined the documents enclosed. *I don't believe this fuckin' shit;* he thought when he found a document with the White House letterhead on it, which stated that Strike Force was planning an assault on Feyzabad. "Fuck," he commented and closed the folder, and slid it back to Colonel Wilson.

"Yeah, as you can see, the mission was compromised before it started," Colonel Wilson pointed out. "They knew we were coming; they just didn't know when. That's why A'zam al Shammari and the VX wasn't there."

"So someone at the White House sold us out?" Captain Hale asked.

"It looks like it," Colonel Wilson answered.

"I think we should concentrate on finding the leak at the White House and plug it," Captain Hale pointed out. "We got lucky this time."

"That we did," Colonel Wilson agreed. "We might not be so lucky the next time."

"Wolverine, if I may be so bold; I think we should start looking into anyone in the White House that knew about the possible Afghanistan operation," Captain Hale was quick to suggest.

"I'll look into the White House problem," Colonel Wilson shot back. "Right now what I need you to do is concentrate on finding Shammari. I want to know exactly where this asshole is hiding, in case the president decides to go after him."

"I'll get right on it," Captain Hale acknowledged. He got up from his seat and left the conference room, closing the door behind him.

A few minutes later, there was a knock on the door. Colonel Wilson looked through the see-through wall and saw Second Lieutenant Samantha Cooltrain, nicknamed Giggles, standing at the door; he motioned for her to enter.

She opened the door and stepped into the conference room. "MI-5 in London has just notified us that their agents in Afghanistan, who were tailing A'zam al Shammari, reported that Shammari has slipped through their surveillance at the Pakistani border. They have no idea where he is, but they believe he was heading for Chitral, Pakistan."

"Has this information been relayed to General Richwood?"

"Yes, it has."

"I'll take it from here Giggles," Colonel Wilson commented. "I'll page you if I should need you."

"I understand," Lieutenant Cooltrain acknowledged and then left the conference room, and closed the door.

Why the hell are you heading to Chitral, Pakistan? Colonel Wilson thought to himself as he got up from his seat. *Better yet, what the fuck are you planning?* He continued to think while he left the conference room. He walked back to his office and found Captain Hale sitting in the chair, in front of his desk. He entered, and Captain Hale jumped to his feet. "As you were Bulldog," Colonel Wilson said while he walked over to his desk and sat down.

"I have the medical report from the doc about Hammer," Captain Hale said while he returned to his seat. "I put it on your desk."

"How is he doing?"

"Not good," Captain Hale sadly replied. "Doc said that due to the condition of his leg injury, Hammer won't be able to return to full combat duty."

"It's that bad?"

"Doc seems to think so. He says that one wrong move could shatter Hammer's leg bone."

"Damn that is bad news. Hammer's a good unit leader. I'll have to talk to General Richwood about finding his replacement." Colonel Wilson paused for a moment before he continued. "When does Hammer get out of the hospital?"

"Tomorrow morning."

"Have Hammer come and see me when he gets released from the hospital."

"I'll pass it on; is there anything else?"

"Not that I can think of at the moment."

Captain Hale got up from his seat and left Colonel Wilson's office. Colonel Wilson opened the report from Lieutenant Shea's doctor and began to read through it.

* * * * *

Washington, D. C.
The White House
Two Weeks Before Election Day

President Ike Matthews sat at his desk in the Oval Office, with the NSA Director and the CIA Director sitting across from him. They were watching the CNN news report on the television about the growing unrest in Colombia. The pictures that were being shown on the television were devastating.

When the news report concluded, President Matthews picked up the television remote control from his desk and turned off the television. A few minutes later, there was a knock on the side door to the Oval Office.

President Matthews got up from his seat and hurried to the side door. He opened the door, and General Richwood entered the Oval Office. "General Richwood, please come in," President Matthews said while shaking hands with the general.

Afterwards, he walked back to his desk and sat down in his chair behind the desk while General Richwood sat in one of the chairs in front of the president's desk. "General, I'm guessing that you're curious as to why I asked you here today, so I'll get right to the point. I'm concerned about the growing unrest in Colombia. I need you to send some Strike Force personnel to the Marine camp we have near the Colombian border and get me some answers. I need to know what's going on down there before I commit to helping President Roberto with this problem."

"Mr. President, I wasn't aware that the Senate Intelligence Committee had approved such a mission," General Richwood commented.

"I'll inform the committee about this later," President Matthews fired back. "For now, we need to keep this between us. Just let me know what you're going to need, and I'll see to it that you get it."

General Richwood jumped to his feet and saluted President Matthews. "Yes, sir, Mr. President, I'll get right on it." General Richwood walked over to the side door and opened it. He stepped into the hallway and closed the door.

President Matthews started to pick up the television remote control from his desk when the intercom on his telephone beeped. He pushed the intercom button on the telephone in front of him. "Yes."

"Mr. President, Colombian Ambassador Cruz is here to see you," President Matthews Secretary, Betty Clark, a lovely middle-aged woman, said over the intercom.

"Very well; show him in," President Mathews said and pushed the intercom button on the telephone, canceling the intercom call.

The door to the Oval Office opened, and Ambassador Cruz entered. President Mathews stood up and walked over to greet the Ambassador while Mrs. Clark closed the door.

"Ambassador, it's nice to see you again," President Mathews said, and they shook hands. "Please, have a seat." He continued to say, motioning to one of the sofas in the middle of the room.

Ambassador Cruz walked over to the sofa and sat down while President Mathews sat down on the other sofa across from him. "Mr. President I'll get right to the point about my visit," Ambassador Cruz began. "President Roberto is concerned about the expansion of your Marine base that is a few kilometers from our border."

"Your president and the Panamanian president both agreed on the location and size of that Marine training base," President Mathews pointed out. "The airstrip was put in recently, so the Marines could bring in supplies and training personnel. All of this is in accordance with our agreement."

"President Roberto is aware of that," Ambassador Cruz calmly said "He's worried that it might be used for something other than training."

"Like what?" President Mathews fired back.

"President Roberto is concerned that your CIA is using the base for the purpose of spying on Colombia," Ambassador Cruz answered, "He wants your assurance that this is not the case."

"I can assure you Mr. Ambassador that the CIA is not using that base to spy on your country," President Mathews said calmly. "There are no CIA personnel on that base, but if someone should attack that base, the Marines will put down the threat with extreme prejudice."

Ambassador Cruz was stunned by President Matthews's statement. He got up from the sofa and said, "Mr. President; I will assure President Roberto that he has nothing to worry about. I thank you for your time, sir."

"Any time Mr. Ambassador," President Matthews commented, and then he too got up from the sofa that he was sitting on. "Please tell President Roberto that he has nothing to fear from the United States."

President Matthews shook hands with Ambassador Cruz and followed him to the door. Ambassador Cruz opened the door and stepped into the reception area. President Matthews stood in the reception area and watched Ambassador Cruz walk down the hallway and disappear out of sight. He looked at Mrs. Clark, who was sitting at her desk. "Betty, get me General Casey at the Pentagon on the telephone." He did not wait for a reply from Mrs. Clark. He stepped back into the Oval Office and closed the door. He walked over to his desk and sat down in the chair behind it.

A few minutes later, the telephone on his desk rang. He picked up the telephone receiver and put it to his ear. "President Matthews," he said in a calm voice.

"Mr. President, this is General Casey, sir."

"General, I need to know how soon you can put a three hundred-man combat force at Camp Freedom in Panama."

"I can have them there in about twelve-hours sir. Sir, is Camp Freedom at risk?"

"Not, to my knowledge. It's just a precautionary measure general. Just have your Marines keep a sharp lookout."

"Yes, sir, Mr. President. I'll get started on it immediately."

"Good," President Matthews commented, and then he returned the telephone receiver to its normal resting place, ending the call. He picked up the television remote control and turn on the television. He flipped through the channels until he found something that he wanted to watch.

* * * * *

Al-Qaeda Safe-House
Chitral, Pakistan

A covered GAZ-66 (4X4) 2,000 kg truck that was carrying A'zam al Shammari and the VX nerve gas; along with six of his faithful followers who were in the back of the truck, pulled off the main road onto a dirt driveway. They continued down the drive until they reached a house that had a large metal building next to it. Shammari got out of the truck just as a man walked out of the house and opened the metal doors on the building. The driver pulled the truck into the building. The man closed the doors and hurried back into the house.

Another man came out of the house and hurried over to where Shammari was standing. "Praise Allah for your safe trip," the man said in Arabic. "You will be safe here. The American satellites can't penetrate the metal building."

"Any news from Feyzabad," Shammari inquired, also speaking in Arabic.

"The Americans attacked a few hours after you left," the man answered. "Most of our friends were killed when the Americans bombed the laboratory."

So, the warning I got from my American friend was accurate, Shammari thought. "Any news from the people that I'm supposed to meet here?"

"Yes, they are on their way and should be here shortly."

"Good, let's get inside," Shammari said when two of his men emerged from the metal building; each armed with an AK-47 assault rifle. "I don't like being out in the open like this for too long," Shammari continued as the two men began walking towards them.

"I understand," the man said. "If you follow me, I will show you to your room."

Shammari followed the man to the front door, and they entered the house, but the two men remained outside. "Not bad," Shammari remarked, still speaking in Arabic.

"Please make yourself at home," the man offered. "You may stay as long as you like."

"We won't be staying long," Shammari commented. "We'll be leaving right after the meeting."

The front door opened, and one of the men who was standing guard entered. "They are here," he reported.

"Show them in," Shammari ordered, and then he turned to the man. "I will need you and the other man to leave until this meeting is over."

"We will be out back if you should need us," the man said and left the room. He and the other man went out the back door just as Shammari's guest entered through the front door.

"Leave us," Shammari ordered. "Have the men patrol the area around the house.

"I will pass on your order," the guard acknowledged, and then closed the door.

"My dear friend, how are you?" Shammari asked, speaking in perfect English. "I hope your trip was a pleasant one," he continued while they shook hands.

"Let's just say it was a long trip."

"Please, let us go into the kitchen and sit at the table," he suggested while he motioned to the kitchen. "I am sure you have much to talk about with me.

"Actually, my friend here is in need of your help," the American said as they walked into the kitchen. "I think that we can help him, and still achieve our goal of striking the United States," he continued while everyone sat at the table. "It may even accelerate our timeline."

"I don't think I caught your friend's name."

"My name is of no importance," the man shot back in English. "I represent General Fresco Juarez, the Commander of the Revolutionary Armed Forces of Colombia. I am here to acquire your assistance in helping us put an end to our struggle against our corrupt government."

"What can I do? I am only one man."

"I met with General Juarez before I came here. He knows that you have the ability to manufacture the VX nerve gas. He asked me to ask you if you would come to Colombia, and make the gas for him."

"How does this general know that I can make this gas?"

"He got the information from a CIA person that we captured," the Colombian man answered. "He also learned that the Americans are using the consulate that they recently built on the Panamanian side of our border as an intelligence hub."

Shammari looked at the American and smiled. "That would be an excellent target if I had enough gas made up, and the means of getting it there."

"General Juarez assured me that he will do whatever it takes to wipe out the Americans at Puerto Obaldia," the Colombian man was quick to point out. "The Americans have been a pain in our side from the beginning. If you agree to help us, General Juarez will see to it that you have everything you need."

"You know the Americans will not take an attack on their consulate lightly," Shammari pointed out. "There will be consequences."

"By the time the Americans figure out what is going on, it will be too late for them to stop us," the Colombian man fired back. "With the Americans out-of-the-way, General Juarez will have the time he needs to take control of Colombia."

"Your plan is bold, but I like it," Shammari commented. "I think it might just work."

"So, you'll help us?"

"Yes, I will help you," Shammari calmly answered. He turned to the American. "I will need an accurate copy of the blueprints for our target."

"I will have them when you get to Colombia," the American said. "How soon can you leave?"

"I can leave within the hour. I will call you when I arrive."

"Very well then," the American said as he got up from his seat. "I will wait for your call," he continued while the Colombian man got up from his seat.

Shammari jumped up from his seat and walked to the door, with the American and the Colombian man following. He opened the door, and the two men exited. Shammari watched the two men walk to their car and climb inside. He stood in the doorway and watched them drive off. "Get everyone ready to move out," he said to one of the men standing guard, and then he closed the door.

Two of Shammari's men came storming through the back door with the two men who lived at the house in tow. "We found these two standing outside by the kitchen window listening in on your conversation," one of Shammari's men reported, speaking in Arabic.

"You should not have done that," Shammari said in Arabic while he removed the Colt forty-five that he had tucked in his pants behind his back.

"We will not tell anyone about what we heard," one of the men pleaded.

"I know," Shammari said, and then he shot both of the men in the head, and they dropped to the floor. Hearing the shots, the remaining guard at the door rushed inside with his AK-47 assault rifle ready for action. "Everything is under control," Shammari assured the guard. "We must leave now. We have a long journey ahead of us," he concluded as he walked to the opened door.

Shammari walked out of the house with the three men following just as his people were backing the truck out of the metal building. Shammari climbed into the front seat while the others jumped into the back of the A GAZ-66 (4X4) 2,000 kg truck. The driver turned the truck around and headed back towards the main road.

Chapter 5

Strike Force Delta Command
Tinker Air Force Base
Oklahoma City, Oklahoma

Colonel Wilson started his day just as he has done since he took command of Strike Force Delta. He was standing in his office looking at the crisis board on the wall. He noticed that Colombia was recently marked a hot spot and a point of interest.

The office door opened, and Captain Hale entered. "Wolverine we just received a pouch from General Richwood. "It's marked your eyes-only."

Colonel Wilson walked over to Captain Hale and took the locked pouch from him. He hurried over to his desk and opened the center drawer. He removed a key from the drawer and opened the locked pouch. He returned the key to the drawer and closed it before sitting down in the chair behind the desk.

Colonel Wilson removed the contents of the pouch and laid it on the desk in front of him. He read the two-page cover sheet carefully and stopped. He looked up at Captain Hale and smiled. He handed Captain Hale the two-page cover sheet while he picked up the telephone receiver from the telephone on his desk. He dialed an extension number and put the telephone receiver to his ear.

"Maverick," a man answered after a couple of rings.

"Maverick, this is Wolverine. I need you and Lieutenant Lakewood in my office."

"On our way," Maverick acknowledged and then the line went dead.

"That man needs to learn some manners," Colonel Wilson remarked while he returned the telephone receiver to its resting place.

"That's Maverick," Captain Hale commented, and then handed the two-page cover sheet back to Colonel Wilson.

"Yeah, I guess you're right." Colonel Wilson chuckled while he laid the cover sheet down on his desk. "You never know what might come out of his mouth." He continued as he picked up the telephone receiver from the telephone on his desk. He dialed the extension number for the hangar maintenance chief at hangar nine, and then he put the telephone receiver to his ear.

"Maintenance."

"Chief, ready a C-130J. I want it ready to go in thirty. Tell the pilot that he is to be ready to take off when my people get there."

"We'll be ready," the maintenance chief acknowledged.

"Good," Colonel Wilson said, and then he returned the telephone receiver to the telephone on his desk, ending the call.

A few minutes later, Second Lieutenant Rick Johnson, nicknamed Maverick, and Second Lieutenant Jackson Lakewood, nicknamed Wild Man, entered Colonel Wilson's office. They walked over to the empty chairs next to Captain Hale and stood at attention.

"Have a seat," Colonel Wilson said.

Lieutenant Johnson and Lieutenant Lakewood sat down and waited for Colonel Wilson to continue.

"An operation has presented itself that will require both of your teams," Colonel Wilson began. "This mission will be called Operation Sparrow. Maverick, your call-sign will be Sparrow-one and Wild Man, you will be Sparrow-two. This operation came straight from the White House so pay attention. We have a lot to go over so let's get started."

Colonel Wilson opened the operational folder and began. Lieutenant Johnson, along with Lieutenant Lakewood and Captain Hale listened while Colonel Wilson went over the mission plan one-step at a time. When he was finished, he closed the operational folder and offered it to Lieutenant Johnson. "Are there any questions?"

"When do we leave?" Lieutenant Johnson asked while he took the operational folder from Colonel Wilson.

"ASAP so Maverick, Wild Man, assemble your units," Colonel Wilson ordered while he got up from his seat. "Your aircraft is waiting at hangar nine. Everything you need for this assignment is on the aircraft. Watch your asses down there."

"Always," Lieutenant Johnson remarked while he and Lieutenant Lakewood got up from their seats. "We'll see you when this is over boss," Lieutenant Johnson remarked.

Colonel Wilson sat back down in his seat while Lieutenant Johnson walked over to the office door with Lieutenant Lakewood following. Lieutenant Johnson opened the door and exited the office. Lieutenant Lakewood closed the door on his way out.

"What do you make of this?" Captain Hale asked. "I mean setting up a listening post so close to the Colombian border."

"I believe that President Matthews is concerned about the shit that's going on in Colombia, and he needs us to help him get some answers," Colonel Wilson answered. "I must admit; I was concerned about it a while back. However, I believe that there's more to this than what the president is telling us. He's holding something back."

"Why do you say that?"

"It's just a hunch I have," Colonel Wilson replied.

The office door opened, and Encryption Specialist, Second Lieutenant Betty Williams, nicknamed Raven, entered carrying a red folder in her hand. "I'm sorry to barge in Wolverine, but I have an urgent message for you from General Richwood. It came in on the Delta Alfa code."

"Delta Alfa," Captain Hale commented. "I thought that code was only used in extreme circumstances."

"It is," Lieutenant Williams said while she laid the red folder down on Colonel Wilson's desk in front of him. "I guess this is one of those circumstances."

Colonel Wilson picked up the telephone receiver from the telephone on his desk. He dialed the number for General Richwood at the Pentagon and put the telephone receiver to his ear. While waiting for General Richwood to answer, he took his computer mouse and clicked on the Delta Alfa icon on his screen.

"Richwood," The general answered.

"General, this is Wilson," Colonel Wilson began. "I just got a Delta

Alfa message from you; please authenticate." Using the computer keyboard, Colonel Wilson typed the authentication code into his computer as General Richwood spoke and then pressed the enter key when the general was finished. "I got it general," Colonel Wilson said when a message appeared on his computer monitor."

"Good," General Richwood acknowledged, and then he abruptly ended the call.

Colonel Wilson returned the telephone receiver to the telephone on his desk, and then he pushed the print document button on his computer keyboard. Seconds later, the printer on the other side of the office came to life and began printing out the message.

When the printer stopped printing, Lieutenant Williams retrieved the document from the printer. She walked over to Colonel Wilson and handed him the document. Afterwards, she left the office and closed the door.

Colonel Wilson sifted through the pages. He wanted to make sure that the printer had printed them out correctly. Satisfied, he used the computer mouse to close the program, which deleted the message from the system.

Captain Hale remained silent while Colonel Wilson read each page. When he was done, he looked at Captain Hale. "We have another operation," he pointed out. "This one comes directly from the president. From here on out in our messages we are to refer to A'zam al Shammari as The Scorpion.

"I think that is a good name for the dickhead," Captain Hale chuckled.

Colonel Wilson cracked a smile and then continued. "We need to find out where A'zam al Shammari is hiding and put this rat down once and for all."

"What if we can't find Shammari?" Captain Hale boldly asked.

"If we don't find him, then we're fucked, and a lot of innocent people are going to die," Colonel Wilson fired back. "I don't care what we have to do; we need to find this asshole. I know he's planning something, and we need to find out what before he strikes."

"Whatever he's planning; you can bet your ass it's not going to be good for us," Captain Hale calmly pointed out. "Especially if it involves the VX nerve gas that we know he's capable of manufacturing."

"Exactly," Colonel Wilson remarked. "I want our people ready to move when the time comes."

"They'll be ready," Captain Hale said while he got up from his seat. "Is there anything else you need?"

"Not at this time," Colonel Wilson answered. "Just keep me informed of anything that comes in about Shammari."

"You got it," Captain Hale acknowledged. He walked over to the office door and opened it. He left the office and closed the door.

Colonel Wilson looked at the crisis board on the wall. "Why are you going to fuckin' Colombia," he muttered. "What's there that you want?"

"Is this a bad time Wolverine?" Lieutenant Shea asked who was standing in the doorway supported by his crutches. "I can come back later."

"Hammer, I didn't hear you come in," Colonel Wilson answered, startled by Lieutenant Shea's sudden appearance.

"I'm sorry for the intrusion Wolverine, but Bulldog said you wanted to see me."

"Yes, I do," Colonel Wilson acknowledged. "Please have a seat."

Lieutenant Shea closed the office door and with the aid of his crutches, he made his way over to the chair in front of Colonel Wilson's desk and sat down.

"I've taken the liberty of speaking to your doctor about your situation."

"Then you know that I'm not coming back to my unit."

"Yes, I do, and that's why we need to talk."

"Talk about what Wolverine. I'm on my way out. It's as simple as that."

"Is that what you want?"

"Of course not, but I'm useless to this unit. I can never go on another mission; let alone train for one."

"What if you could stay? Would you consider it?"

"Of course I would. What are you up to Wolverine?"

"Hammer, I would like you to consider staying on here and take charge of selecting and training new personnel," Colonel Wilson answered. "I have no doubt that you're the right man for this job. I've already talked this over with your doctor and General Richwood. The job is yours if you want it."

"I'm honored that you and General Richwood think that I can do this. Of course, I want the job. When do I start?"

"When your doctor releases you, report to Bulldog, and he'll get you settled in. If you should have any problems, let Bulldog or myself know."

"I won't let you or General Richwood down," he said while he got up from his seat. Lieutenant Shea made his way to the office door and opened the door. He hobbled his way out of Colonel Wilson's office and closed the door.

Colonel Wilson turned his attention back to the operational plan for Operation Scorpion that was lying on his desk in front of him. He began going back over the operational plan to familiarize himself with every detail of the plan. He wanted to be certain that he understood what President Matthews wanted him to do.

When he was finished, he picked up the operational orders from his desk and put it in his briefcase. He closed his briefcase and then got up from his seat. He walked over to the wall safe that was in his office and opened it. He placed the briefcase inside the safe and closed the door. He locked the safe and turned the handle to make sure it was locked. He then walked back over to his chair behind his desk and sat down. *Something doesn't fit Mr. President* Colonel Wilson thought to himself. *What are you not telling me?*

* * * * *

Camp Freedom, Panama
Thirty Kilometers From The Colombian Border

The C-130J Hercules aircraft that was carrying Lieutenant Johnson and Lieutenant Lakewood, and their Strike Force team members touched down on the runway. The aircraft taxied for a few minutes before coming to a complete stop. The pilot shut down the aircraft's engines and lowered the back cargo door.

Lieutenant Johnson and Lieutenant Lakewood, as well as the entire Strike Force team, were dressed in full combat gear with their HK-416N assault rifles. They departed the aircraft carrying the equipment that they had brought with them.

An M-35 two-and-a-half ton cargo truck pulled up and stopped next to the Strike Force team. A Marine sergeant got out on the passenger side and walked over to them. "Who's in command here?" The sergeant asked.

"I am," Lieutenant Johnson quickly answered.

"Wolverine sent us, sir. We will take you to where you will be staying while you're here," the Marine sergeant said.

"Let's get our gear loaded on the truck," Lieutenant Johnson ordered.

The Strike Force team loaded their gear onto the truck and then climbed in, and the truck drove off. A few minutes later, the truck pulled up in front of the barracks where the Strike Force team would be staying and stopped. The Marine sergeant and the driver got out and walked to the back of the truck. They helped Lieutenant Johnson and Lieutenant Lakewood and the other members of the Strike Force team from the back of the truck.

"This is where you and your people will be staying, sir," the Marine sergeant pointed out while the Strike Force team unloaded their gear from the back of the truck. "It's not much, but it's the best we could do on such short notice."

"It'll do just fine sergeant," Lieutenant Johnson commented.

"If you should need anything, there's a telephone inside that you can use," the Marine sergeant informed Lieutenant Johnson. "Just dial zero to get the camp's switchboard operator.

"Thanks, Sergeant," Lieutenant Johnson said. "I'm sure we can handle it from here."

The Marine sergeant and the driver walked to the front of the truck and climbed in. The driver fired up the truck's diesel engine, and seconds later, they drove off.

"Okay people, let's get our gear inside," Lieutenant Johnson ordered.

Lieutenant Johnson was the first to enter the barracks with Lieutenant Lakewood not far behind. He scanned the room and noticed that the inside of the barracks wasn't much different than what they were accustomed to. The rest of the Strike Force team entered a few seconds later and put their equipment on the floor next to the door.

Lieutenant Johnson noticed that there were two rooms at the back of the barracks. "Dizzy, I want you and Witch Doctor to set up the sat-com in the room on the left," Lieutenant Johnson ordered.

"Roger that," Dizzy acknowledged. "We'll have a com-link to headquarters up and running in a few minutes."

"Very well," Lieutenant Johnson acknowledged. "The rest of you grab a bunk and relax while you can."

Lieutenant Johnson and Lieutenant Lakewood walked to the back of the barracks.They entered the room across from where Dizzy and Witch Doctor were setting up the satellite radio, and found two desks in the room, with a telephone sitting on one of them.

"I wonder if that telephone works," Lieutenant Lakewood commented while he walked over to the desk. He picked up the telephone receiver and put it to his ear. "Yep, it works," he said when he heard a dial tone. He returned the telephone receiver to its resting place and sat down in the chair behind the desk. "Any idea how long we'll be down here?"

"I haven't a clue," Lieutenant Johnson answered and sat down behind the other desk next to where Lieutenant Lakewood was sitting.

Lieutenant Lakewood was startled when the telephone on the desk in front of him began to ring. He looked at Lieutenant Johnson.

"Well, answer the fuckin' phone," Lieutenant Johnson fired back.

Lieutenant Lakewood picked up the telephone receiver and put it to his ear. "Yes," he said. He listened for a few moments and then returned the telephone receiver to its resting place.

"Well," Lieutenant Johnson inquired. "Who was it?"

"It was operations," Lieutenant Lakewood answered. "They're sending a Humvee to take you to the airfield to meet someone,"

"Who?" Lieutenant Johnson fired back.

"They didn't say," Lieutenant Lakewood answered. "All they said was to tell you to be out front in five minutes."

"Well, I better go and find out what the fuck this is all about," Lieutenant Johnson said while he got up from his seat. "Post a guard at each entrance in full combat dress, and let no one in here until I get back."

"I'll get right on it," Lieutenant Lakewood acknowledged.

Lieutenant Johnson walked out of the room and exited the building. A Humvee pulled up; he jumped into the passenger's seat, and they drove off. The Humvee drove to the airfield and stopped next to a Gulfstream G550 twin-engine jet aircraft that was sitting next to a hangar.

"Your party is waiting for you onboard the aircraft," the driver pointed out. "I'll be waiting here for your return."

Lieutenant Johnson nodded his head in acknowledgment and climbed out of the Humvee. He walked over to the aircraft and entered. His eyes lit up when he saw Lieutenant Samantha Cooltrain sitting in one of the seats.

Lieutenant Cooltrain, a twenty-three-year-old red-haired woman, smiled when they made eye contact. "It's nice to see you again, Maverick."

"That it is," Lieutenant Johnson commented while he sat down across from Lieutenant Cooltrain. "I must admit that this is a surprise."

"I'm here on business Maverick," Lieutenant Cooltrain shot back. "So let's get started."

"Okay, let's get to it," Lieutenant Johnson fired back.

"You're an asshole."

"I might be, but we both know you love this asshole."

Lieutenant Cooltrain smiled. "That I do, but this is not the time or the place for our personal feelings. Like I said, I'm here on business. There's been a slight change in your operational plans."

"Go on; I'm listening."

"Wolverine believes that our code may have been compromised and that someone could be listening to our transmissions," Lieutenant Cooltrain began. "As a precautionary measure, I was sent down here with the new codes and new operational orders. Also, I have the codes and frequencies that the CIA and NSA are using in this area. It's all here in this briefcase," she concluded, referring to the metal briefcase sitting next to her on the floor.

Lieutenant Johnson reached for the briefcase, and Lieutenant Cooltrain grabbed his hand. "Rick I'm sorry I called you an asshole," she whispered. "You know I love you."

"I know you do Samantha, and I love you too," he whispered. "You were right; I was out of line, and I apologize."

Lieutenant Cooltrain smiled and released the grip she had on Lieutenant Johnson's hand. "You are to send a message back to Strike

Force Delta Command that you have received the Apple Pie that they sent. They will then send you the combination to the briefcase," she said while she got up out of her seat. "Also, Wolverine said to trust no one outside the unit."

Lieutenant Johnson picked up the briefcase and got up out of his seat. He looked at Lieutenant Cooltrain and smiled. Without warning, he took her into his arms, and they passionately kissed.

"I'll see you when you get back," Lieutenant Cooltrain said while she broke their embrace. "Maverick, please be careful."

"Don't worry love. I'll be back before you know it."

Lieutenant Johnson departed the aircraft with the metal briefcase in hand and walked over to the Humvee. He hopped in, and they drove off. A few minutes later, the Humvee stopped in front of the building where the Strike Force team was housed. He jumped out of the Humvee, and the driver drove off.

The guard at the entrance opened the door, and Lieutenant Johnson entered. He hurried back to the office where Lieutenant Lakewood was waiting. He walked over and laid the metal briefcase down on top of his desk, and sat down.

"That must have been some meeting," Lieutenant Lakewood commented.

"What the fuck are you talking about?" Lieutenant Johnson fired back.

Lieutenant Lakewood cracked a smile. "You have lipstick on your mouth," he answered while he offered Lieutenant Johnson a tissue.

"Not another word," Lieutenant Johnson said and snatched the tissue out of Lieutenant Lakewood's hand and wiped the lipstick off his mouth.

"What's up with the metal briefcase?" Lieutenant Lakewood asked while he tried to keep a straight face.

"Dizzy, come in here," Lieutenant Johnson shouted ignoring Lieutenant Lakewood's question.

Seconds later Dizzy appeared in the doorway. "What's up Maverick?"

"I want you to send Strike Force Delta Command a message," Lieutenant Johnson began. The message is to read; *we have received the Apple Pie that you sent.* Bring me the reply as soon as you get it."

"You mean they sent us some Apple Pie?"

"No, you fuckin' moron, it's a code," Lieutenant Lakewood fired back.

"Oh," Dizzy said while he scratched the top of his head. "I knew that."

"Hurry up Dizzy; we don't have all fuckin' day," Lieutenant Johnson fired back.

"I'll get right on it," Dizzy said, and then hurried back to the radio room.

"Witch Doctor, get in here," Lieutenant Johnson shouted.

Seconds later, Witch Doctor appeared in the doorway. "You rang?"

Lieutenant Johnson hand signaled Witch Doctor that he wanted him to sweep the entire building for listening devices. Witch Doctor nodded his head in acknowledgment and headed back to the radio room to get his radio detection meter. When he turned on the meter, it lit up like a Christmas tree. He found the listening device and disabled it before he checked the rest of the room, and found another. He disabled it and continued his search.

Satisfied that there were no more listening devices in the room, he walked into the other room that Lieutenant Johnson and Lieutenant Lakewood were using as an office, and the radio detection meter lit up again. He put the two disabled listening devices on Lieutenant Johnson's desk and checked the room thoroughly, and found two more listening devices in the room. He disabled each of them and laid them down on Lieutenant Johnson's desk next to the other two that he had found in the radio room.

"Watch what you say until I finish my sweep," Witch Doctor whispered. "I'll be right back."

Lieutenant Johnson nodded his head that he understood, and Witch Doctor left the room. He checked the rest of the building and found three more listening devices. Witch Doctor disabled them and returned to Lieutenant Johnson's office. He laid the disabled listening devices down on Lieutenant Johnson's desk next to the others.

"Did you get them all?" Lieutenant Johnson asked.

"I'm sure I did," Witch Doctor answered. "Give me a few minutes, and I'll have it to where no one will be able to listen in on us."

"Get it done," Lieutenant Johnson ordered.

"I'm on it," Witch Doctor acknowledged and left the room.

"How the hell did you know?" Lieutenant Lakewood curiously asked.

"I didn't," Lieutenant Johnson answered. "It was just a hunch."

"Do you think it has something to do with us being here?"

"I don't know about that, but I do believe that someone wants to know why we're here." Lieutenant Johnson stopped talking when Witch Doctor entered the room carrying a black box.

Witch Doctor put the black box in the corner of the room and turned on the power switch. "The building is secured," Witch Doctor reported. "I have placed dampers around the building and in all the rooms, including this one. No one is going to listen in on us anymore."

Dizzy entered the room and walked over to where Lieutenant Johnson was sitting. "I have a reply from Strike Force Delta Command," he said while he laid the message down on top of the metal briefcase that was in front of Lieutenant Johnson.

Lieutenant Johnson entered the combination and opened the metal briefcase. He removed three notebooks from the briefcase. One had the CIA written on the front of it. It contained the codes and frequencies that the CIA was using to communicate with their agents who were operating in the area. The second notebook had the NSA written on the front of it. It contained the codes and frequencies that the NSA was using to communicate with their agents who were operating in the area. The third notebook had Operation Sparrow written on the front of it. It contained the new codes that they were to use to communicate with Strike Force Command.

"I want the two of you to monitor every communication from the CIA and NSA," Lieutenant Johnson said while he handed the CIA and NSA notebooks to Witch Doctor. "I want to know what these assholes are up to," he continued while he handed the new Operation Sparrow codebook to Dizzy. "Now get to it."

"We're on it," Witch Doctor said, and then he and Dizzy left the room with Dizzy closing the door on their way out.

Lieutenant Johnson removed the folder that was in the metal briefcase and laid it down on the desk. He picked up the disabled listening devices that Witch Doctor had found and tossed them inside the briefcase. He closed the metal briefcase and locked it before he tossed the briefcase into the corner.

"What the hell was that all about?" Lieutenant Lakewood asked.

"No reason," Lieutenant Johnson answered. He opened the folder from the briefcase and began to read through its contents. When he finished, he closed the folder. "You need to read this," he said while he offered the folder to Lieutenant Lakewood.

Lieutenant Lakewood took the folder from Lieutenant Johnson and quickly read its contents. Lieutenant Johnson got up from his seat and left the office; and closed the door.

Chapter 6

Under the cover of darkness, the covered GAZ-66 (4X4), 2,000 kg truck, entered the city. A'zam al Shammari sat in the front of the truck with the driver. Five of Shammari's followers were in the back of the truck with several medium-size, steel canisters that contained the VX nerve gas. There was hardly any traffic on the narrow streets; making it easy to navigate through town. It wasn't long before they arrived at the loading area on the pier next to an Iranian freighter where two men were waiting.

A'zam al Shammari got out of the truck while his followers got out of the back of the truck with their AK-47 assault rifles ready for action. He walked over to the two men. "Good morning," he said in Farsi.

"Do you have a cigarette?" One of the men asked in Farsi.

Shammari removed an unopened package of American made Marlboro cigarettes from his shirt pocket and handed it to the man. The man opened the package, and then he put the pack in his shirt pocket. "I'll smoke these later," he said while he shook hands with Shammari. "All clear," he shouted and several men emerged from their secured hiding places nearby.

"I see you were prepared," Shammari commented.

"You and your people need to get onboard," the man pointed out. "My people will load your cargo, and dispose of your vehicle."

"Please be careful," Shammari said. "This cargo is very dangerous."

"We will," the man assured Shammari.

Shammari and his followers walked up the gangplank while the medium-sized, steel cylinder canisters that contained the VX nerve gas was hoisted onto the ship. "Easau, see to it that the canisters are secured properly to the deck of the ship," Shammari ordered.

"Yes," Easau acknowledged and hurried to where the canisters of VX nerve gas was being loaded.

Shammari cracked a smile as he and the men with him went inside the ship. His American friend had sent him a message informing him that a CIA surveillance team was watching the docks. He was certain that they were watching his every move, and that before the ship got underway, the CIA in Langley, Virginia would know that he had boarded an Iranian freighter; giving the CIA the illusion that he was heading for Iran.

Thirty Minutes Later

When the captain of the freighter got word from his first mate that the ship was ready to depart, he gave the order to get underway. Shammari stood on the bridge with the captain, and together they watched the crew as they sprang into action. It wasn't long before the ship was under its own power, and slowly pulling away from the pier.

The captain ordered maximum speed when the ship entered the Arabian Sea. Shammari was shaken when he felt the ship begin to shutter. *I hope the propellers don't fall off this old bucket;* he thought while he watched the land disappear, and all he could see was water.

The captain walked over to Shammari and handed him an envelope. "We'll be traveling at this speed until we reach the rendezvous point," He said in perfect English. "At this speed, we should be there in four or five days," he continued as he handed Shammari the envelope. "The contents of that envelope will explain everything."

"I did not know you spoke English," Shammari pointed out, speaking in English.

"I learned English from my mother. Now, if you want, I could have one of my crew show you to your cabin. My first mate has informed me that your people have settled into their quarters."

"Yes, I think that would be an excellent idea."

The captain motioned to one of his crew members on the bridge, and Shammari followed him off the bridge, and into the belly of the ship.

* * * * *

Langley, Virginia
William Hastings residence

William Hastings sat on the couch in his living room trying to relax while he watched television. He had only been back from his assignment in Afghanistan for a few weeks, but it felt as though he had just returned home. Even though, he had been with the CIA for nearly ten years, the death and destruction that he witnessed firsthand while he was in Afghanistan still haunted him.

He smiled when the news of President Mathews' defeat to Martian Elliot in the election the day before came on the news. "Good-by asshole," he mumbled. "I never liked your incompetent ass. I'm sure Elliot can't be any worse than you."

He turned the television off and got up from the couch. He walked to the kitchen to get a cup of coffee when the cell phone in his shirt pocket began to ring. He removed the cell phone from his shirt pocket and flipped it open, and put it to his ear. "Hastings," he said.

"Mr. Hastings, this is Mary from The director's office," a woman's voice said. "The director would like for you to report to his office at thirteen thirty. He said to bring your go bag with you."

"Tell The director that I'll be there," Hastings said, and then he flipped the cell phone closed to cancel the call. "Another fuckin' assignment," he muttered while he put his cell phone back into his shirt pocket.

Hastings walked to his bedroom to get the suitcase that he always kept packed in case he had to leave in a minutes noticed. He carried the suitcase out to his car and put it in the trunk. He walked back into his house and checked one last time to be certain that everything was turned off. He set the alarm to his house and locked the front door on his way out. He walked over to his car and climbed in behind the wheel, inserted the key into the ignition and turned on the car. He carefully backed the car out of the driveway and drove off.

William Hastings lived only a few miles from the CIA Headquarters, so it didn't take him long to get there. When he arrived, he parked his car in the secured parking lot. He locked his car and proceeded to the entrance. He went through the security checkpoint and continued to the director's office.

He entered the director's office and walked up to the desk where a young lady was sitting typing something on her computer. "You must be Mary?" He asked.

"The young lady stopped what she was doing and looked at William Hastings. "You must be Mr. Hastings."

"That I am."

"The director is waiting for you," She said while she picked up the telephone receiver and put it to her ear, and then pushed the intercom button on the telephone in front of her.

"Yes," The director said when he answered the intercom call.

"Sir, Mr. Hastings is here."

"Send him in," The director ordered, and then he canceled the intercom call.

"The director will see you now," she said while she returned the telephone receiver to its resting place and got up from her seat.

Mary walked over to the door and opened it. William Hastings entered the director's office, and she closed the door.

CIA Director, Robert Müller, got up from his seat behind his desk and walked over to William Hastings, and they shook hands. "I'm sorry for the short notice on this one Bill," Director Müller said while he returned to his seat behind his desk. "But something has come up."

"I figured it was another assignment," Hastings commented while he sat in the chair, in front of Director Müller's desk. "I must say, sir; I'm surprised that you wanted to see me personally."

"This is not a normal assignment," Director Müller pointed out. "I needed a good man for this job, and you came highly recommended to me from several people."

"I'm flattered," Hastings remarked.

"Bill, I'll get right to the point. I'm sending you to the consulate at Puerto Obaldia, Panama to take over the job of Station Chief there."

"Station Chief!" Hastings said, surprised at his new assignment. "I'm honored sir; but why me?"

"You've earned it Bill," Director Müller pointed out. "Bill, things are starting to heat-up down there, and I need someone in charge that I can count on to get me the information I need."

"How bad is it?"

"I'm not sure yet. All I know is that there's been a lot of radio chatter between General Juarez and his troop commanders along the border."

"He's planning something."

"Yes, he is, but what, I don't know."

"What does President Matthews have to say about this?"

"President Matthews doesn't give a shit about anything. Like the president before him, all he's concerned about it finishing up the last few days he has left in office. It's going to be up to us to get the new president up-to-speed on what's going on down there when he takes office."

"I understand, sir. When do I leave?"

"Right now; there's a jet waiting for you at Langley Air Force Base. Bill, watch your ass down there."

"I'll keep my eyes open," Hastings acknowledged and got up from his seat. He left Director Müller's office and closed the door.

Hastings hurried back to where he parked his car and unlocked the driver's side door. He climbed in behind the wheel and started his car, and backed out of his parking space. He drove out of the CIA Headquarters and headed toward Langley Air Force Base.

William Hastings arrived at the main gate to Langley Air Force Base in record time. He showed the guard at the gate his credentials. The guard motioned to the Humvee that was parked off to the side, and two men got out dressed in full combat dress with their M-4 carbine rifles in hand.

"Pull your vehicle over to the side next to the Humvee," the guard instructed Hastings. "Leave your keys in the vehicle. The two men in the Humvee will take you to where you need to go."

Hastings did as he was instructed to do. He parked his car and turned it off, and popped the trunk before he got out. He walked to the back of his car and removed his travel bag from the trunk, and then closed the trunk. He walked over to the Humvee and got into the backseat. The two men got into the front seat, and they drove off.

A few minutes later, the Humvee stopped in front of a Gulfstream G550 twin-engine jet aircraft. Hastings grabbed his bag and got out of the Humvee. He boarded the aircraft while the Humvee drove off.

"Hello, Mr. Hastings," the young woman who was standing in front of Hastings said. "Just take a seat and make yourself comfortable; we'll be taking off shortly."

Hastings sat down and fastened his seat belt. He went to reach for a magazine when his old friend Michael Lawrence boarded the aircraft. Lawrence noticed Hastings and walked over, and sat down across from him.

"How's it going Mike?" Hastings asked. "I see they finally kicked your ass out of Afghanistan.

"I'm good," Lawrence replied while he sat down, and fastened his seat belt. "I've been reassigned to the station at Puerto Obaldia Panama; what about you?"

Hastings cracked a smile. "I was assigned the Station Chief post at Puerto Obaldia Panama. I guess that means I'm going to be your boss."

"Yeah, I guess so," Lawrence reluctantly commented.

The Gulfstream G550 twin-engine jet aircraft fired up its jet engines and began to move. Seconds later, the aircraft began to pick up speed and leave the ground.

* * * * *

Eight Days Later
Oklahoma City, Oklahoma

Colonel Wilson had no sooner cleared the main gate to Tinker Air Force Base, when his cell phone in his shirt pocket rang. He removed his cell phone and looked at the caller ID as he pulled his black colored Cadillac Escalade into the visitors' parking area. He parked the Escalade in the first space he saw that was empty, and then turned off the engine. He opened his cell phone and pushed the talk button before putting it to his ear. "What's up?"

"I need to see you," a man's voice said. "I have something that I know will interest you," the man continued. "How soon can you meet me at the Federal Building?"

"I can be there in about twenty minutes."

"Good; I will alert security to expect you. When you get here, tell security that you're here to see Mr. Samson."

"I'll see you when I get there Mr. Samson," Colonel Wilson said, and then he closed his cell phone to end the call. He then powered down the cell phone and returned it to his shirt pocket. He started up the Escalade and backed out of the parking space, and headed back to the main gate.

He drove out of the main gate and headed toward the Federal Building in Oklahoma City. When he arrived at the Federal Building, he pulled into the visitors' parking area and parked. He got out of the Escalade and closed the door. He walked to the entrance to the Federal Building and entered.

Colonel Wilson walked over to a security officer who was standing off to the side of the security check in area. He removed his military credentials from his back pants pocket and presented it to the security officer. "I'm here to see Mr. Samson."

"Yes, he's expecting you Mr. Wilson. If you'll follow me, I'll take you to the conference room where he's waiting for you."

Colonel Wilson followed the security officer down the hallway. They stopped in front of a door, and the security officer opened the door. 'I'll be right here when you're done," he said as Colonel Wilson stepped inside. "I'll escort you back to the lobby when you're done," he continued, and then he closed the door.

"What's up with all this cloak and dagger shit?" Colonel Wilson asked while he walked over to the table where Mr. Samson was sitting.

"Believe me Wilson it's necessary," Mr. Samson answered while Colonel Wilson sat in a chair at the table. "I don't need anyone asking questions about our meeting."

"Okay. Now, what's up?"

"As I'm sure you know by now, eight days ago, a CIA surveillance team in Ormara, Pakistan reported that A'zam al Shammari and six of his al-Qaeda followers, along with the VX nerve gas, boarded a freighter bound for Iran."

"Yes, I read the report."

"What you don't know is that the freighter never went to Iran. Instead, it went to Bandarbeyla, Somalia."

"So, what you're saying is that Shammari did not go to Iran; he's in Somalia?"

"He wasn't on the freighter, nor was the VX nerve gas when the freighter reached Bandarbeyla."

"Then where in the hell is he? Better yet, where's the VX?"

"No one knows. It's believed that the Iranian freighter rendezvoused with another ship somewhere in the Indian Ocean. That would explain why the ship arrived at Bandarbeyla two days late."

"I got a bad feeling about this," Colonel Wilson commented. "Shammari could pop up anywhere in the world without any notice. He can rip us a new ass, and before we figure out what happened, he could disappear again. One thing's for sure, no matter where he shows up at; innocent people are going to die. I have no doubt that he is on a mission; and that he has already chosen his target."

"Wilson, I wish I could help you, but I've been told to stay away from this one."

"I understand," Colonel Wilson said as he got up from his seat. "I appreciate you giving me the heads-up on this one. I assure you; no one will know that we had this talk."

"Watch where you step Wilson," Mr. Samson warned as he got up from his seat. "I got a bad feeling about this one."

"So do I," Colonel Wilson remarked while he walked over to the door. He opened the door and stepped out into the hallway, and closed the door. He followed the security officer down the corridor to the main lobby and exited the federal building.

He hurried back to the visitors' parking area where his Cadillac Escalade was parked. He got into the Escalade and closed the door. He started the Escalade and backed out of the parking space. *Something just isn't right about this;* he thought as he pulled onto the ramp to the interstate.

Colonel Wilson drove back to Tinker Air Force Base and stopped at the main gate. He showed the guard his credentials and was allowed to continue. He turned into the visitors' parking area and parked his Escalade next to a Humvee. He got out of his Escalade and got in the Humvee on the driver's side. He took his cell phone out of his pocket and turned it on before he started up the Humvee, and headed back to the Strike Force facility.

When Colonel Wilson arrived at the main gate to the Strike Force facility, he showed his identification badge to the guard and was allowed to continue on his way. He parked the Humvee in front of the main building and got out. He entered the building and hurried to his office. He walked over to his desk and sat down in his chair.

He turned on his computer monitor and waited for it to warm up before he logged onto the system. He opened his e-mail program to see if he had received any messages while he was out. *Well, so much for that,* he thought when he discovered that he had no new messages. He closed the e-mail program and logged off the system, and powered-down the computer monitor. He started to get up from his seat when Captain Hale entered his office.

"Wolverine, I have the latest from Camp Freedom in Panama," Captain Hale said, referring to the folder he was holding in his hand.

"Anything new about this person they refer to as the American or the visitor?" Colonel Wilson inquired as he returned to his seat.

"They're still trying to figure it out," Captain Hale answered while he walked over to Colonel Wilson's desk and handed Colonel Wilson the folder.

"You know; it could be the person they call the American and the visitor are the same person," Colonel Wilson pointed out as he put the folder down on his desk. "They could be trying to confuse us."

"Or, it could be that they are two separate people," Captain Hale was quick to point out as he sat down in the chair that was in front of Colonel Wilson's desk. "Anyway, whoever this visitor is, they're due to arrive in Colombia soon."

"Wolverine, I'm sorry for the intrusion, but we have a problem," Operations Specialist First Lieutenant Kate Stanton, nicknamed Barbie because of her blonde colored hair and her Barbie shaped figure, said; who was standing in the doorway to Colonel Wilson's office.

"What kind of a problem?" Captain Hale was quick to ask before Colonel Wilson could utter a word.

"A large portion of northern Colombia has just gone dark," Lieutenant Stanton answered as she stepped into Colonel Wilson's office. "Our satellites are picking up nothing from that area."

"How can that be?" Colonel Wilson demanded to know. "Is there something wrong with our equipment?"

"I've checked everything here, and our equipment is in proper working order," Lieutenant Stanton answered.

"What about the CIA and NSA satellites," Colonel Wilson asked.

"They're experiencing the same problem with their satellites as we are. Wolverine, someone down there has gotten their hands on some military-grade satellite jammers; similar to the ones we use around the perimeter of our compound here."

"Do we know of any satellite jammers that are unaccounted for?" Captain Hale curiously asked.

"Five days ago six satellite jammers and two mobile command stations were reported stolen from Fort Bliss in Texas," Lieutenant Stanton answered.

"Why haven't I heard about this before now?" Colonel Wilson snapped.

"I just found out about this a few minutes ago," Lieutenant Stanton fired back. "I was told that the CID (Army Criminal Investigation Command (USACIDC) were looking into the theft before the AI (Army Intelligence) stepped in and took over the investigation because of a suspected link to an international terrorist organization."

"You mean al-Qaeda?" Captain Hale asked.

"They didn't say."

"That's just fuckin' great," Colonel Wilson remarked.

"I guess we know where to start looking for the missing hardware," Captain Hale pointed out.

"Is there anything else you need to report?" Colonel Wilson calmly asked Lieutenant Stanton.

"No, I think that covers it for now," she answered.

"Let me know the minute anything changes," Colonel Wilson ordered.

"No problem," Lieutenant Stanton acknowledged, and then she left Colonel Wilson's office and closed the office door on her way out.

"This satellite problem might present a problem for us," Colonel Wilson pointed out to Captain Hale. "I don't like not being able to see what's going on down there. I want you to look into this and find out all you can about what's going on with the investigation at Fort Bliss."

"I'll get right on it," Captain Hale said as he got up from his seat. "I'll let you know the minute I come up with something," he continued while he walked to the office door. He opened the door and exited Colonel Wilson's office.

Let's see what Maverick has for me today; Colonel Wilson thought as he opened the folder on his desk and began to read through the report that Captain Hale had given him.

* * * * *

North Pacific Ocean
Twenty Nautical Miles Off The Coast Of Juradó, Colombia

The Liberian freighter that was carrying A'zam al Shammari and several medium-size, steel cylinder canisters of VX nerve gas; along with six of his faithful followers, dropped the ship's anchor. "We dare not get any closer," the captain said to Shammari in Arabic. "It is safer out here," he continued. "The patrol boats that patrol this area will not come out into international waters. Arrangements have been made for a fishing boat to meet us here and take you and your people to shore."

"Is that safe?" Shammari asked, speaking in Arabic.

"The patrol boats do not mess with the fishing boats," the captain answered. "You have nothing to worry about. The boat should be here shortly."

"I get the impression that you have done this before?"

"A few times."

"So, we wait?"

"Yes, but not for long." The captain answered as he pointed to a boat that was approaching the freighter.

"Is that our boat?"

"We will know in a minute," the captain answered. "They should be signaling us shortly." The captain was silent and waited for the approaching boat to flash the proper signal with their signaling light. "Yep, that is your boat," the captain continued when the approaching boat flashed the correct signal.

"I am grateful for all you have done for us," Shammari said as he walked over to the captain.

"May Allah keep you safe on the next leg of your journey," the captain said as he shook hands with Shammari.

Shammari walked over to his long-time faithful friend Easau, who was standing on the other side of the bridge, and together they watched as a medium-sized fishing boat approached. "Our long journey is almost at an end my friend," he said to Easau in Arabic. "Allah has blessed us with another safe journey."

"That he has," Easau remarked. "May he watch over us in this new land?"

Shammari looked at Easau and smiled. "I have no doubt that he will."

Shammari walked off the bridge, and Easau followed him down to the deck of the ship while the fishing boat positioned itself alongside the freighter. They watched while the medium-sized, cylinder canisters that contained the VX nerve gas was hoisted down onto the deck of the fishing boat; and then properly secured. "Easau, round up our people; it's time for us to leave."

The captain ordered the ship's ladder to be lowered while Shammari waited for Easau to return. When Easau returned with the rest of the group, he handed Shammari an AK-47 assault rifle. Shammari hung the rifle on his shoulder, as did the rest of his people. They followed Shammari down the ladder and boarded the fishing boat at the bottom of the ladder.

"I'm glad to see that you made it," a man said in English, who was standing behind Shammari.

I know this voice; Shammari thought while he turned around to see who was speaking to him. He was surprised to see the Colombian man that he had met with at the safe house in Chitral, Pakistan standing a few feet away from him. "What a pleasant surprise," Shammari said in English as he shook hands with the Colombian man. "I was not expecting you to greet us on our arrival. Is there a problem?"

"No problem. I just thought it would be best if I met you when you and your people arrived," the Colombian man answered.

"Have you heard from the American?"

"He is waiting for us at the base camp. He has the documents that you requested, and we have the lab equipment that you will need to continue your work.

"Excellent."

"General, we need to get everyone below, and get going so we can avoid the patrol boats," the captain of the fishing boat hollered down from the bridge in Spanish."

"I understand, Captain," the Colombian man hollered back in Spanish. "You may leave when ready."

"You are a general?" Shammari surprisingly asked in English.

"I did not know that you spoke my language," the Colombian man answered in English.

"I do not speak Spanish, but I know what general means."

"Come, let us get below deck. It is too dangerous for us to stay up here. I will explain everything to you when we get below."

Shammari and his men followed the Colombian man into the lower deck of the fishing boat, and one of the fishermen topside secured the entryway.

"I am General Fresco Juarez; Commander of the Revolutionary Armed Forces of Colombia," the Colombian man announced. "I apologize for the deception, but it was a necessary security measure to ensure my safety, as well as yours."

"Why did you not tell me who you were when we met in Pakistan?"

"I wanted to meet you in person without drawing any attention to either of us. You are too important of an ally for me to have trusted the meeting to one of my subordinates."

Shammari cracked a smile. "I would have done the same thing myself. We think alike; you and I."

"We are going to accomplish many good things together," General Juarez pointed out.

Maybe; Shammari thought. He grabbed onto the table next to him when he felt the fishing boat move as it pulled away from the freighter. Seconds later, the fishing boat began to pick up speed and head towards Juradó.

With the fishing boat leaving the area, the captain of the freighter ordered his crew to prepare the ship to get underway. The ladder and the ship's anchor were raised back to their normal resting places and secured properly before the ship began to pick up speed and continued up the coast to its final destination.

Chapter 7

General Richwood finished going over the latest reports from the Strike Force team at Camp Freedom when the office door suddenly opened, and President Mathews entered. General Richwood quickly jumped to his feet and stood at attention.

"Have a seat," President Mathews said while he closed the door.

General Richwood returned to his seat while President Mathews walked over and sat down in one of the chairs in front of the general's desk.

"Any news about where Shammari and his companions are heading?" President Mathews asked.

"At this time, no one is sure of anything," General Richwood replied. "I'm certain Mr. President that whatever Shammari is up to it has to be something important, or he wouldn't have left his safe-haven in Pakistan."

"Yes, but what?"

"We don't know yet. We're still looking into it. Sir, it's going to take some time to figure this out."

"When it comes to al-Qaeda general, time is one thing we don't have," President Matthews was quick to point out. "Put Colonel Wilson on this. I don't care what it takes, or what he has to do, but get me some answers."

"Yes, Mr. President," General Richwood acknowledged.

"Anything new from our boys at Camp Freedom?" President Mathews inquired.

"Nothing new," General Richwood replied.

"General, can Strike Force monitor the situation down there from Strike Force Command?"

"Yes, they can."

"Our boys have been down there long enough. Bring them back home ASAP. Let the CIA and NSA handle it down there for a while," President Matthews said while he got up from his seat.

General Richwood jumped up from his seat and snapped President Matthews a salute. "I'll issue the recall order immediately, sir."

President Matthews walked over to the door and stopped. He turned around to face General Richwood and said, "General if I don't see you again before I leave office, I want you to know that it has been a pleasure working with you." He turned back around and opened the door. Without waiting for General Richwood's reply, President Matthews left the general's office and closed the door.

"It has been a pleasure working with you to Mr. President," General Richwood mumbled while he returned to his seat. He picked up the telephone receiver from the telephone on his desk and put it to his ear while he dialed Colonel Wilson's telephone number.

"Wilson," Colonel Wilson said with a sharp tone in his voice.

"Wilson, President Matthews wants you to recall Sparrow ASAP. He wants the CIA and NSA to run things down there."

"Yes, sir, I'll issue the recall immediately." Before Colonel Wilson could say another word, the line went dead. "I hate it when he does that," Colonel Wilson remarked while he returned the telephone receiver to the telephone on his desk. "The man never says goodbye before he ends a call."

"I take it that was General Richwood on the telephone," Captain Hale said, who was sitting in the chair in front of Colonel Wilson's desk.

Colonel Wilson looked at Captain Hale and nodded. "President Matthews has ordered Sparrow back home. He's going to let the CIA and NSA take over the surveillance operation."

"Wolverine, you and I both know that something is brewing down there," Captain Hale was quick to point out. "When the shit hits the fan down there, we're going to wish we kept our people there."

"I don't like it any more than you do Bulldog, but we have our orders from the president," Colonel Wilson shot back. "We have to abide by his decision and follow his orders. I'm sure President Matthews has his reasons." Colonel Wilson hesitated for a few seconds before he continued. "I want you to issue the order to recall our people at Camp Freedom. We'll figure the rest out later."

"I'll get right on it," Captain Hale acknowledged while he got up from his seat. "I want to go on the record, and point out that I believe this is a mistake." He continued to say while he walked over to the office door.

"So noted," Colonel Wilson remarked while Captain Hale opened the door and stepped out of the office, and closed the door.

Three Days Later

Colonel Wilson was sitting behind his desk enjoying a cup of coffee when Lieutenant Johnson entered his office and closed the door. "Bulldog said you wanted to see me," He said while he walked over to the chair in front of the Colonel's desk and sat down. "He said it was important."

"I wanted to talk to you about your final report from Camp Freedom before I submit it to General Richwood."

"It's all there in my report."

"Bullshit Maverick," Colonel Wilson fired back. "This report has more holes in it than a piece of Swiss cheese. I'm not sending this to General Richwood. I want to know what's not in this report."

"The content of my report is what I know for sure. I left a few things out because I have no proof. All I have is a theory, not facts, and I could be wrong."

"What's your theory Maverick?" Colonel Wilson demanded to know.

"I believe that the person known as the visitor is A'zam al Shammari. I think that he has teamed up with General Fresco Juarez and his rebel army in Colombia and that Shammari and Juarez are planning an attack using the VX nerve gas that we know Shammari can manufacture." Lieutenant Johnson answered. "However, I can't prove any of this; it's just a theory that I came up with."

"A damn good theory I would say," Colonel Wilson added. "But what's the target?"

I'm not sure," Lieutenant Johnson answered. "My guess would be somewhere along the Panamanian and Colombian border for starters. We have two prime targets on the Panamanian side of the border."

"So you think that Shammari and Juarez have joined forces and that they are planning to launch an attack against us?" Colonel Wilson asked.

"What better way to start an international incident so that they can go after their real target."

"Do you have any idea what their real target might be?" Colonel Wilson asked.

"I haven't figured that out yet," Lieutenant Johnson answered. "I'm certain that if Shammari and his al-Qaeda companions have anything to say about it; it's going to be a big event."

"It sure would be nice to know where they're going to strike and when," Colonel Wilson commented.

"I wish I could tell you, but I have no clue," Lieutenant Johnson answered.

"I want you to put this theory of yours in your report," Colonel Wilson said. "Maybe General Richwood can come up with something."

"I'll have my revised report on your desk by the end of the day," Lieutenant Johnson said while he jumped to his feet. He hurried over to the office door and opened it. He left the office and closed the door.

Shortly after Lieutenant Johnson left Colonel Wilson's office, Captain Hale entered. "Where's Maverick off to in a big hurry?" Captain Hale inquired while he closed the office door.

"I told him to revise his final report from Camp Freedom and include his theory about why A'zam al Shammari would be in Colombia."

"Shammari is in Colombia? Does he have any proof of this?"

"Not really; Maverick believes that A'zam al Shammari is in Colombia and has teamed up with General Juarez and that they're planning their first strike along the Panamanian and Colombian border."

"That makes sense to me," Captain Hale commented.

"Yes, but proving it isn't going to be easy, and the clock is ticking."

"Does President Matthews know about this new development? Has he taken any precautionary measures?"

"President Matthews is on his way out of office, and he probably doesn't give a fuck what's going to happen anyway," Colonel Wilson calmly said.

"I think that we still need to find Shammari and put his murdering ass down for good," Captain Hale commented. "The world would be a lot safer without him in it."

"Well, that's not going to happen anytime soon while Matthews is in office," Colonel Wilson pointed out. "Maybe this new president will take the Shammari threat more seriously and deal with the problem."

"Yeah, maybe," Captain Hale remarked.

"Are you making any headway on who compromised our last mission in Afghanistan?" Colonel Wilson asked. "Do you have any idea who was behind it?"

"Not yet," Captain Hale answered. "I did, however, find out that the CIA director had William Hastings, and Michael Lawrence transferred from Afghanistan to the consulate at Puerto Obaldia Panama. The director made Hastings Station Chief."

"Why is that important?" Colonel Wilson curiously asked. "Do you think Hastings and Lawrence had something to do with the mission being compromised?"

"No, I don't think they were involved," Captain Hale replied. "I just thought it was odd that the two of them would be transferred to the same post on the same day."

"Yes, I see your point."

"I'll keep looking into this," Captain Hale assured Colonel Wilson. "Is there anything else you need?"

"No, just keep me posted on your progress."

Captain Hale got up from his seat and left the office. He ran into Lieutenant Johnson, who was heading to Colonel Wilson's office in a hurry. "Woo cowboy; where the fuck is the fire?" Captain Hale asked.

"Sorry Bulldog," Lieutenant Johnson said. "I just wanted to get this revised report to Wolverine, so he could get it out to General Richwood."

"Slow down, Wolverine will still be there when you get there," Captain Hale said and walked away.

Lieutenant Johnson continued at a normal pace to Colonel Wilson's office. He stood in the doorway and knocked before he entered the room. "I have revised my report like you asked me to do." He said while he walked over to Colonel Wilson's desk and placed the folder that contained his report down on the desk in front of Colonel Wilson.

"Thanks, Maverick; I'll let you know if I should have any questions about your report."

"You know where to find me," Lieutenant Johnson commented and left Colonel Wilson's office.

Colonel Wilson opened the folder and began to read over Lieutenant Johnson's revised report. When he was finished, he closed the folder. He looked up and saw Lieutenant McDonald standing in the doorway. "How long have you been standing there?"

"Not long," Lieutenant McDonald answered. "I was wondering if you had a few minutes to spare."

"Sure; what do you need?"

"I understand that you have Bulldog looking into who might have compromised our last mission in Afghanistan," Lieutenant McDonald said while he entered the office and closed the door. He walked over to Colonel Wilson's desk and sat down in the chair, in front of the desk. "We have finally finished translating all the documents that we seized from that raid. I think I know who compromised our mission."

"Go on; I'm listening," Colonel Wilson said anxiously. "Who do you think it was?"

"I'm certain that Bill Riley; the CIA Station Chief in Kabul, Afghanistan sold us out," Lieutenant McDonald continued. "I have proof that Riley was selling al-Qaeda information. The bad news is he was killed in Kabul two days ago by a car bomb."

"Are you sure about this?" Colonel Wilson surprisingly asked.

"Yes, I am," Lieutenant McDonald answered. "I have no doubt in my mind," he continued while he sat the folder that he had in his hand down in front of Colonel Wilson. "It's all there in that folder."

"That would explain why William Hastings and Michael Lawrence were transferred to the consulate at Puerto Obaldia Panama," Colonel Wilson commented. "The CIA director must have found out about this, and he's trying to cover it up."

"I want to go on the record and state that I know William Hastings and Michael Lawrence very well; they are both good men," Lieutenant McDonald pointed out.

"Is it possible that they knew what Riley was doing?"

"I can't find any evidence to support that they knew anything," Lieutenant McDonald answered. "However, knowing the two of them, it's possible that one or both of them might have figured it out."

"I want you to say nothing to anyone about this. I will talk to General Richwood and see how he wants to handle this."

"I understand," Lieutenant McDonald acknowledged and got up out of his seat. "Is there anything else?"

"Yes, there is; do me a favor and stop by Bulldog's office and tell him I want to see him."

"I sure will," Lieutenant McDonald said and headed toward the door. He opened the door and left Colonel Wilson's office.

Colonel Wilson opened the folder that Lieutenant McDonald had given him and read each page carefully. He had just finished reading the last page when Captain Hale entered the office.

"Popeye said you wanted to see me."

"Yes, I did; close the door and have a seat."

Captain Hale closed the office door and walked over to the chair in front of Colonel Wilson's desk, and sat down. "What's up?"

Colonel Wilson handed Captain Hale the folder that Lieutenant McDonald had given him. "Read that and tell me what you think."

Captain Hale opened the folder and read through its contents. When he was done, he sat the folder down on Colonel Wilson's desk. "I must say; Popeye has done his homework. I guess I can stop investigating this; looks like we found our traitor."

"I want you to keep investigating this just to be certain that we have the right person."

"You think this information was a plant?"

"It's possible," Colonel Wilson answered, "That's what I want you to find out. I want to know how this Bill Riley knew about that operation."

"You think someone here told him?"

"I think it would be worth looking into don't you?" Colonel Wilson asked.

"I'll keep looking, and I'll let you know what I find out," Captain

Hale said and got up from his seat. "If you'll excuse me, I have a few things that I need to take care of."

"Bulldog, close the door on your way out."

Captain Hale walked over to the door and opened it. He left Colonel Wilson's office and closed the door.

Colonel Wilson picked up the telephone receiver from the telephone on his desk. He dialed the pager number for his personal assistant, Second Lieutenant Samantha Cooltrain while he put the receiver to his ear. He waited for the pager to answer his call before he returned the telephone receiver to his telephone.

Less than a minute later, Lieutenant Cooltrain entered Colonel Wilson's office and walked over to his desk. "You rang."

Colonel Wilson grabbed the folder from his desk that contained Lieutenant Johnson's revised report and handed it to Lieutenant Cooltrain. "Take that to Raven and have her code the folder's contents, and then take it to communications and have it sent to General Richwood a-sap,"

"Is there anything else you need?"

"No, just get that report sent to General Richwood."

Colonel Wilson sat in his seat and watched as Lieutenant Cooltrain exited his office and closed the door. He looked at the crisis board on the wall. *Shammari, if you 're in Colombia, I'll find your ass.* He thought. He got up from his seat and hurried out of his office.

∗ ∗ ∗ ∗ ∗

Twenty kilometers from Puerto Obaldia on the Colombian side of the border, CIA operatives, Diego Romero and Jose Martinez, dressed in jungle camouflage clothing and armed with M4-A1 assault rifles, laid on the ground and watched through their night-vision binoculars from a distance as the Revolutionary Armed Forces of Colombia set up a defensive perimeter around their camp.

"They've never set up camp this close to the border before," Martinez said to Romero. "Something big is brewing."

"Yeah, but what?" Romero asked.

"Whatever it is; it can't be good," Martinez answered.

Romero and Martinez watched several trucks arrive at the camp and offloaded men and supplies. A few minutes later, an old US Army Jeep pulled up in front of what appeared to be the command tent. They were both surprised to see General Fresco Juarez, Commander of the Revolutionary Armed Forces of Colombia and A'zam al Shammari, get out of the Jeep and go inside.

"So, Shammari is in Colombia," Romero remarked. "I got a bad feeling about this."

"I don't like it either, but we need to get closer to that camp, and see if we can find out what the two of them are up too," Martinez pointed out.

Romero nodded, indicating he understood what Martinez had said, and they began to move towards the camp, careful not to alert the sentries guarding the perimeter that someone was approaching.

The moonless night assisted Martinez and Romero in slipping past the perimeter sentries without being detected. They continued to move closer to the camp when Martinez suddenly hand signaled Romero to stop. He pointed down to the ground and showed him the trip wire that he spotted in front of them. Romero gave Martinez the thumbs-up sign, and they continued on, stepping over the trip wire.

Martinez and Romero quietly entered the camp and hurried to what they thought was the supply tent, being careful not to get caught in the process. They slipped past the guard that was posted at the entrance and entered. Martinez was quick to realize that they were not in a supply tent. After inspecting a couple of crates, Martinez and Romero had no doubt that the tent was being used to store weapons and ammunition.

They began taking a quick inventory of what was in the tent until Martinez and Romero heard some soldiers talking in their native tongue outside the entrance. They took cover behind some crates at the back of the tent in case one of them entered the tent and quietly listened; understanding everything the soldiers were saying.

After a few minutes, Martinez and Romero knew what General Juarez and the Revolutionary Armed Forces of Colombia was doing in the area. Martinez knew that they had to get out of there and report what they had discovered. He took out his knife and cut a slit in the back of the tent. They exited the tent and hurried out of the camp.

A few kilometers, down the road a six-man night patrol, armed with AK-47 assault rifles spotted Martinez and Romero running down the road. A warning shot was fired into the air, and Martinez and Romero were ordered to halt. They stopped briefly and turned around firing two three-round bursts from their M4-A1 rifles, dropping four of their pursuers. The two remaining soldiers stopped pursuing Martinez and Romero and waited for reinforcements to arrive before they continued their pursuit.

When Martinez and Romero arrived at the spot where they had left their vehicle, their pursuers were right behind them and gaining ground. Martinez quickly removed the camouflage from around the vehicle while Romero opened fire with his M4-A1 rifle on the advancing soldiers, hoping to buy some much-needed time for their escape.

"Let's get the fuck out of here," Martinez shouted in Spanish.

"Right behind you," Romero acknowledged, also speaking in Spanish.

With bullets bouncing off their vehicle, Martinez jumped in on the driver side and started up the vehicle while closing his door. Meanwhile, Romero got in on the passenger side. Martinez put the vehicle in gear and sped off while Romero closed the passenger side door. Martinez stepped on the gas and picked up speed. He headed south, away from the border. After a few moments, he turned on the headlights, so he could see the road better.

"Did I hear them right back there?" Romero asked. "Those bastards are planning to attack the consulate at Puerto Obaldia?"

"Yes, you did," Martinez answered.

"We need to let Langley know what's going on," Romero pointed out. "Those poor bastards at Puerto Obaldia won't stand a chance in hell."

"See if you can get someone on the satellite radio," Martinez said as he looked in his rear-view mirror and noticed that no one was following them.

"You know damn well that our station won't answer," Romero shot back.

"Use the emergency code," Martinez instructed Romero.

Romero grabbed the satellite radio from the back seat. "Damn it," he said when he noticed a bullet hole in the satellite radio. "The fuckin' radio has a bullet hole in it. We're not calling anyone on this."

"Oh shit," Martinez said, noticing that a tree had fallen across the road. He slammed on the car breaks, bringing the vehicle to a screeching halt.

Suddenly, automatic rifle fire erupted from the tree line on both sides of the road, riddling their vehicle with a wall of bullets, killing Martinez and Romero.

"Stop firing," someone yelled out in Spanish, and the gunfire stopped.

Several members of the Revolutionary Armed Forces emerged from their cover and moved toward the vehicle. They pulled the bodies of Martinez and Romero from the vehicle and began searching through its contents. The lieutenant in command watched while his soldiers ransacked the vehicle.

"What is this?" A soldier remarked in Spanish when he pulled the satellite telephone from the pocket of Romero's dead body. The soldiers flipped open the satellite phone and turned it on. He smiled when it powered up and saw that it was in working order. He put the satellite telephone to his ear and heard someone on the other end was speaking in English. He ran over to the lieutenant and showed him what he had found.

"Was this on when you found it?" The lieutenant asked while taking the satellite telephone from the soldier.

"No, sir, I turned it on to see if it worked."

The lieutenant put the satellite telephone to his ear and heard someone speaking in English. He quickly threw it down on the ground and stomped it with the heel of his boot. He backed up and pulled out his forty-five sidearm, and fired three rounds into the satellite phone.

"Did I do something wrong, sir?" The soldier asked.

"It was an honest mistake," The lieutenant answered while he picked up the satellite telephone and made sure that it no longer worked. "Just be more careful next time."

"Yes, sir," the soldier acknowledged and went back to help his comrades search the vehicle.

"Don't turn anything on," the lieutenant yelled out. "If you find something, bring it to me."

A Jeep pulled up with a colonel seated on the passenger side. The lieutenant quickly ran over to the Jeep to make his report. He showed the colonel the satellite telephone and explained why there were bullet holes in it.

"Oh," the colonel said while he took the shot-up satellite telephone from the lieutenant. "I want you to get this mess cleaned up, and then get back to your patrol area."

"Yes, sir," the lieutenant acknowledged. He saluted the colonel and hurried off, barking orders to his men.

The colonel ordered the driver to turn the Jeep around, and head back to their camp. When they entered the camp, the driver stopped the Jeep in front of the command tent. The colonel jumped out and hurried inside, with the satellite telephone in hand. He walked up to the table where General Juarez and A'zam al Shammari were sitting and snapped to attention. "General, we have a problem," he reported while saluting the general.

"Did our perimeter patrol catch the two intruders that fled our camp?" The general asked in Spanish while returning the colonel's salute.

"Yes, sir, they did," the colonel answered in Spanish. "This was found in their vehicle," he continued, placing the satellite telephone down on the table in front of the general. "The person on the other end was speaking English. Fearing that it might give our location away, the lieutenant put a couple of rounds in it."

"Continue making final preparations; the operation continues as planned," General Juarez instructed the colonel. "We've come too far to postpone our plans."

"Yes, sir," the colonel replied. He saluted General Juarez and left the command tent.

"Is there a problem?" Shammari asked in English.

"No problem," General Juarez answered in English. "My people have neutralized the threat. There is nothing to worry about my friend."

"Do you think the Americans know where we are?" Shammari inquired.

"I doubt it. With the help of our American friend, we have blocked their satellites from spying on us. Do not worry. There is no way the Americans know what we are planning."

"I hope you are right about this," Shammari remarked as he got up from his seat. "I had better go and make sure the gas is ready to be transported," he concluded, and then he walked out of the tent.

Chapter 8

Puerto Obaldia, Panama

The sun was beginning to make its way over the horizon, bringing daylight to Puerto Obaldia, a small Panamanian coastal town near the Colombian border. With the rise in border crossings from Colombia, a hundred Panamanian National Border Service personnel set up an immigration check station at the border crossing. Their sole purpose was to protect Panama's borders by not allowing any contraband in or out of Panama.

The United States Consulate sat on a hill a few miles outside of town. It was surrounded by a twelve-foot stone wall with razor wire on top. Dusk to dawn security lights, motion detectors, and wireless surveillance cameras were placed every thirty feet on the inside perimeter of the wall.

The only entrance to the consulate was the main gates. There was one inbound and one outbound gate, which were made from one-inch thick iron rods. The gates were operated electronically from inside the security building located between the two gates. The external windows on the security building contained three-inch thick bulletproof glass, and the information counter inside was also enclosed with three-inch thick bulletproof glass.

During regular business hours, visitors were required to check in with the security office before they were granted access to the consulate. Four members of the consulate's Marine Security Force dressed in full battle dress, including their M16-A4 rifles, provided security. After hours, the security office was manned by two members of the Marine Security Force also dressed in full combat dress with their M16-A4 assault rifles.

While a visitor was being processed in the security office, two additional members of the Marine security force, also dressed in full combat dress with their M16-A4 assault rifles, checked their vehicle to ensure that it was safe to continue on into the consulate.

Once a visitor was cleared to proceed into the consulate; they were given a visitor's pass, which they had to wear on their person at all times. They were instructed to park their vehicle in the east side parking lot and use the east entrance to enter the consulate.

Consulate staff members who live in town gained access to the consulate by showing their ID badge at the main entrance and had the proper decal sticker displayed on the windshield of their vehicle. Once the routine vehicle security check was completed, they were then allowed to continue to the staff parking lot, located in the back of the consulate, and enter the building through the back entryway.

Local vendors that supplied the consulate had to go through the same security checks as the consulate staff personnel. After receiving clearance to proceed, they made their deliveries at the loading docks located in the back of the consulate.

The west side parking lot was fenced in with a twelve foot electrified fence, equipped with a remote-controlled gate and reserved for the consulate's diplomatic vehicles. Access to the parking lot was the entrance on the west side of the consulate.

The driveway from the security office to the front entrance of the consulate was constructed in a horseshoe design with a beautiful water fountain in the middle. The front entryway, which was rarely used, was used by official visitors.

On the rooftop, there was a helicopter landing pad along with satellite communication dishes and security lights on the roof's perimeter. Motion detectors and wireless surveillance cameras were used on the rooftop for added security.

The Ambassador, Roger Meeks, along with his wife and three children, occupied the third floor of the consulate when they were staying there. The third floor could only be accessed by an elevator, which ran from the first floor to the roof. To gain access to the residence, a security code had to be entered into the keypad next to the control panel that operated the elevator.

The residence was equipped with a full-size kitchen, a good size dining room, and three large bedrooms, with its own bathroom for the children. The Master bedroom was a good size room with its own private his and her bath.

The second floor was where the Communication Center was located. It was adjacent to the NSA offices. The CIA offices occupied the remainder of the second floor. The only access to the second floor was an elevator on the west side of the consulate. A special key-card was needed to use the elevator.

Security was not as tight on the first floor. However, when the Ambassador was at the consulate conducting business, two members of the Marine Security Force, dressed in their Marine dress uniform, with a forty-five caliber sidearm on their hip, stood guard at the entrance to the Ambassador's office located on the southeast side of the consulate.

The consulate administration offices occupied the east side of the building. The surveillance room was located on the west side of the consulate next to the Marine Security Force barracks that housed seventy-five Marines; equipped with their own kitchen and dining area. The surveillance room could only be accessed by entering the correct code on the keypad next to the entrance door.

The formal dining hall, used only for special events and parties, was located in front of the main kitchen in the middle of the consulate.

As the sun began to gain strength, the town began to come alive as its residents prepared for another day. Local shop vendors were opening their stores for business, preparing for the day ahead. Traffic on the road to the consulate was moving at a moderate pace as the local residents who worked at the consulate made their way to work.

By mid-afternoon, the town was thriving; until fighting between a band of the Revolutionary Armed Forces of Colombia operating on the Colombian side of the border and the Colombian Army broke out a few miles from the border. The border crossing was quickly locked-down. The entire Panamanian National Border Service personnel stationed at Puerto Obaldia was on full alert in case the fighting should spill across the border.

The US Consulate was also locked-down, and the Marine Security Force was put on alert. They were dressed in full combat dress with their weapons ready for action. The front gates were secured; no one could enter or leave the consulate.

As the sun began to set, the fighting on the Colombian side of the border stopped, and the sound of gunfire could no longer be heard. A few hours later, the border crossing was reopened. As an added security measure, extra personnel had been assigned at the border crossing, and patrols along the border were increased.

It was a moonless night; a cool breeze was coming off the Caribbean Sea, a welcome relief after a hot, sunny day. The usual sounds of the local wildlife could be heard, making their presence known in the darkness; otherwise, it was a quiet night.

When all nonessential personnel that worked at the US consulate had gone home for the evening, the front gates were secured for the night. The roof top lights were switched on, illuminating the entire rooftop. With the aid of wireless surveillance cameras and motion detectors, it was thought to be impossible for an intruder to gain access to the rooftop undetected.

Marine guards who were assigned to nightly patrols began their routine of patrolling the grounds. They were in full combat dress, with their M16-A4 assault rifles ready, and prepared to repel or detain any intruder whom they might find on the grounds. They were authorized to take whatever action; they deemed necessary to keep the grounds secured.

Two experienced radio and surveillance personnel manned the surveillance room. Their only task was to monitor the live surveillance cameras feed and motion detectors. If an alarm should go off, or if the surveillance cameras should pick up something that was out of the ordinary, they were to report the incident to the Marine guards patrolling the consulate grounds over their wireless radio.

Although the sound of gunfire could no longer be heard, everyone at the consulate was still a little jumpy. The Communication Center on the second floor was busy translating the radio traffic that had been intercepted earlier. Once translated, it was transmitted to NSA headquarters in Fort Meade, Maryland, and the CIA headquarters in Langley, Virginia by satellite. Copies were also delivered to NSA

Operations Chief, James Dillon and the CIA Station Chief, William Hastings.

After receiving his copy of the transcripts, William Hastings sat behind his desk and went over every page of the report carefully. Afterwards, he picked up the telephone receiver from the telephone on his desk and dialed the extension number for NSA Operations Chief, James Dillon.

"Dillon," a voice said on the other end.

"Jim, Bill here. Have you read the transcripts yet?"

"Yeah Bill, I just got done reading it."

"What do you make of it?"

"What bothers me the most is that the fighting was so close to the border this time," Dillon replied. "I think something is up, and I got a bad feeling that whatever it is, it's heading our way."

"I agree," William Hastings acknowledged. "My agents in the field have told me the same thing. I'm waiting for Langley to..." The door to Hastings' office suddenly opened, and CIA Operative Michael Lawrence entered. "Jim I'll have to call you back," Hastings continued and then returned the telephone receiver to its resting place.

"I have an urgent message from Langley," Lawrence said as he walked over to William Hastings' desk. "It just came in a few minutes ago," he continued as he handed Hastings the message.

Hastings took the message from Lawrence, opened it, and read the message contents. "This doesn't make any sense," he mumbled aloud.

"What's up?" Lawrence asked.

Hastings looked at Lawrence bewildered. "I've been ordered back to Langley for a debriefing on the situation here. I'm leaving first thing in the morning. I should be back in a couple of days."

"Do you think Langley knows something that we don't know?" Lawrence asked.

"It's possible," Hastings replied. "But until I find out what's going on at Langley, I want you to inform our people working in the field that we will not be transmitting for the next couple of days. Also, as a precautionary measure, we will be changing over to code delta. They are not to act on any transmissions that they might receive in the old code. I want you to get this done immediately, and I want confirmation that our people have received the message."

"I'll get right on it," Lawrence acknowledged, and left the office.

Hastings started to pick up the telephone receiver from the telephone on his desk when his office door suddenly opened, and James Dillon entered. "We need to talk," he said as he closed the door. Dillon walked over to Hastings's desk and sat in the chair, in front of it. "Bill is there something going on that you're not sharing with me?"

"No, there's not," Hastings replied. "I just got word that I'm ordered back to Langley for a debriefing on the situation here. As a precautionary measure, I've ordered all CIA operations in the area halted until I get back from Langley. This is a CIA matter, and it doesn't concern you."

"I see," Dillon said as he stood up. "Have a nice trip," he continued and then left the office, slamming the door behind him.

Hastings sat behind his desk bewildered by Dillon's reaction to what he had just said. Meanwhile, Michael Lawrence entered his office and typed up the message that William Hastings wanted sent out. He then walked to the communications room. The Marine Security Guard at the door, dressed in full combat dress and armed with his M16-A4 assault rifle, opened the door, and Lawrence entered.

Lawrence walked over to one of the radio operators and handed him the coded message. "I need this sent out immediately. I'll wait for confirmation."

The radio operator took the message from Lawrence, and without delay, he sent the message. A few minutes later, each CIA operative that was operating along the border acknowledged receipt of the message from Lawrence.

With his task completed, Lawrence left the communication room. The Marine Security Guard closed the door, and Lawrence returned to his office. He sat behind his desk, picked up the telephone receiver from the telephone on his desk, and dialed the extension number for William Hastings.

"Hastings," William Hastings said when he answered the call.

"Lawrence here; the message has been sent out, and confirmation has been received."

"Good," Hastings acknowledged

"Sir, if it's okay with you, I'd like to take a couple of days off, so I can go visit some friends of mine in Panama City."

"Yes, take a couple of days off. If you hurry, you might be able to catch a ride with the ambassador and his family. They're heading back to Panama City," Hastings said. "Just be back here when I return," he concluded, and then the line suddenly went dead.

"Asshole," Lawrence said aloud. Lawrence opened his laptop computer on his desk. He opened the e-mail program and began typing. When he was finished, he sent the e-mail and waited for a reply. A few minutes later, the recipient acknowledged receiving Lawrence's e-mail.

Lawrence closed the e-mail program and then shut down his laptop computer. He put it in its carrying bag and zipped up the bag. He got up from his desk with the bag in hand and left his office, locking the door behind him. He headed up to the roof and arrived just in time to climb on board the Sikorsky CH-53 Sea Stallion helicopter before it lifted off, and headed towards Panama City.

∗ ∗ ∗ ∗ ∗

US Embassy
Bogotá, Colombia

NSA Operations Chief, Carmelita Martinez, A lovely thirty-five-year-old woman of Spanish-American descent, sat at her desk in her office at the US Embassy in Bogotá, Colombia. She couldn't help but worry about the agents that were working on a case near the Panamanian border.

Rosalyn Vasquez, Martinez's assistant and fellow NSA agent, also of Spanish-American descent, entered the office and closed the door. "A message has come in from our agents in the field," She said as she walked over to Carmelita's desk and handed her the message she was holding in her hand.

Carmelita read the entire message and then smiled. "They're chasing down a lead about a major weapons shipment by the border," she pointed out. "They hope to be back here in a couple of days."

"Do they have any idea what's going on around the border?" Rosalyn curiously asked.

"They don't say," Carmelita answered. "I guess we'll have to wait until they get back. I'm sure…" Carmelita abruptly stopped when there was a knock on the door.

The door opened, and thirty-six-year-old CIA Station Chief, John Marrow, entered, and closed the door. "I'm sorry Carmelita; I thought you were alone. I can come back later."

"No, that's okay," Carmelita shot back. "We can talk in front of Rosalyn."

"Do you have anyone operating by the Panamanian Border?" Marrow asked.

"I may have," Carmelita cautiously commented. "What's up?"

"I'm not sure," Marrow replied. "I just received an e-mail from a friend of mine at the Consulate in Puerto Obaldia. He says that there could be something brewing along the border. No one is sure of anything yet; it's just speculation."

"What's Langley saying about this?" Carmelita asked.

"Nothing; if they know anything, they're not telling anybody," Marrow pointed out. "Look, I got to go. Just let your people know to be extra careful up there. I'll see you ladies later." John Marrow quickly left the room without waiting for a response, and closed the door.

He hurried back to his office and entered. He closed the door and walked over to his desk. He sat down and quickly typed in his password to gain access to his computer. A few seconds later, he began printing out the documents he had received from Michael Lawrence at the Consulate in Puerto Obaldia.

When Marrow was finished printing out the documents, he logged off his computer and got up from his desk. He walked over to the printer and retrieved the printed documents. He then walked back to his desk and sat down. He took a large brown envelope from the desk center drawer and put the documents inside. He sealed the envelope shut and left the office, with the envelope in hand.

Marrow walked to the ambassador's office and entered. "Good morning beautiful," he said to Jennifer Masterson, the ambassador's personal secretary. "I need to see the ambassador." He informed her as he closed the door.

"I'll let the ambassador know you're here," Jennifer Masterson said and then pushed the intercom button for the ambassador.

"Yes," Ambassador Haskell answered.

"Mr. Ambassador I'm sorry for the intrusion," Masterson said. "Mr. Marrow wishes to see you."

"Send him in."

Marrow entered the ambassador's office with the large brown envelope in hand. Robert Haskell, the US Ambassador to Colombia, was sitting at his desk drinking a cup of coffee with his wife, Joan.

"John, how nice it is to see you again," Joan said as she and Ambassador Haskell stood up. "How's your wife Julie doing? Has she had the baby yet?"

"I talked to her last night, and she's fine," Marrow replied as he walked over to the ambassador's desk. "The doctor said it'll be a couple of more months before the baby comes."

"Well, I best leave the two of you alone, so you can talk about whatever it is that you came here to talk about." Joan kissed Ambassador Haskell on the cheek and left the office, closing the door behind her.

"Okay, John, what's up?" Ambassador Haskell asked as he returned to his seat behind his desk.

"Mr. Ambassador I need to get this package to the president ASAP," Marrow said, referring to the envelope he was holding in his hand. "I was hoping that you could help me."

"If it's that important, why don't you send it to your director?"

"The president needs to see this information now, not next week," Marrow shot back.

"You do realize that your director is going to have your ass for going over his head? Are you sure you want to do this?"

"The president needs to know what I know, regardless of the consequences," Marrow snapped back.

"Do you mind if I look it over?" Ambassador Haskell asked.

"Please do." Marrow said as he handed the ambassador the envelope. "I'm sure you'll see the importance of getting this to the president." He continued to say as he sat down in the chair, in front of the ambassador's desk.

Ambassador Haskell put the envelope down on his desk, opened it, and carefully removed its contents. He quickly glanced over the material. When he was finished, he put everything back into the envelope. He looked at Marrow and said, "I must say this is some compelling stuff. I agree with you; the president needs to see this. I will see to it that the president gets this as quickly as possible. You have my word on it."

"Thank you, Mr. Ambassador," Marrow said as he got up from his seat. "I appreciate your help in this matter." Marrow paused for a moment and then asked, "Is there any way you can do this without telling the president where you got this information from?"

"I promise you that no one will know this information came from you," Ambassador Haskell assured Marrow as he stood up.

Satisfied that he had gotten his point across to the ambassador, Marrow left the Ambassador's office and closed the door while Ambassador Haskell sat back down behind his desk. Ambassador Haskell pushed the intercom button on his telephone and waited.

"Yes, Mr. Ambassador," Jennifer Masterson, said over the intercom."

"I need you to get a diplomatic courier in here ASAP," Ambassador Haskell said and then pushed the intercom button, canceling the intercom call. He removed a diplomatic pouch from his desk and put the envelope that John Marrow gave him inside. He locked the pouch and put it on his desk in front of him.

Ambassador Haskell picked up the telephone receiver and dialed the extension number for the embassy's transportation department.

"Transportation," someone said when the call was answered.

"This is Ambassador Haskell; I need a car brought around front. I have someone coming down that needs to go to the airport."

"Yes, Mr. Ambassador. I'll have a car brought around immediately."

"Thanks," Ambassador Haskell said, and then he canceled the call. Afterwards, he dialed the phone number to the airport hangar where the diplomatic jet was housed.

"Yes," A female voice said.

"This is Ambassador Haskell; I need to talk to the pilot."

"Hang on and I'll get him for you."

"Yes, Mr. Ambassador," the pilot said. "What can I do for you?"

"Is the jet ready?" Ambassador Haskell asked.

"It's all fueled up and ready to go," the pilot answered. "All we have to do here is pull it out of the hangar, and warm-up the engines."

"Get it ready for takeoff," Ambassador Haskell ordered. "I have a courier that needs to go to Washington."

"We'll be ready to leave when the courier arrives," the pilot assured Ambassador Haskell.

Ambassador Haskell hung up the telephone and sat at his desk. He was startled when there was a knock on his office door. The door opened, and Agent Andrew Kilgore of the Diplomatic Security Service, entered the office and closed the door.

"Andrew, it's nice to see you again," Ambassador Haskell said as he stood up.

"I was told that you needed a diplomatic courier," Agent Kilgore said as he walked over to Ambassador Haskell's desk.

"Yes, I do," Ambassador Haskell commented and picked up the diplomatic pouch from his desk. "I need you to deliver this pouch to President Elliot, and no one else," He instructed Agent Kilgore and then handed him the pouch.

"I understand," Agent Kilgore acknowledged. "Do I wait for a reply from the president?"

"Not necessary, just make sure the president gets this."

"No problem," Agent Kilgore assured Ambassador Haskell. "I'll leave for Washington right away."

"Andrew, tell no one what you're doing," Ambassador Haskell warned Agent Kilgore. "Watch your back on this one."

"I will keep an eye out Mr. Ambassador. You can count on me."

"There's a car waiting out front to take you to the airport," Ambassador Haskell pointed out. "The jet is fueled and waiting."

"Yes, sir," Agent Kilgore acknowledged and left Ambassador Haskell's office with the diplomatic pouch in hand, and closed the door. He left the embassy and climbed into the back seat of the SUV that was waiting, and closed the door. A few seconds later, the SUV drove off toward the airport.

Chapter 9

Newly elected, President Martin Elliot, had only been president for a few days, but it felt like months. He sat at his writing desk in the Presidential Residence drinking his morning cup of coffee. He opened the right-side top drawer of his desk and took out the folder that he had received the night before from a special diplomatic-courier from Ambassador Haskell in Bogotá, Colombia. He placed the folder in front of him, opened it, and began to go over its contents for the second time. When he finished reading the documents, President Elliot closed the folder.

"You're up early," the First Lady, Amanda Elliot said, who was standing behind him. "I thought you were going to sleep in today?"

"I couldn't sleep," he replied while he turned his swivel chair around to face her. "What time is it?"

Amanda looked at her watch and replied, "It's six thirty-five."

"Great," President Elliot said and got up out of his chair. "Let's go have some breakfast."

He picked up the folder from his desk and followed Amanda into the dining room of the Presidential Residence. They arrived just as the cook was entering with their breakfast.

"Good Morning Mr. President and Madam, First Lady," the cook said.

"A beautiful morning it is," Amanda commented and sat down.

"Yes, it is," President Elliot agreed. He sat down at the table next to Amanda and then put the folder down on the other side of the table.

"I have prepared your usual breakfast this morning," the cook said while he placed their meal on the table in front of them. "I hope it's suitable for you both?"

"It'll be fine," Amanda assured him.

"It looks delicious Frank," President Elliot added.

"Thank you, sir," the cook said, and then left the room.

President Elliot and Amanda began eating their breakfast. Amanda couldn't help but notice that the president was unusually quiet. "You're awful quiet this morning," she said to break the silence. "What's up?"

"Nothing," he replied. "Now if you don't mind, I'd like to finish my breakfast."

"Well, excuse the hell out of me," Amanda snapped back. "I hope you get rid of whatever bug crawled up your ass."

President Elliot looked at Amanda stunned. "I'm sorry," he said, "I didn't mean to snap at you. I just have a lot on my mine right now."

"Does it have something to do with the folder that you're carrying around?" Amanda asked.

"You know I can't tell you one way or the other," President Elliot answered. "Now, if you'll excuse me, I got to go," he continued to say while he stood up. "I don't want to be late for my morning security briefing." President Elliot kissed Amanda on the lips and picked up the folder, and then left the Presidential Residence.

* * * * *

The Situation Room

White House Chief of Staff, Howard Gordon, was busy setting up the Situation Room for the morning intelligence briefing with President Elliot.

National-Security Adviser, John Haig was the first to arrive, followed by Secretary of State, George Maxwell, and NSA Analyst, Maria Carlos; with Secretary of Defense, Mark Roberts and Secretary of the Navy, John Forsythe arrived shortly Afterwards.

"Good morning, Howard," CIA Deputy Director Karen Hicks said when she entered the room.

"Good morning, Deputy Director," Gordon acknowledged.

General Richwood and Vice President Conrad were the last to arrive. Everyone took a seat at the conference table in the middle of the room.

When President Elliot entered the room, everyone jumped to their feet. Howard Gordon left the room, and the Marine guard outside closed the double-doors.

"Have a seat," President Elliot said, and then he sat down at the conference table, and placed the folder down on the table in front of him. "I would like to start by saying that I'm disappointed in the way that the CIA and NSA have failed to keep me informed about the situation along the Panamanian-Colombian border. Do either of you know what's going on down there?"

"Mr. President, there's not much to report," CIA Deputy Director Karen Hicks was quick to respond. "Other than a few incidents on the Colombian side of the border between the Colombian Army and the Revolutionary Armed Forces of Colombia, there's nothing to report."

"I agree with Deputy Director Hicks," NSA Analyst, Maria Carlos added. "The NSA is confident that the Panamanian border is secure."

"You really believe that?" President Elliot asked.

NSA Analyst, Maria Carlos, and Deputy Director Hicks nodded their heads in agreement. "Yes, sir, we do," Deputy Director Hicks answered.

"Well, I don't," President Elliot shot back. "I have reason to believe that General Juarez and his army are going to attack one of two targets on the Panamanian side of the border. I would bet money that our consulate at Puerto Obaldia is the primary target because of the intelligence hub that the NSA and CIA have put there."

"Mr. President, that will never happen," NSA Analyst, Maria Carlos pointed out. "General Juarez doesn't have the resources to attempt such an attack."

"I think he does," President Elliot snapped back. "Juarez has already blinded our satellite coverage of the area. Until we know his intentions, we need to secure the consulate at Puerto Obaldia."

"I agree with the president," Secretary of Defense, Mark Roberts added.

"So do I," Secretary of the Navy, John Forsythe Jumped in. "Mr. President, we could put one of our carrier groups off the coast of Panama, near the Colombian border. A show of force may make General Juarez think twice before coming across the border."

"It could also piss him off enough to cross the border anyway," Secretary of State, George Maxwell pointed out. "It may even raise a stink with the UN Security Council."

"Piss on the UN Security Council," President Elliot shot back. "Let's put a carrier group in the Caribbean Sea and one in the Pacific Ocean off the coast of Panama, near the Colombian border in international waters; each accompanied by a Marine Amphibious Unit."

"Mr. President, a show of force that size may be asking for trouble," NSA Analyst, Maria Carlos jumped in.

"Look people, this isn't a debate session," President Elliot snapped back. "I have made up my mine on this issue. John, how soon can you get this done?"

"Three to four days," Secretary of the Navy, John Forsythe, answered.

"Good," President Elliot acknowledged. "Are there any more questions? President Elliot waited for a few minutes before continuing. "Thank you all for coming. Have a nice day."

Secretary of the Navy, John Forsythe was the first to get up from his seat and head for the door. He opened the double-doors and left the room. Everyone else was quick to follow while President Elliot remained seated. He noticed that General Richwood, and Vice President Conrad were standing at the door talking. "General Richwood, could I have a word with you?"

"Yes, Mr. President," General Richwood replied.

Vice President Conrad left to return to his duties, and General Richwood sat across from President Elliot at the conference table.

"Marine," President Elliot called out.

"Yes, Mr. President," The Marine guard answered when he appeared in the doorway and saluted President Elliot.

"Close the doors, please," President Elliot instructed the Marine and then saluted him back.

"Yes, sir," The Marine guard acknowledged and closed the double-doors, and remained outside.

"General, you didn't have much to say during the meeting," President Elliot pointed out. "Everyone else looked disappointed in my decision except you."

"Mr. President I'm a soldier," General Richwood proudly said. "A soldier follows orders; he does not question them."

"I'm going to show you something that very few people have seen," President Elliot said while he slid the folder across the table to General Richwood. "Perhaps you should take a look at this and tell me what you think."

General Richwood opened the folder and began to examine its contents. When he finished, he closed the folder. "If this information is correct, we might have a major problem along the Panamanian border," He commented and slid the folder back to President Elliot. "We might know the where, but not the when," General Richwood went on. "This could also be a diversion tactic. Someone could want us to look at the wrong target area so they can strike their actual target."

"Do you think that's what the CIA and NSA think?" President Elliot asked.

"That's what I would think," General Richwood pointed out. "But Mr. President, I don't think we should ignore this."

"General, the previous president told me about a unit called Strike Force Delta. I was told that you have direct contact with this unit."

"Yes, sir, I do."

"Who is the Strike Force Delta commander?"

"That would be Colonel John Wilson, sir."

"I want you to summon Colonel Wilson to Washington ASAP. He is not to know that I want to see him. Our meeting must remain a secret."

"He's here in Washington, sir. I was going to meet with him later this afternoon. I could have him brought here if you wish."

"No, that won't be necessary," President Elliot said as he stood up. "I'll handle it from here."

"Yes, Mr. President," General Richwood said while he jumped to his feet.

President Elliot walked over to the double doors and opened them.

He left the Situation Room and walked to the side entrance to the Oval Office. He opened the door and entered, and closed the door. He walked over to his desk and sat down in his chair behind the desk. He opened the top right-side drawer of his desk and put the folder on Colombia inside. He took out his key from his pants pocket and locked the drawer, and then returned the key to his pocket. He then reached under the center drawer and pushed a button, indicating to his Personal Assistant, Mrs. Joan Wyatt, who was sitting at her desk in the reception area, that he was in the Oval Office and ready to receive visitors.

* * * * *

The Hay-Adams Hotel
Washington, D. C.

Colonel John Wilson sat on the bed in his hotel room wrapped only in a towel. He looked out the window and watched as the rain began to come down harder. "Fuckin' rain," He mumbled while he put on a pair of sweat pants and a pocket T-shirt. He walked over to the chair next to the bed and sat down. He took a clean pair of socks from his bed and put them on his feet, and then he put on his tennis shoes. Shortly Afterwards, there was a knock on his door. "Who is it?" He asked while he jumped to his feet.

"Sir, I'm here to pick you up," a man's voice replied.

Colonel Wilson hurried over to the nightstand next to the bed. He opened the drawer and got out his M-9 nine- millimeter Beretta. He released the safety and loaded a round into the firing chamber. "Pick me up for what?" Colonel Wilson asked while he walked over to the door.

"Sir, if you open the door, I can explain."

Colonel Wilson looked out the peephole in the door and saw a man standing there in an expensive three-piece suit. He quickly flung the door open and pointed his Beretta at the man's head. "Start fuckin' explaining," Wilson said, cocking the firing hammer to its ready position. "I'm listening."

"Sir, I'm going to show you my credentials," the man said and then slowly reached into his jacket pocket. He pulled out a wallet from his pocket and opened it up, exposing his badge and his I D. "John Haskell, Secret Service."

"Haskell," Colonel Wilson mumbled. "Are you related to Ambassador Haskell?"

"He's my uncle."

"Oh," Wilson commented.

Satisfied that Agent Haskell was no threat, Colonel Wilson put the firing hammer back to its safety position and lowered his pistol. "Please come in," Wilson said, trying to defuse the situation. Agent Haskell stepped inside, and Colonel Wilson closed the door. "Sorry about that... I've been... well... a little on the edge lately, if you know what I mean."

"Like I said; I'm here to pick you up," Agent Haskell commented. "I have a car waiting downstairs."

"Let me get my uniform on, and I'll be ready," Colonel Wilson pointed out.

"What you're wearing will do," Agent Haskell fired back. "We must be going," he insisted.

Colonel Wilson put the Beretta back into the nightstand drawer and left the room. Agent Haskell followed Colonel Wilson out and closed the door. They walked to the elevator and entered. Haskell released the door lock on the elevator. The doors closed and began to move downward.

When they arrived at the first floor, they exited the elevator and entered the lobby, where three other Secret Service agents were waiting. Agent Haskell and Colonel Wilson followed one of the agents to a car that was waiting for them outside. The other two agents remained in the lobby.

Agent Haskell and Colonel Wilson quickly got in the back of the car, and the agent closed the door. The driver put the car into gear and drove off, and the agent returned to the hotel lobby.

The rain was coming down by the buckets full; making it difficult for the driver to see the lines on the road. The driver was doing his best to maneuver the car safely.

"I thought you were taking me to the Pentagon," Colonel Wilson said to Agent Haskell when the driver turned onto Pennsylvania Avenue

"You're not going to the Pentagon," Haskell replied.

Before Colonel Wilson could ask his next question, the driver pulled into the driveway to the White House and stopped the vehicle at the gate. The guard opened the gate, and they continued.

The driver stopped the car under a closed-in canopy. Moments later, Wilson's door opened, and he exited the vehicle. Colonel Wilson followed the person that was standing there into the White House, where two Secret Service men were waiting.

The two Secret Service men escorted Colonel Wilson down a corridor, and they stopped in front of a door. One of the Secret Service men knocked on the door, and then opened it. He entered the room with Colonel Wilson following close behind. The other Secret Service man closed the door and remained outside.

Colonel Wilson looked around in total dismay. He'd never been to the White House before, but from pictures and the movies, he realized that he was standing in the Oval Office.

"The president will be with you shortly," The Secret Service man said. He then left the room and closed the door.

Seconds later, the side door to the oval office opened. President Elliot entered and closed the door. Colonel Wilson quickly snapped to attention; the president walked over to him, and they shook hands. "Have a seat colonel," President Elliot said. He then walked over to his desk and sat down behind it while Colonel Wilson took a seat in front of the president's desk.

"Mr. President, I must apologize for the way I'm dressed," Colonel Wilson was quick to point out. "I had no idea I was coming here to meet with you."

"There's no need to apologize," President Elliot assured Colonel Wilson. He took out his key to the top right-side drawer of his desk from his pants pocket and unlocked the drawer. President Elliot removed the folder that he had received from Ambassador Haskell in Colombia and placed it on top of his desk, and then returned the key to his pocket. "Colonel, I'll get right to the point," President Elliot continued. "I have a problem, and I need your help."

"Yes, sir, Mr. President," Colonel Wilson acknowledged. "I'll do whatever I can, sir."

"Colonel, I want you to look over these intelligence reports that Ambassador Haskell in Colombia sent to me," President Elliot began while he picked up the folder and placed it down on the desk in front of

Colonel Wilson. "I need your professional opinion on this."

Colonel Wilson looked at President Elliot confused and opened the folder. He took his time and read each page carefully. When he was finished, he closed the folder.

"Colonel, I hope you see the dilemma I'm faced with."

"Mr. President, there's nothing in this folder that I didn't report before you took office," Colonel Wilson said while tapping on the folder. "Sir the previous president should have briefed you on this."

"I see," President Elliot commented. "Well, he didn't; this is the first I've heard of this."

"Mr. President, what do you need from me?"

"I want you to send some of your people down there and see if you can find out what General Juarez and this A'zam al Shammari are up to before it's too late. You're to report your findings to me and me only."

"I understand Mr. President," Colonel Wilson acknowledged, "I can have a team down there in about eight hours. I should have a report on the situation there within twenty-four hours after that."

"Your people are to avoid any conflict with General Juarez's Army and the Colombian Army; but, make it clear to them that they are authorized to use deadly force to defend themselves."

"I understand, sir."

"Your people won't be down there on their own. I have ordered a carrier group to be placed on the Atlantic and Pacific side of Panama, near the Colombian border in international waters; each accompanied by a Marine Amphibious Unit. Help won't be far away if you should need some. Do you have any questions?"

"No, Sir."

"Your personal belongings have been packed up and loaded onto your aircraft," President Elliot said while he stood up, "There's a car waiting to take you to Andrews. The Secret Service Agent outside will escort you to the vehicle."

"You can count on us Mr. President to get the job done," Colonel Wilson assured President Elliot and got up from his seat.

Colonel Wilson left the Oval Office and closed the door. He followed the Secret Service Agent that was waiting for him outside the Oval Office. He exited the White House and walked over to the vehicle that was waiting. The driver opened the door to the back seat and stood at attention, and Colonel Wilson entered. Wilson was surprised to see General Richwood sitting in the back seat. The driver closed the door, then walked around to the driver's side and got in, and they drove away.

"I must say general, I'm surprised to see you," Colonel Wilson began. "I was starting to get the impression that you were avoiding me."

"I've been busy finding a replacement for Lieutenant Shea."

"General, this might not be a good time to send me a replacement. I mean with what's going on, I don't think it's a good idea to add a new member to the unit. I'm going to have my hands full. I don't have the time to train someone new."

"I know it's short notice, but it's not open for debate. I've assigned a First Lieutenant by the name of Jonathan Nash to your unit. I believe he served under you in Afghanistan."

"Yes, I remember Lieutenant Nash; he's a good soldier. When can I expect him?"

"He's waiting for you on the aircraft. He'll be flying back with you."

Colonel Wilson sat in silence and enjoyed the ride. When they approached the main gates to Andrews, the sentries at the gate motioned for them to continue without stopping. Colonel Wilson got the impression that the guards had recognized their vehicle, and they were expecting them.

Not long Afterwards, the vehicle stopped a few feet from the Gulfstream G550 twin-engine jet aircraft that was sitting on the runway waiting to take off. The driver got out and walked to the back of the vehicle. He opened the door and stood at attention, and Colonel Wilson exited the vehicle. Wilson walked over to the awaiting aircraft and entered. He quickly glanced around and noticed twenty-six-year-old First Lieutenant Jonathan Nash sitting in one of the seats.

Lieutenant Nash jumped to his feet when he saw Colonel Wilson. "I must say, sir; it's good to see you again."

"You don't need to call me sir anymore. Everyone in this unit is equal," Colonel Wilson was quick to point out. "We don't go by rank here." Colonel Wilson sat down in one of the seats and fastened his seat restraint. "I suggest you have a seat. We will be taking off shortly," He informed Lieutenant Nash, noticing the red light at the front of the aircraft was flashing, indicating that the pilot was preparing to take off.

Lieutenant Nash sat down next to Colonel Wilson and fastened his seat restraint. Soon Afterwards, the aircraft began to move and then leave the ground. Once the aircraft leveled off at its cruising altitude, the red light at the front of the aircraft changed to solid green, indicating that it was safe for them to walk around the aircraft.

"The most important thing you need to know is that from here on out, I will be addressed as Wolverine, and you will be addressed as Condor. Is that clear?"

"Roger that," Lieutenant Nash acknowledged.

"I suggest you learn everyone's nickname as quickly as you can because we don't use our real names.

"I understand Wolverine."

"Did General Richwood give you your new ID?

"Yes, he did. It's in my wallet."

"That's good because you won't be able to get on the base or our compound without it."

"What do I do with my military ID?"

"Give it to me. I'll put it in my safe."

Lieutenant Nash took out his wallet and removed his military ID card, and handed it to Colonel Wilson.

"Do you have any questions?" Colonel Wilson asked.

"Not at this time," Lieutenant Nash answered.

"One last thing; we don't wear uniforms, so I suggest you change into some civilian clothing. We'll be landing shortly."

Without saying another word, Lieutenant Nash removed his seat restraint and jumped to his feet. He walked to the back of the aircraft and began changing into his civilian clothes while Colonel Wilson got up from his seat and walked to the front of the aircraft.

He removed the satellite telephone from the holder on the wall and put the antenna for the satellite telephone into its proper position. He pressed zero and put the satellite phone to his ear, and waited for the operator at Strike Force Delta command to answer. "This is Wolverine; I need a secure line to the hangar nine maintenance chief." Colonel Wilson could hear a click as the operator transferred his call, and after a few rings, the maintenance chief answered. "Chief, this is Wolverine; I need a C-130J fueled for maximum range and standing by a-sap. Get a flight crew ready and standing by. My people will be there with their equipment within the hour.

"We'll be ready."

Colonel Wilson ended the call and dialed the number for Captain Hale, and put the satellite telephone back to his ear. After the second ring, Captain Hale answered his telephone. "Bulldog, this is Wolverine. I will be landing shortly, and I want Popeye and Crazy Horse to meet me in the conference room when I arrive. In the meantime, I want you to have their strike teams assemble in hanger nine in full combat dress, along with their equipment for a halo jump."

"I'll get it done," Captain Hale acknowledged.

"I'll explain everything when I get there," Colonel Wilson said, and then he ended the call. He placed the antenna for the satellite telephone into its normal resting place and returned the satellite telephone to the holder on the wall. He checked to make sure it was secured before he walked back to his seat and sat down, and fastened his seat restraint. Lieutenant Nash finished changing into his civilian clothes and returned to his seat, and sat down. He fastened his seat restraint and waited for the aircraft to land.

A few minutes later, the aircraft began to descend. Not long Afterwards the aircraft touched down and taxied on the runway for a few minutes before the aircraft came to a complete stop, and the pilot shut down the engines.

"Don't worry about your gear," Colonel Wilson said while he removed his seat restraints. "It'll be taken to your quarters for you," he continued as he got up from his seat.

Lieutenant Nash nodded his head to acknowledge that he understood while he removed his seat restraints and got up from his seat. They disembarked from the aircraft and walked over to the Humvee that was waiting for them. They got into the back, and the Humvee drove off, heading toward the Strike Force Delta facility.

The Humvee stopped at the main gates. The guards were each dressed in full combat dress and armed with an HK-416N assault rifle. One of the guards checked everyone's identification card that was in the Humvee before he allowed them to continue. When their Humvee stopped, Colonel Wilson exited, and Lieutenant Nash followed him into the building. They did not walk far when they stopped in front of a door where another guard, dressed in full battle dress and armed with an HK-416N assault rifle, was standing. The guard opened the door, and

Colonel Wilson entered, with Lieutenant Nash following.

They walked down the hallway and stopped in front of a door, and entered. "Take a seat," Colonel Wilson said while he walked over to the desk at the back of the room and sat down behind the desk.

Lieutenant Nash walked over and sat down in the chair, in front of the desk where Colonel Wilson was sitting. The door opened, and a tall, middle-aged black man entered the room and walked over to where Colonel Wilson and Lieutenant Nash were sitting.

"Condor you remember Sambo don't you?" Colonel Wilson asked.

"I certainly do," Lieutenant Nash replied while getting up from his seat. "How the hell have you been?" He asked while he shook hands with Sambo. "The last time I saw you, you were medevacked out of Afghanistan. I'm glad to see that you're back on your feet again."

"Thanks, it wasn't as serious as it looked."

"Sambo, I want you to show Condor to his quarters, and then introduce him to the rest of the unit in the morning."

"No problem Wolverine," Sambo said.

Lieutenant Nash got up from his seat and followed Sambo out of Colonel Wilson's office. Colonel Wilson waited a few minutes before he got up from his seat and left his office. He walked to the conference room and entered. First Lieutenant Mathew McDonald, nicknamed Popeye and Second Lieutenant Roger Milestone, nicknamed Crazy Horse, jumped to their feet and stood at attention.

"As you were," Colonel Wilson said while he walked over and sat down in the chair at the head of the table, and waited while Lieutenant McDonald and Lieutenant Milestone returned to their seats before he continued. "I'm sure you're wondering why I called this meeting, so I'll get right to the point," Colonel Wilson began. "President Elliot has asked us to check out the situation at the Panamanian border near the border town of Puerto Obaldia. We believe that General Juarez and the Revolutionary Armed Forces of Colombia are dangerously close to the Panamanian border on the Colombian side. The president wants us to find out what they're up to."

"Surely if there's something brewing down there our satellite surveillance would have picked up on it by now," Lieutenant McDonald was quick to point out.

"It's believed that they're using satellite jammers," Colonel Wilson said. "Our satellites are blind in that area."

"If that's the case, then we could be looking for a needle in a haystack," Lieutenant Milestone commented.

"No one said it was going to be easy," Colonel Wilson snapped back. "The president wants us to go down there and look around, and that's just what we're going to do. I'm confident that if there's anything going on down there, you'll find it." Colonel Wilson paused for a brief moment before continuing, "This mission is code named Operation Sierra. Popeye, you, and your team will be inserted by halo jump at designated point X-Ray, two klicks from the Colombian border. Once you're on the ground, you will proceed to the target area marked on your map that will be in your mission brief. Crazy Horse, you and your team will be inserted by halo jump at designated point X-Ray-1. Once you're on the ground, you will proceed to the target area marked on your map that will be in your mission brief. Also, you will check in with Strike Force Command when you first arrive, and you will send in progress reports every day."

"What are the rules of engagement?" Lieutenant McDonald asked.

"If fired upon, you are to defend yourselves," Colonel Wilson was quick to reply. "Don't take any unnecessary risks."

"When do we leave?" Lieutenant Milestone asked.

"A C-130J is standing-by. Your team and your equipment are on the aircraft waiting for you. You will receive your mission brief while en-route to your drop zones. Are there any more questions?" Colonel Wilson waited for a few moments before continuing. "Good hunting gentlemen."

Lieutenant McDonald and Lieutenant Milestone jumped to their feet. "Yes, sir," they said in unity.

Colonel Wilson remained seated while Lieutenant McDonald and Lieutenant Milestone left the conference room.

Chapter 10

Strike Force Delta Command
Tinker Air Force Base
Oklahoma City, Oklahoma

Colonel Wilson was sitting at his writing table in his quarters with his laptop in front of him, writing an overdue letter when he was interrupted by a knock on the door. He closed the lid on the laptop and got up from his seat, and walked over to the door. When he opened it, he saw Second Lieutenant Samantha Cooltrain, nicknamed Giggles, standing in the doorway. "Sorry to bother you, but we have a situation; you're needed in the Operation Center."

Colonel Wilson followed Lieutenant Cooltrain out of his quarters to the Operation Center and entered. "Bulldog, sit-rep," he said while walking over to Captain Hale.

"We lost communications with the consulate in Puerto Obaldia, Panama about fifteen minutes ago," Captain Hale reported. "They just stopped transmitting. We've been trying to reestablish communications with them, but no one down there is answering."

"What's our satellites picking up?" Colonel Wilson inquired.

"Nothing," Captain Hale answered. "It's as if no one is there."

"That's impossible," Colonel Wilson fired back. "The satellites should be picking up something."

"I agree Wolverine; they should, but the satellites are not picking up anything, not even their body heat signatures."

"Have our people landed yet?"

"They're still in the air," Captain Hale answered.

"I want Crazy Horse and his people to land near the consulate. They are to proceed to the consulate with caution and find out what the hell is going on." Colonel Wilson ordered. "Popeye and his people are to remain on standby at this time."

"I'll get right on it," Captain Hale remarked and walked over to one of the communications operators. A few minutes later, Captain Hale walked back to where Colonel Wilson was standing. "Your new orders have been sent and received. Crazy Horse and his team should be on the ground shortly."

"All we can do now is wait," Colonel Wilson commented.

"Shouldn't we notify General Richwood about the present situation?" Captain Hale asked.

"Notify the general about what," Colonel Wilson fired back. "I think we should wait until we have figured out what's going on down there. We need more information before we start waking up the brass, so we'll wait." Colonel Wilson paused for a moment to think before he continued. "Barbie, I want our satellites re-tasked, so we have an uninterrupted feed of the area."

"I'm on it," Operations Specialist, First Lieutenant Kate Stanton acknowledged. "The satellites will be repositioned shortly. We'll have a coverage area of three-hundred miles in any direction. If there's anything out there, we'll know about it."

"Good," Colonel Wilson acknowledged. He looked at the electronic plotter map on the wall and noticed that a group of ships was about seventy-five miles from the coast of Panama in the Caribbean Sea. "Bulldog, where did that group of ships come from?"

"They were on a humanitarian mission in Jamaica; helping them with recovery from the hurricane that blew through there last week," Captain Hale answered. "They left Jamaica about twelve hours ago, heading south in a big hurry. The command ship is the USS Bataan, LHD-5, code name Papa Bear. The group is carrying an entire Marine Expeditionary Unit (MEU)."

"How soon will Papa Bear be in range of the Panamanian coast?" Colonel Wilson inquired.

"At their present speed, about forty-five minutes."

"Roger that," Colonel Wilson acknowledged. He turned his attention to the screen that was displaying the live satellite feed of the area around the Consulate at Puerto Obaldia. *I got a bad feeling about this;* he thought.

Thirty Minutes Later

Second Lieutenant Milestone, nicknamed Crazy Horse, and his team landed safely on the ground at their target area, two kilometers from the US Consulate at Puerto Obaldia, Panama. They did a complete weapons and equipment check before proceeding toward the consulate with Lieutenant Milestone leading the way.

When the consulate was in sight, Lieutenant Milestone signaled for his team to stop. He took out his binoculars and scanned the area. *This is strange;* he thought to himself when he noticed that the consulate perimeter was lit up, but there were no Marines patrolling the consulate grounds.

Lieutenant Milestone put his binoculars back into its carrying case and continued to make his way closer to the consulate, with the rest of his team following close behind. When they reached the front gates to the consulate, he discovered that there were no Marines guards guarding the main gates and that the entrance gate was partially opened. "What the fuck," he mumbled. *Where are the Marines guards?* He thought to himself

"This doesn't feel right," one of the team members called Cowboy, who was next to Lieutenant Milestone pointed out. "I got a bad feeling about this."

"Listen up," Lieutenant Milestone said over his radio headset. "It's not known what we're going to find inside so be on your toes."

Lieutenant Milestone readied his HK-416N assault rifle and entered the consulate grounds. The rest of his team followed close behind him with their HK-416N assault rifles ready. He stopped at the entrance to the security building and looked inside, but all he could see was darkness. He shined his flashlight inside and saw two Marines lying on the floor. At first glance, they appeared not to have been shot, but it was clear to Lieutenant Milestone that both Marines were dead. He tried the door and found it unlocked. "Cowboy, I want you and Snake to go around to the other side and check the entrance door there," Lieutenant Milestone ordered. "Let me know what you find."

Cowboy nodded his head in acknowledgment, and he and Snake hurried to the other side of the security building, with Snake leading the way. When they reached their destination, Snake tried the door and found it unlocked. "The door is unlocked," Snake reported over his radio headset. "What are your orders?"

"Stay where you are," Lieutenant Milestone replied over his radio headset. "We'll breach from this side."

"Roger, standing by," Snake acknowledged over his radio headset.

Lieutenant Milestone hand signaled one of the team members called Jelly Bean to enter the security building, and he entered. Lieutenant Milestone stood in the doorway, ready to enter the building when Jelly Bean suddenly dropped to his knees and started to cough uncontrollably and then gasp for air, followed by vomiting. Lieutenant Milestone took a deep breath of fresh air and entered the building. He grabbed Jelly Bean by the back of his uniform and quickly pulled him out of the building and slammed the door shut. He laid Jelly Bean down on the ground a few feet from the building.

"I need help over here," Lieutenant Milestone yelled out.

Ice Man, the team's medical technician, hurried over to Jelly Bean and crouched down next to him. "What the hell happened in there?" Ice Man asked while he began to examine Jelly Bean.

"I'm not sure," Lieutenant Milestone answered.

After a quick examination of Jelly Bean, Ice Man looked at Lieutenant Milestone confused. "I think Jelly Bean was gassed," he sadly said.

"Can you do anything for him?" Lieutenant Milestone asked, hoping for the best.

"Crazy Horse, Jelly Bean is dead," Ice Man replied.

Lieutenant Milestone was shocked by what he had just heard. "I want everyone to put on their gas masks," he ordered, and then he put his M-42 gas mask on over his headset while the rest of the Strike Force team did the same. "Cowboy, I want you and Snake to check out the perimeter," He said over his radio headset. "Do not enter any of the buildings; is that clear?"

"I understand," Cowboy acknowledged over his radio headset.

"We'll check out the perimeter and let you know what we find."

"Be careful," Lieutenant Milestone said over his radio headset. "Keep me posted."

"Yes, dad," Snake remarked over his radio headset. "We'll stay out of trouble."

"Just do what the fuck I said without the smart-ass remarks," Lieutenant Milestone fired back over his radio headset. "Crazy Horse out," he concluded.

The radio headset went silent. Everyone knew that Snake's remarks had pissed-off Lieutenant Milestone.

"Ice Man, do you have your biological and chemical gas detection meter with you?" Lieutenant Milestone asked.

"I never go anywhere without it; it's in my backpack," Ice Man replied. He removed his backpack and pulled out the biological and chemical gas detection meter. He attached the three-foot lead to the meter and walked over to the entrance door to the security building. "All I have to do now is get this lead inside the building, and turn it on."

"And how do you propose to get that lead inside the building?" Lieutenant Milestone asked.

"Well, I'm not going the fuck in there," Ice Man fired back. He pulled his combat knife out and began to pry up the weather seal on the bottom of the door. He then slid the lead through the opening until all three-foot of it was inside the building. He turned on the biological and chemical gas detection meter and waited.

"I should have had you do this before I sent Jelly Bean inside," Lieutenant Milestone commented. "My negligence got him killed."

"Crazy Horse, that's bullshit, and you know it," Ice Man shot back. "You're one of the best team leaders I've ever served with. Don't start second guessing yourself now. We were sent here to do a job, so let's get down to business here."

Before Lieutenant Milestone could say another word, the biological and chemical gas detection meter beeped several times. Ice Man looked at the meter display and shook his head in disbelief.

"What is it?" Lieutenant Milestone asked. "What's the meter reading?"

"It's VX nerve gas and a very high concentration of it too," Ice Man answered. "It has the same chemical compound that Popeye and his team ran into on that raid they did in Afghanistan a few months ago. The one where al-Qaeda was doing experiments on biological and chemical gasses."

"Yeah, I remember," Lieutenant Milestone acknowledged. "If I'm not mistaken, they took out that lab and everyone in it."

"That's what we thought," Ice Man commented. "I hate to be the one to say it, but this has al-Qaeda written all over it."

"You can bet your ass that if al-Qaeda is behind this, this was just a field test." Lieutenant Milestone pointed out. "I'd lay good money on it that al-Qaeda has a bigger target in mind and that the clock is ticking."

"It's going to be hard to prove your theory," Ice Man pointed out.

"I'm sure if we look in the right places, we'll find our proof," Lieutenant Milestone pointed out.

Lieutenant Milestone stopped talking when he noticed Cowboy and Snake returning from their reconnaissance of the perimeter.

"Report," Lieutenant Milestone ordered.

"We found the perimeter guards lying on the ground dead," Cowboy reported. "They show all the signs that they have been subjected to some kind of biological or chemical gas. We looked inside the consulate through the windows and found no movement inside. All we saw were bodies lying on the floor."

"Ironman, get your ass over here with the radio," Lieutenant Milestone said over his radio headset.

"On my way," Ironman acknowledged over his radio headset.

Moments later, Ironman arrived where Lieutenant Milestone was waiting. He wasted no time in setting up the antenna for the satellite radio. He set the satellite radio to the proper frequency and handed Lieutenant Milestone, the satellite radiotelephone receiver.

Lieutenant Milestone put the satellite radiotelephone receiver to his ear. "Eagle Nest this is Beach Ball, over."

"Beach Ball this is Eagle Nest go ahead, over."

"Eagle Nest, I'm declaring a Tango One Alfa, over."

Colonel Wilson, who was listening to Lieutenant Milestone's report, hurried over to the communication operator and put on a headset. "Beach Ball, this is Wolverine, over," he said into the headset microphone.

"Go ahead, Wolverine; this is Crazy Horse, over."

"How bad is it? Over."

"It's bad Wolverine. I have one man down, with a lot more in the building that we can't get into. We have detected the presence of VX nerve gas. I'm afraid the body count on this one is going to be high, over."

"Hold your position Crazy Horse. I'll get help to you ASAP, over."

"Roger Wolverine, Beach Ball, out," Lieutenant Milestone acknowledged and handed Ironman the satellite radiotelephone receiver.

Colonel Wilson took off the headset and laid it down in front of the communication operator. "Bulldog, have Popeye and his team land at Crazy Horse's position," Colonel Wilson ordered. "Inform Popeye that the presence of VX nerve gas has been detected and that he is to assume tactical command of both units when he arrives."

"Right away," Captain Hale acknowledged.

Colonel Wilson walked over to the blue telephone on the wall, a direct secured line to General Richwood. He picked up the telephone receiver and put it to his ear. Seconds later, General Richwood picked up. "General, we have a Tango One Alfa situation at the Consulate in Puerto Obaldia, Panama," He reported. "I have a team on the ground and another one landing in a few minutes."

"How bad is it?" General Richwood asked.

"It's bad general," Colonel Wilson answered. "I'm afraid that once we clear the building the body count is going to be high. The presence of VX nerve gas has been detected. General, I would like your permission to contact Papa Bear to see if they can render any assistance?"

"Permission granted," General Richwood answered. "I'll notify the president about the situation in Puerto Obaldia. Keep me informed."

"Yes, sir," Colonel Wilson acknowledged, and then returned the telephone receiver to its resting place. "Bulldog, what's the status of Popeye and his team?"

"They'll be on the ground shortly," Captain Hale answered.

"Roger that," Colonel Wilson acknowledged, and walked over to a computer terminal and looked up the code name for the Consulate in Puerto Obaldia, Panama. *Alcatraz* he thought to himself. *Where the hell do they get these code names from?* He hurried over to the communications operator in charge of the Navel fleet communications. "Get me Papa Bear, priority one."

"Papa Bear, this is Eagle Nest; we have a priority one message, over," the communications operator began.

"Eagle Nest, this is Papa Bear; we are ready to receive your priority one message, over," the radio operator aboard the USS Bataan said.

"Roger Papa Bear, message as follows, Alcatraz has a Tango One Alfa situation with VX. We have a team on the ground that needs your assistance immediately. Team leader Popeye has assumed tactical command of the situation, over."

"Eagle Nest, we copy message as follows, Alcatraz, has a Tango One Alfa situation with VX, and you have a team on the ground. Popeye has assumed tactical command of the situation, authenticate, over."

"I authenticate, Golf, Zulu, Bravo, Six, over."

"Roger Eagle Nest, message received. Stand-by, over."

"Eagle Nest standing-by."

Colonel Wilson stood next to where the communications operator was sitting. He put on a headset and waited for the USS Bataan to resume transmitting.

"Eagle Nest, this is Papa Bear. Do you copy, over?"

"Yes, Papa Bear, we copy, over."

"Eagle Nest, we are sending Tango Charlie three-one to Alcatraz. Do you copy, over?"

"Yes, we copy Papa Bear. Have Tango Charlie three-one contact Beach Ball before landing, over."

"Roger, Eagle Nest, We will pass that along to Tango Charlie three-one, over and out," the radio operator aboard the USS Bataan concluded.

"Roger, Papa Bear, Eagle Nest, out."

Colonel Wilson took off the headset and laid it down in front of the Navel fleet communications operator. "All we can do now is wait," he mumbled and walked away. He walked across the room to the other communications operator who was talking to Lieutenant Milestone at the consulate. The communications operator handed Colonel Wilson a headset, and he put it on. "Crazy Horse, this is Wolverine, do you copy, over," Colonel Wilson said into the headset microphone.

"Wolverine, this is Crazy Horse, over."

"Crazy Horse, help is on the way. Their call sign is Tango Charlie three-one, over."

"Roger that," Crazy Horse acknowledged. "Do you have an ETA? "

"Not at this time," Colonel Wilson answered. "All we know is that they're on their way, over."

"Roger that," Crazy Horse said. "We'll keep a sharp eye out for them, over."

"Crazy Horse, Popeye will assume tactical command of the situation there when he and his team arrive. They should be there shortly, over."

"I understand," Crazy Horse acknowledged. "Crazy Horse, out."

Colonel Wilson took off the headset and handed it to the communications operator. He looked at the monitor on the wall and watched the live satellite feed of the area. "Bulldog, I'll be in my office. Keep me posted on the situation at Puerto Obaldia." Without waiting for a reply, Colonel Wilson left the Operation Center and closed the door.

* * * * *

US Consulate
Puerto Obaldia, Panama

First Lieutenant McDonald, nicknamed Popeye, and his team safely parachuted onto the consulate grounds, not far from where Lieutenant Milestone and his team was waiting. Lieutenant McDonald's team quickly discarded their parachutes and put their M-42 gas mask on, and assembled where Lieutenant McDonald had landed.

Lieutenant McDonald and his team ran over to where Lieutenant Milestone and Ironman were waiting. "Sit-rep, Crazy Horse," Lieutenant McDonald ordered.

"Popeye, it's a fuckin' mess here."

"Yeah, I heard," Lieutenant McDonald commented. "I also heard about Jelly Bean; he was one hell of a soldier."

"That he was," Lieutenant Milestone agreed.

"Popeye, Tango Charlie three-one wants to talk to you," Ironman said and handed Lieutenant McDonald the satellite radiotelephone receiver.

Lieutenant McDonald took the satellite radiotelephone receiver from Ironman. He put it to his ear and pushed the send key. "Tango Charlie three-one this is Popeye, go ahead, over."

"Popeye, this is Tango Charlie three-one; we will be arriving at your location shortly, over."

"Tango Charlie three-one, this is Popeye; we copy; we'll see you when you get here, over and out," Lieutenant McDonald concluded and handed Ironman the satellite radiotelephone receiver.

A few minutes later, the first of three Boeing Vertol CH-46 Sea Knight helicopters from the USS Bataan landed. A Marine captain and a gunnery sergeant, both dressed in full combat dress, with their M16-A4 assault rifles in hand and wearing the M-42 gas mask emerged from the rear of the helicopter and hurried over to where Popeye and Crazy Horse were standing. "Are you Popeye?" The Marine captain asked Lieutenant McDonald."

"Yes, I am," Lieutenant McDonald replied. "Captain, I need a squad of your men to assist my people in securing the main gates. I want the rest of your Marines deployed along the perimeter wall. No one is to enter the consulate for any reason. We suspect a poisonous gas has been released inside the building."

"You got it," the captain fired back. "Gunny, get it done."

"Yes, sir," the gunnery sergeant acknowledged and saluted the captain. The captain quickly returned his salute.

"Popeye, I have two more inbound choppers about ten mikes out," the captain said while the gunnery sergeant ran back to the other Marines, barking out orders. "There's a haz-mat team on board one of them."

"When your haz-mat team lands, have them begin clearing the building," Lieutenant McDonald instructed the captain. "Tell them to be extra careful. This VX is some nasty shit."

"I'll get right on it," the captain acknowledged and walked away, heading back to his Marines.

"Popeye, I wonder if he knows that he outranks you?" Lieutenant Milestone asked.

"Well, if he doesn't, let's not tell him," Lieutenant McDonald shot back. "Wolverine put me in command of this mess here, and that's good enough for me."

Lieutenant McDonald and Lieutenant Milestone watched the Marines relieve their team members who were guarding the main gates to the consulate. The team members carefully picked up Jelly Bean's body and walked over to where they were standing.

They watched while two more CH-46 Sea Knight helicopters landed with more Marines and the haz-mat team onboard. Everyone quickly disembarked from the helicopters, and the helicopters took off, heading back out to sea. The haz-mat team quickly began to set up their command tent close to the main entrance to the consulate. They put on their Level A protective clothing and then entered the consulate.

A few minutes later, a Sikorsky CH-53 Sea Stallion helicopter landed not far from where Lieutenant McDonald and the rest of the Strike Force members were standing. A man dressed in civilian clothing emerged from the helicopter and walked over to them. "Which one of you is Popeye?" He asked.

"I am," Lieutenant McDonald answered.

"I have a message for you from Wolverine," the man said and handed Lieutenant McDonald the envelope that contained the message.

Lieutenant McDonald took the envelope from the man, opened it, and read the message. "Alright, people listen up. We've been ordered back to Panama City. Let's get Jelly Bean's body, and our gear loaded onto the chopper."

The Strike Force members did as Lieutenant McDonald had ordered and then climbed on board the Sikorsky CH-53 Sea Stallion helicopter. Shortly Afterwards, the helicopter took off and headed North toward Panama City.

Chapter 11

President Elliot was awakened when the telephone on his nightstand began ringing. He sat up on the side of the bed and turned on the lamp that was on his nightstand. He picked up the telephone receiver from the telephone on the nightstand and put it to his ear. "Yes," he said.

"Mr. President, we have a situation at the Consulate in Puerto Obaldia, Panama," General Richwood informed the president.

"What's wrong?"

"It is believed that VX nerve gas was released in the consulate a few hours ago," General Richwood answered. "Colonel Wilson has boots on the ground there, and they're reporting that the situation there is critical."

"Are there any survivors?"

"At this time, it is believed that there are no survivors." General Richwood sadly replied. "Sir, the body count on this one is going too high."

"What about Ambassador Meeks and his wife and three children; were they there?"

"They were headed back to Panama City accompanied by a CIA officer."

"Thank you, General," President Elliot sadly commented. "I want you here ASAP."

"Yes, Mr. President; I'm on my way, sir."

President Elliot canceled the call and waited for a dial tone, and then he dialed the number for his White House Chief of Staff, Howard Gordon. After a few rings, Gordon picked up. "Howard, we have a situation at the Consulate in Puerto Obaldia, Panama. I want everyone in the Situation Room in one hour."

"Yes Mr. President," Gordon acknowledged.

Without saying another word, President Elliot canceled the call and dialed zero for the White House operator. "I need to talk to Ambassador Meeks at the embassy in Panama City," the president said when the operator answered.

"Sir, do you realize what time it is there?"

"I don't give a rat's ass what time it is there," President Elliot snapped. "Get the ambassador on the phone."

"Yes, Mr. President; right away, sir."

President Elliot heard a few clicks while his call was being put through to the embassy in Panama City. It wasn't long before Ambassador Meeks came on the line. "Roger, have you heard about the situation at the Consulate in Puerto Obaldia?"

"Yes, Mr. President; I just heard about it. I've ordered the embassy locked-down and the Marine Security Force here is searching every inch of the embassy."

"Let me know if you find anything."

"Yes, Mr. President."

"Roger, be extra careful down there."

"Yes, sir, I will."

President Elliot canceled the call and returned the telephone receiver to its normal resting place.

"What was that all about?" The first lady, Amanda Elliot, asked.

"My worst nightmare."

Amanda Elliot sat up in bed, shocked by President Elliot's answer. "Is it that bad?"

"Yep, I'm afraid so," President Elliot answered while he got dressed. "You might as well go on back to sleep. There's no sense in you losing sleep over this too." President Elliot finished getting dressed and kissed Amanda Elliot on the lips. "I don't think I'll be back for breakfast.

I'll try to make lunch if I can."

"I'll see you when I see you," Amanda commented with a smile on her face.

President Elliot smiled back at Amanda and left the room. He walked to the kitchen and got a clean cup out of the cabinet, and then opened the refrigerator and got out a soda. He then opened the freezer part of the refrigerator and put some ice into the glass. He walked over to the kitchen table and sat down. He poured the soda into the glass and took a drink.

"I thought you left," Amanda said, entering the kitchen undetected.

"I was just trying to kill a few minutes," President Elliot remarked. "I thought you went back to sleep."

"Come on Martin; you know, after all these years, I can read you like a book," Amanda was quick to point out while she sat at the table across from President Elliot. "What's really bothering you?"

"Something has happened at our consulate in Puerto Obaldia, Panama," President Elliot began. "From what little General Richwood told me, it appears to be a terrorist attack."

"Oh my," Amanda uttered, surprised at what she had just heard. "Are there any survivors?"

"First reports indicate that there are no survivors," President Elliot answered. "Luckily, Roger and his family were on their way back to Panama City; they were the lucky ones."

"My god Martin, what are you going to do?"

"That's just it; I don't know," President Elliot fired back. "If I'm not careful, this could start another war, a war that this country doesn't need right now."

"Martin Elliot," Amanda said while taking President Elliot's hands into hers. She looked him in the eye before continuing. "The people of this great nation elected you to be their president because they believe in you. You must do what you feel is the right thing to do for the people."

"That's what I love about you," President Elliot said and then smiled at Amanda. "You always know what to say to cheer me up."

"That's my job as First Lady and your wife," Amanda was quick to point out.

President Elliot and Amanda were both startled when the doorbell rang. "Come in," President Elliot said and released his grip on Amanda's hands and smiled at her.

The door to the Presidential Residence opened, and Secret Service agent; John Baylor entered. He walked over to where President Elliot and Amanda were sitting. "Mr. President, everyone is assembled in the Situation Room."

"Well, duty calls," President Elliot remarked and kissed Amanda Elliot softly on her lips. "Thanks for the pep talk."

"I'll send you my bill later," Amanda said and then smiled.

President Elliot followed agent Baylor out of the Presidential Residence, and another Secret Service agent, who was standing outside, closed the door. He followed agent Baylor down the hallway to the Situation Room. The Marine guard snapped to attention and saluted President Elliot.

When President Elliot entered the Situation Room, everyone stopped talking and jumped to their feet. He walked over to the conference table in the middle of the room and sat down while the Marine guard closed the double-doors. "Have a seat gentleman," President Elliot waited for everyone to return to their seats before he continued. "I'm glad to see the heads of the CIA and NSA have decided to join us for this meeting."

"Mr. President, I thought it be best if I attended this meeting since the CIA dropped the ball on this one," NSA Director, Jack Parkinson remarked.

"The CIA didn't miss anything," CIA Director, Robert Müller fired back. "There was no indication that something like this was going to happen at Puerto Obaldia. I lost a lot of valuable people in this attack."

"Enough," President Elliot shouted and slammed his hand on the table. "Blaming each other for this is not the answer. What's done is done. We need to figure out who did this, and where they're hiding."

"Mr. President, before I came here I talked with the Marine colonel in command of the Marines who were sent to Puerto Obaldia," John Forsythe; the Secretary of the Navy began. "When his haz-mat team finished their sweep of the building, they found four large gas cylinders in the mechanical room that was hooked into the ventilation system. Upon inspection of the gas cylinders, they found VX Nerve Gas residue; the same kind of gas that al-Qaeda was doing experiments on in Afghanistan."

"So what you're saying is that this is a terrorist attack?" President Elliot asked.

"Yes, sir, it looks that way," Secretary Forsythe sadly replied. "Also, Mr. President I would like to add that stamped on the bottom of each gas cylinder used in this attack was the words Made-In-Colombia."

"Mr. President, based on what Secretary Forsythe has just said. I believe that General Juarez has teamed up with A'zam al Shammari and his al-Qaeda cell," Robert Müller, Director of the CIA pointed out. "Our latest intelligence reports indicated that General Juarez was close to the Panamanian border."

"Jack, what's your opinion on this?" President Elliot asked.

"I think it's worth looking into," Jack Parkinson; Director of the NSA replied.

"I agree with Director Parkinson," Secretary of Defense; Mark Roberts jumped in. "We need to get to the bottom of this and fast before they strike again."

"I say, send in our bombers and carpet-bomb along the Colombian border on the Colombian side, and be rid of these people once and for all," Vice President Conrad remarked.

"Are you nuts?" Secretary of Defense; Mark Roberts asked. "Are you trying to start a war?"

"I'm not trying to start anything," Vice President Conrad answered. "I just think it's time we put our foot down and end this; they attacked us first."

"I've heard enough," President Elliot jumped in. "We're not bombing anyone yet. Robert, Jack I strongly suggest that the two of you put your differences aside and work on this together, and get me some answers. I want hard, indisputable evidence about who was behind this."

"Yes Mr. President," CIA Director, Robert Müller acknowledged while at the same time NSA Director, Jack Parkinson nodded his head that he understood what President Elliot had said.

"John," I want the carrier groups to position themselves fifteen miles off the coast of Colombia, in international waters. They are to remain on the highest alert at all times," President Elliot ordered John Forsythe; the Secretary of the Navy. "Our Navel forces are authorized to use deadly force if fired upon."

"I will send the order out immediately," Secretary of the Navy, John

Forsythe assured President Elliot.

"What are we going to tell the American people?" Secretary of Defense; Mark Roberts asked. "There's no way we can keep this quiet. It's all over the news about what happened."

"I will have Press Secretary, Jill Summers prepare a statement to the effect that what happen at the Consulate in Puerto Obaldia was a terrible accident and not an act of terrorism," President Elliot answered. "The last thing we need is a mass panic. Are there any questions?" President Elliot waited a few seconds before continuing. "Good, then let's get started on this. The minute any of you find out anything, I want to know about it immediately."

Vice President Conrad jumped to his feet and hurried over to the double-doors. He opened the doors and left the Situation Room, with CIA Director, Robert Müller and NSA Director, Jack Parkinson not far behind him. Secretary of Defense; Mark Roberts and Secretary of the Navy, John Forsythe left shortly afterwards, with Secretary of State, George Maxwell not far behind them. General Richwood, Chairman of the Joint Chiefs of Staff, remained seated at the conference table next to President Elliot.

"Marine," President Elliot called out.

"Yes, Mr. President."

"Close the doors."

"Yes, sir, Mr. President," the Marine Guard acknowledged and closed the double-doors.

"General what would you do about this if you were me?"

"Mr. President, my opinions don't matter."

"They do to me," President Elliot fired back. "Hypothetically general, what would your next move be? How would you proceed with this?"

"Well, sir… first off… I wouldn't send in our bombers and carpet-bomb along the Colombian border as Vice President Conrad has suggested."

"I agree; please continue."

"Well, I would send in a couple Strike Force teams into Colombia and track down General Juarez and A'zam al Shammari, and put them down once and for all."

"General, how would you justify such an operation with the

Colombians?"

"We have justification to go in there after them because the gas cylinders used in this attack were made in Colombia."

"I see that you and I are on the same page here," President Elliot remarked. "I agree with everything you just said."

"You do?" General Richwood curiously asked.

"Yes, I do," President Elliot answered as he got up from his seat. "That's why I'm authorizing you to have Colonel Wilson send in some Strike Force teams and do whatever it takes to find these bastards and put them down for good."

"Yes, sir," General Richwood said while he jumped to his feet. "I'll get right on it, sir." He saluted President Elliot and walked over to the double-doors, and opened them. He exited the Situation Room. "As you were Marine," the general said when the Marine guard snapped to attention and saluted General Richwood.

President Elliot returned to his seat and removed the telephone receiver from the telephone on the table in front of him. He dialed the extension number for Press Secretary, Jill Summers while he put the telephone receiver to his ear. After a few rings Press Secretary, Jill Summers answered. "Jill, I'm in the Situation Room, and I need to see you right away."

"Yes, Mr. President; I'm on my way, sir."

President Elliot returned the telephone receiver to the telephone on the table and waited. A few minutes later, Press Secretary, Jill Summers entered the Situation Room, and the Marine guard closed the double-doors.

"Mr. President, I checked my voicemail right after you called, and I had several voice messages from news correspondents," Press Secretary, Jill Summers said while she walked over to the table where President Elliot was sitting. "They're asking about the incident at our consulate in Puerto Obaldia, Panama," she continued as she sat down across from the president. "They want to know if it was an act of terrorism."

"That's the reason why I asked you to come here," President Elliot began. "I need you to prepare a statement to the effect that what happen at the Consulate in Puerto Obaldia was a terrible accident and not an act of terrorism."

"Mr. President, Vice President Conrad told me that it was a terrorist attack. Sir, I'm not comfortable with lying to the press about this."

"I need you to do this for me. I need you to buy me some time so I can get to the bottom of this."

Mr. President, if the truth gets out about this, and I know it will; you're going to take a lot of heat for this, and my credibility with the press will be seriously damaged."

"Jill, I need you to do this for me. If it wasn't in the best interest of the country, I wouldn't be asking."

"I don't like it, but I'll do it," Press Secretary Summers said as she got up from her seat. "I just hope you know what you're doing sir."

"Thanks, Jill," President Elliot said as he got up from his seat.

Press Secretary, Jill Summers walked over to the double doors and opened them, and left the Situation Room. A few minutes later, President Elliot walked out of the room. The Marine guard snapped to attention and saluted him. President Elliot just kept walking and headed towards the Oval Office.

* * * * *

Panama City, Panama.

The Sikorsky CH-53 Sea Stallion helicopter carrying the Strike Force team from Puerto Obaldia, Panama landed at an old hangar at the Tocumen International Airport, located fifteen miles from Panama City, Panama. They proudly walked off the Sea Stallion helicopter, carrying Jelly Bean's body on a stretcher. They were met by an Army Honor Guard of six soldiers and a captain, all dressed in their dress uniforms. "Which one of you is Popeye?" The captain asked.

"I am," Lieutenant McDonald answered.

"Sir, we're here to take your fallen soldier back home," the captain pointed out.

The Honor Guard took possession of the stretcher that contained Jelly Bean's body. The Strike Force team stood at attention and watched the Honor Guard carry Jelly Bean to the C-130J Hercules aircraft that was waiting with its engine's running, and entered. The back cargo door closed and a few minutes later; the C-130J Hercules aircraft took off and climbed into the clear sky.

"Good-bye my friend," Lieutenant Milestone sadly said. "We will definitely miss you."

"That we will," Lieutenant McDonald agreed while they stood there and watched as the C-130J Hercules aircraft disappeared into the sky. "Alright people, let's get our gear off the chopper."

The Strike Force team removed their gear from the helicopter and then watched the Sikorsky CH-53 Sea Stallion take off and fly away.

Moments later, a Humvee pulled up and a Marine captain got out on the passenger side and walked over to where Lieutenant McDonald and Lieutenant Milestone were standing. "Who's in command here?" He asked.

"I am," Lieutenant McDonald quickly answered.

"Wolverine sent me, sir. You and your people will be staying in that hangar until you're ordered out," he said, pointing to the hangar in front of them. "It's not much, but it's the best we could do on such short notice."

"Thanks, captain," Lieutenant McDonald said. "I'm sure we can handle it from here."

"Also, Bulldog and his people will be landing here shortly." The captain pointed out. "The tower will call you before they land." The captain walked back to the Humvee; he climbed in on the passenger side, and the Humvee drove away.

"Alright, let's get our gear into the hangar," Lieutenant McDonald ordered.

The Strike Force team carried their equipment into the hangar and put it on the floor next to the door. Lieutenant McDonald entered, with Lieutenant Milestone following close behind him. Lieutenant McDonald quickly scanned the hangar and saw that the inside of the hangar was set up as a barrack, not much different than what they were accustomed to. Upon further inspection, he noticed that there were two rooms at the back of the hangar. "Ironman, I want you and Terminator to set up the sat-com in the room on the left," Lieutenant McDonald ordered.

"Roger that," Ironman acknowledged. "We'll have a com-link to headquarters up and running in a few mikes."

"Very well," Lieutenant McDonald acknowledged. "The rest of you take a bunk and relax while you can."

Lieutenant McDonald and Lieutenant Milestone walked to the back of the hangar and entered the room next to the one where Ironman and Terminator were setting up the satellite radio. They found two desks in the room, with a telephone sitting on one of them.

"I wonder if that telephone works," Lieutenant Milestone commented while he walked over to the desk. He picked up the telephone receiver and put it to his ear. "Yep, it works," he said when he heard a dial tone, and then returned the telephone receiver to its resting place. Lieutenant Milestone laid his HK-416N assault rifle down on the desk and sat down in the chair behind the desk. He took off his radio headset and placed it down on the desk in front of him. "Any idea what Wolverine's planning for us?"

"I haven't a clue," Lieutenant McDonald answered while he laid his HK-416N assault rifle down on the desk next to where Lieutenant Milestone was sitting and then sat down. "One thing's for certain; we're not going back home anytime soon," he continued to say while he took off his radio headset and put it down on the desk in front of him. "I don't think our job here is done yet."

Lieutenant Milestone was startled when the telephone on the desk in front of him began to ring. He looked at Lieutenant McDonald.

"Well, answer the fuckin' phone," Lieutenant McDonald fired back.

Lieutenant Milestone picked up the telephone receiver and put it to his ear. "Yes," he said and listened for a few moments before returning the telephone receiver to its resting place.

"Well," Lieutenant McDonald inquired. "Who was it?"

"It was the tower," Lieutenant Milestone answered. "They said that two C-130J aircraft are approaching and will be landing shortly."

"Well, we better go meet Bulldog," Lieutenant McDonald said while he got up from his seat and headed for the door.

"I'm right behind you," Lieutenant Milestone commented while he too got up from his seat and hurried to catch up with Lieutenant McDonald.

Lieutenant McDonald and Lieutenant Milestone left the office and walked to the hangar entrance. They watched the two C-130J Hercules aircraft touchdown and taxi to the empty hangar next to where they were standing before shutting down their engines.

The back cargo door on one of the C-130J aircraft opened and Captain Hale, nicknamed Bulldog walked down the ramp. The other C-

130J aircraft lowered its back cargo door, and the Strike Force, mobile command personnel, began unloading their equipment from the aircraft and into the empty hangar next to where the Strike Force assault teams were housed. Two UH-60L Black Hawk helicopters were also being offloaded from the C-130J aircraft that Captain Hale had exited from and moved into the same hangar.

Seconds later, two, AM-35 two-and-a-half ton trucks from the US Marine training camp, located a couple of miles from the airport, pulled up next to the two C-130J aircraft. The Marines, dressed in full combat dress with their M16-A4 assault rifles, disembarked from the trucks. The Marine lieutenant in command of the Marines ran over to Captain Hale. "Orders, sir," the lieutenant said while he snapped to attention.

"Lieutenant, I want your Marines to secure the area while these birds are being unloaded," Captain Hale ordered. "Afterwards, you are to secure the perimeter around the hangars. No one but my people is to have access to this area."

"Yes, sir," the lieutenant replied and then ran back to the other Marines barking out orders.

Captain Hale walked over to where Lieutenant McDonald and Lieutenant Milestone were standing.

"What's up?" Lieutenant McDonald asked.

"I'll brief you both inside," Captain Hale answered and walked inside the hangar with Lieutenant McDonald and Lieutenant Milestone following close behind him.

The Strike Force assault teams inside the hangar was surprised to see Captain Hale. Everyone watched Lieutenant McDonald and Lieutenant Milestone escort Captain Hale to the office at the back of the hangar. They entered the office, and Lieutenant Milestone closed the door.

Captain Hale walked over to one of the desks in the room and sat down behind it. "Pull up a chair; we have a lot to go over." Lieutenant McDonald and Lieutenant Milestone each grabbed a chair and sat down before Captain Hale continued. "The President needs more information about the incident at Puerto Obaldia. For now, he's telling everyone that it was an accident."

"What happened at Puerto Obaldia was no accident," Lieutenant Milestone fired back. "We all know that A'zam al Shammari was behind this attack. We've suspected for weeks that Shammari and Juarez were working together."

"The president needs proof," Captain Hale pointed out. "First, we need to find these idiots and get to the bottom of this. All we know for sure is that the gas cylinders used in this attack were made in Colombia."

"Maybe someone wants us to think that General Juarez and Shammari were behind this to take our eyes off the real target," Lieutenant McDonald commented.

"That's why we need to find out if General Juarez and Shammari were behind this," Captain Hale was quick to point out. "I brought the mobile command unit and two Black Hawk helicopters with me. We will be coordinating the mission from here."

Lieutenant McDonald and Lieutenant Milestone listened while Captain Hale explained their upcoming mission in detail.

Chapter 12

US Embassy
Panama City, Panama

CIA operative, Michael Lawrence was sound asleep in his room in the guest quarters at the embassy. He was awakened when someone knocked on the door to his room. Lawrence got out of bed and put his pants on, and walked over to the door. Still half-asleep, he opened the door and was surprised to see one of the Marines from the embassy's security force dressed if full combat dress, with his M16-A4 assault rifle, slung over his shoulder.

"What's up with the combat gear?" Michael Lawrence asked while he rubbed his eyes.

"The embassy is on lockdown."

"For what?"

"Mr. Stone wishes to see you, so get dressed," the Marine said without answering Michael Lawrence's question. "I'll wait out here for you."

"I know how to get to Mr. Stone's office. I don't need an escort to take me there."

"You do today; now get dressed."

Realizing that arguing with the Marine was pointless, Michael Lawrence hurried back over to where the rest of his clothes were and got dressed. He walked back to the doorway where the Marine was waiting and stepped out into the hallway. He closed the door and followed the Marine down the hallway.

The Marine stopped in front of the entrance door to CIA Station Chief, George Stone's office. He knocked on the door before he opened it and motioned for Michael Lawrence to enter. Michael Lawrence entered the office, and the Marine closed the door and stood outside in front of the door.

Forty-four-year-old CIA Station Chief, George Stone was sitting behind his desk reading the latest report on the incident at the US Consulate in Puerto Obaldia, Panama. He had just finished reading the report when Michael Lawrence entered his office.

"What's up with all the security?" Michael Lawrence inquired while he walked over to the chair in front of Stone's desk and sat down.

"You haven't heard?"

"Heard what?"

"You better read this," George Stone said as he handed the report to Michael Lawrence. "We have a serious problem."

Michael Lawrence quickly read the report and sat there in silence for a few seconds. "There were no survivors?"

"None," George Stone sadly answered. "Publicly, the president is calling this an accident. He's looking for answers as to how this could have happened and by whom."

"The who part is simple," Michael Lawrence remarked. "Shammari and that idiot Juarez has to be behind this."

"I agree, but the director wants proof. He..." George Stone stopped talking when the door to his office opened, and CIA operative Kate Livingston; a red-haired thirty-year-old woman entered, and closed the door. "Kate, it's nice to see you again," George Stone said as he and Michael Lawrence got up from their seats. "I thought Deputy Director Hicks was coming down with you?"

"She stayed at the airport with the jet while it's being refueled. She sent me here to pick up Lawrence. I have a car waiting outside to take us to the airport."

Michael Lawrence looked at George Stone. "Is that why you sent for me?"

"Yes, it is," George Stone answered. "I just learned about this a few minutes before I sent the Marine after you. You've been reassigned to the Embassy in Bogotá, Colombia. Deputy Director Hicks will brief you on the way down there."

"It must be important if the director sent Deputy Director Hicks down here," Michael Lawrence was quick to point out.

"It is," Kate Livingston fired back. "So if you don't mind, we need to be going."

"You better do as the lady says," George Stone added. "The Marine outside will escort you both back to your room so you can gather your things. Watch your backs down there. I got a feeling that things are going to get a little wild; if you know what I mean."

"Yes, sir, I'll take good care of Kate."

"In your fuckin' dreams lover boy," Kate Livingston snapped.

"Try not to kill each other down there," George Stone remarked.

Without saying another word, Kate Livingston and Michael Lawrence stepped out of CIA Station Chief, George Stone's office, and the Marine closed the door. They followed the Marine back to the room where Michael Lawrence was staying. The Marine opened the door, and Michael Lawrence hurried inside. He quickly gathered his things and rushed back to where the Marine and Kate Livingston were waiting.

They followed the Marine to the main entrance and exited the embassy. Another Marine from the embassy's security force, also dressed in full combat dress, with his M16-A4 assault rifle, slung over his shoulder, stood by a black SUV with the back door opened. Michael Lawrence opened the back hatch on the SUV and placed his belongings in the back while Kate Livingston climbed into the back seat. When he was done, he closed the hatch and joined Kate Livingston in the back seat. The Marine closed the door, and the SUV sped off.

A few minutes later, the SUV arrived at the airport and stopped alongside a Gulfstream G550 twin-engine jet aircraft. Michael Lawrence got out of the SUV and hurried to the back of the SUV to gather his belongings while Kate Livingston got out and closed the door. He opened the back hatch on the SUV, collected his things, and closed the door, and the SUV drove off. Michael Lawrence and Kate Livingston walked to the aircraft, with Lawrence leading the way.

Michael Lawrence entered the Gulfstream G550 twin-engine jet aircraft, with Kate Livingston following close behind him. He was quick to notice thirty-year-old CIA Deputy Director, Karen Hicks sitting at a table at the front of the aircraft. She was wearing a tight-fitting skirt with a matching blouse. Her blonde color hair appeared to be wrapped in a tight bun and was secured to the back of her head with a hairpin.

"Have a seat Lawrence," Deputy Director Hicks suggested. "We'll talk when we get airborne."

Michael Lawrence sat down in a seat and fastened his seat restraints while Kate Livingston sat across from him and did the same.

The flight crew closed the door, and the pilot gave the jet engines some power, and the aircraft began to move to the runway. When they were cleared for takeoff, the pilot brought the jet engines to maximum power, and the aircraft began to move down the runway, and pick up speed. A few seconds later, the Gulfstream G550 twin-engine jet aircraft left the ground and climbed to its assigned altitude.

"Lawrence, we can get started now," Deputy Director Hicks said when the aircraft leveled off at its cruising altitude. "We don't have much time, so let's get to it."

Michael Lawrence and Kate Livingston removed their seat restraints and got up from their seats, and walked to the front of the aircraft. Lawrence sat down at a table across from Deputy Director Hicks while Kate Livingston sat down next to Deputy Director Hicks.

"I have a few questions for you about what happened at the consulate at Puerto Obaldia," Deputy Director Hicks began while she opened the folder on the table in front of her. "Director Müller sent Kate and I down here to investigate the Puerto Obaldia incident," she continued. "It is believed that the attack was executed with the help of someone inside the consulate. There are some things I need to go over with you before we land at Langley."

"Stone told me that I was reassigned to Bogotá," Michael Lawrence was quick to point out. "I don't understand; what's going on here?"

"That's what Stone was told," Kate Livingston answered while Deputy Director Hicks looked through the folder. "The director felt that the less anyone knew about our investigation, the better."

"The one question everyone wants answered is why did you leave the consulate at Puerto Obaldia hours before the attack occurred?" Deputy Director Hicks inquired. "It just seems strange that you left there hours before the attack."

"Wait a minute; you don't think that I had anything to do with this?

Are you accusing me of being involved in this attack?"

"No one is accusing you of anything," Deputy Director Hicks fired back. "It just seems odd that you left the consulate the same night of the attack."

"Hastings got a message ordering him back to Langley for a debriefing, and to halt all operations until he got back. He told me I could take a few days off, so I decided to go to Panama City and relax a little." Michael Lawrence paused to get control of his emotions before he continued. "Hastings was the one who suggested that I catch a ride with the ambassador and his family who were leaving for Panama City. If I hadn't, I'd be dead too."

"You're sure that Hastings got a message from Langley?" Deputy Director Hicks asked while she looked through the folder in front of her again and removed the message log sheet from the consulate for the day in question.

"Yes, I am," Lawrence fired back. "I took the message to him myself."

Deputy Director Hicks looked at the message log sheet. "Where did you get this message from that you say was for Hastings?"

"I picked it up in the com-center with the rest of our messages," Lawrence answered. "It was lying in our basket."

"Fortunate for you there is no one alive at the consulate that can dispute your claim," Kate Livingston pointed out.

"What the hell do you mean by that?"

"There's no record that a message was sent by Langley or received by the consulate for Hastings," Deputy Director Hicks was quick to point out. "We have no way of verifying your story."

"This is bullshit," Michael Lawrence said as he got up from his seat.

"Sit down," Deputy Director Hicks snapped. "We're not done here."

"Yes, we are," Michael Lawrence fired back. He reached into his inside jacket pocket and removed his credentials, and slammed them down on the table in front of Deputy Director Hicks. "Kiss my ass; I'm done." He walked to the back of the aircraft and sat down.

"What do you think?" Deputy Director Hicks asked Kate Livingston.

"I think someone planted that message for Hastings knowing that they would follow protocol, and shut down operations in the area," Kate Livingston pointed out. "Plus, it's evident that they knew how to get around our security at the consulate."

"So you believe Lawrence's story."

"Yes, I believe he's telling the truth."

"You could be right about Lawrence," Deputy Director Hicks agreed. "Let's see how he does on the polygraph when we get back at Langley." Deputy Director Hicks picked up Michael Lawrence's credentials from the table and handed them to Kate Livingston. "Give these back to Lawrence, and tell him I didn't mean to press him so hard."

"What about our investigation into the attack on Puerto Obaldia?" Kate Livingston asked as she got up from her seat with Michael Lawrence's credentials in her hand.

"We keep looking and hope we find the answers before they attack again."

Kate Livingston walked to the back of the aircraft and sat down across from Michael Lawrence. She handed him his credentials and smiled. "She didn't mean to be so hard on you."

"She's got some nerve accusing me of lying," he commented as he put his credentials back into his inside jacket pocket.

"She's just trying to get to the truth before anyone else dies," Kate Livingston assured Michael Lawrence as she got up from her seat. "Try to relax a little. We'll be landing in Langley in a couple of hours."

Kate Livingston walked back to the table where Deputy Director Hicks was sitting while Michael Lawrence picked up a magazine that was lying on the seat next to him and began to thumb through the pages.

* * * * *

Twenty kilometers from Puerto Obaldia Panama on the Colombian side of the border, General Fresco Juarez, Commander of the Revolutionary Armed Forces of Colombia, was sitting in the command tent listing to the news reports about the incident at the US Consulate in Puerto Obaldia, Panama on his short-wave radio. He was furious when he heard that President Elliot claimed that the incident at the US Consulate in Puerto Obaldia, Panama was a terrible accident, and not an act of terrorism. "Accident my ass," General Juarez said in Spanish to the colonel that was sitting across from him.

"The American president will pay for his ignorance soon enough," A'zam al Shammari said in English, who was sitting next to the colonel. "We need to stick to our plan. There's no way the Americans know where we'll strike next. By the time they figure that out, it will be too late for them to stop us."

General Juarez looked at A'zam al Shammari and smiled. Before he could respond to A'zam al Shammari's comment, the sound of some of his men shouting outside the command tent got his attention. "Go see what's going on out there," General Juarez said to the colonel in Spanish.

"Yes, sir," the colonel acknowledged in Spanish and got up from his seat. He hurried outside to see what was going on. "What's all the commotion about," he demanded to know,

"We caught those two following our supply trucks," a lieutenant answered, pointing to the two men who had a burlap bag over their head, and being held at gunpoint in front of a Jeep that was parked next to the command tent. "The papers that we found on them, identify them as American reporters from CNN," the lieutenant continued while handing the colonel the documents that were found on the two men.

The colonel took the documents from the lieutenant and looked at them. Without uttering a word, he hurried back into the command tent. "General, one of our patrols captured two American reporters who were following our supply trucks," the colonel reported, speaking in Spanish. The colonel put the papers that were found on the two Americans in front of General Juarez. "What should we do with these American spies?"

"Take them to the interrogation tent," General Juarez replied in Spanish. "I will personally interrogate them myself shortly."

"Yes, sir," the colonel acknowledged. He saluted General Juarez and left the command tent to carry out the general's orders. "Bring those two American dogs to the interrogation tent," the colonel said to the lieutenant.

"Yes, sir," the lieutenant acknowledged.

The lieutenant, along with four men, and the two captured Americans, followed the colonel to the interrogation tent and entered.

Once inside the interrogation tent, the burlap bags were removed from the American captives' heads. One of the reporters was strapped into a chair in the middle of the room while the other was chained to one of the posts on the inside of the tent.

With their task completed, the lieutenant and his four men left the interrogation tent. The lieutenant assigned two men to stand guard at the tent's entrance, in case they were needed while he and the other two men returned to their duties.

A few minutes later, General Juarez and A'zam al Shammari entered the interrogation tent. Everyone inside the tent snapped to attention and saluted the general. General Juarez snapped a quick salute back at them and walked over to the reporter who was strapped into the interrogation chair.

The reporter looked at General Juarez. "Who the fuck are you?" He asked in English.

General Juarez slapped him hard across his face in anger. "You might be a smart-ass now, but that will change," he said in English.

"Fuck off," the reporter who was strapped into the interrogation chair shot back. "You'll get nothing out of us."

"Oh, I think I will," General Juarez commented and then walked over to the other reporter who was chained to the post. "One of you will tell me what I want to know before we're finished with you." The general walked back over to the man who was strapped into the interrogation chair. "Now tell me, why were you following my trucks?"

"Blow me."

General Juarez stepped back, and the interrogator began beating the reporter with a two-foot piece of insulated rubber hose. After a few long minutes, the general motioned the interrogator to stop. General Juarez walked over to the reporter who was strapped into the interrogation chair and grabbed him by his hair. He flung his head back hard on the chair's headrest. "Tell me, why were you following my trucks?"

The man moaned in pain but didn't say anything. General Juarez released the grip that he had on his head, and the reporter slumped forward.

"Can't you see that you're fuckin' killing him," the other man who was chained to the post shouted. "We weren't following your trucks. We were on our way back to Bogotá, and we got lost."

"You expect me to believe that?" General Juarez fired back.

"It's the truth," the man who was chained to the post shouted back.

General Juarez pulled out his pearl handled forty-five caliber sidearm from its holster. He loaded a round into the firing chamber, cocked the firing hammer back, and put the barrel against the head of the reporter who was strapped into the interrogation chair. He looked directly at the other man who was chained to the post. "Tell me the truth or I'll put a bullet in this man's head."

"Like I said, we were on our way back to Bogotá, and we got lost."

"Wrong answer," General Juarez commented and pulled the trigger on his forty-five caliber pistol, instantly killing the reporter who was strapped into the interrogation chair.

"I'm telling you the truth," the man who was chained to the post shouted.

General Juarez pointed his forty-five caliber pistol at him. "You shouldn't have gotten lost then," he said just before he fired three rounds into his chest, killing him instantly. General Juarez walked over to the dead reporter who was hanging lifeless from the pole. "Liar," he said, and then laughed. He returned his forty-five caliber pistol to its holster.

"General, you know there's a good chance that the Americans know where we are," A'zam al Shammari pointed out.

"Yes, I suppose you're right," General Juarez admitted.

"Sir, should I increase the perimeter guards?" the colonel suggested, speaking in Spanish.

Before General Juarez could respond to the colonel's suggestion, the lieutenant entered the tent. He walked over to the general, snapped to attention, and saluted the general.

"Yes, lieutenant," General Juarez said in Spanish while he returned the lieutenant's salute.

"General, we have received a message from our camp at Carepa," the lieutenant announced, speaking in Spanish. "Everything is ready, sir."

"Good, the general acknowledged. "Colonel, have the men break camp," General Juarez ordered. "I want to be ready to leave within the hour."

"Yes general," the colonel acknowledged. "Lieutenant, with me."

"Yes, sir," the lieutenant acknowledged and followed the colonel out of the interrogation tent.

A few minutes later, General Juarez and A'zam al Shammari left the interrogation tent and walked back to the command tent. When they entered the tent, they found their American friend sitting at the table looking at the identification papers that were taken from the American reporters.

"Do you know those men?" A'zam al Shammari inquired, speaking in English.

"They're not reporters for CNN," the American answered. "They're NSA agents."

"They are dead NSA agents now," General Juarez was quick to point out.

"I heard your people talking about moving to the camp at Carepa," the American said as he got up from his seat.

"Yes, we are," General Juarez said. "I want the two of you to remain here and break down the lab. I will leave some soldiers here to assist you."

"My people and I will take care of dismantling the lab," Shammari pointed out. "We won't be far behind you."

"I will still leave some of my soldiers here just in case you need them," General Juarez insisted. "I will see both of you in Carepa," he concluded, and then he left the tent.

"The general seems a little excited," Shammari commented.

"Yeah, a little bit too excited if you ask me," the American agreed. "If he's not careful, he could screw-up this entire operation and get us all killed."

"What do you suggest we do?"

"I say pack up your lab, and we make our way across the border and lay low there until this is over."

"Yes, I agree," Shammari acknowledged. "I best get my people moving on packing up the lab."

Shammari left the command tent while the American removed a satellite telephone from his back pocket. He extended the antenna and powered-up the satellite telephone. He pushed a number on the sat-phone and put it to his ear. "The package is in play," he said when someone answered his call. "My friend and I are heading for the border.

I will check-in when we get settled somewhere." He ended the call and returned the antenna to its secure resting place. He put the satellite telephone in his back pocket and sat back down behind the table.

Chapter 13

US Embassy
Bogotá, Colombia

Robert Haskell, the ambassador to Colombia, and his wife Joan was eating their daily lunch together in the dining room of the Ambassador's Residence while they watched the world news on the television. They were waiting for Press Secretary, Jill Summers to brief the press on the incident at the US consulate at Puerto Obaldia, Panama.

When Press Secretary Summers appeared on the television set, they listened carefully as she explained what had happened at the US consulate at Puerto Obaldia, Panama. Ambassador Haskell sat in his chair without saying a word. After Press Secretary Summers had finished reading the official statement, Ambassador Haskell picked up the television remote control and turned off the television. "There's more to this than what she's saying," Ambassador Haskell commented.

"You don't think that it was an act of terrorism, do you?" Joan asked.

"It's hard to say," Ambassador Haskell replied. "I'm sure if it was, someone would have claimed responsibility for it by now."

"I suppose you're right," Joan said.

"I'm sorry dear, but I got to get back to my office," Ambassador Haskell said while he got up from his chair. "I have a lot to do this afternoon." He kissed Joan on the lips before continuing. "I'll see you tonight." Ambassador Haskell exited the dining room and walked to his office. When he entered the reception area, Jennifer Masterson, his personal secretary, was sitting behind her desk. Without saying a word, Ambassador Haskell entered his office and closed the door. He walked over to his desk and sat down in his chair.

There was a knock on his door, and the door opened. "Mr. Ambassador, could I have a moment of your time?" Jennifer Masterson asked.

"Sure," Ambassador Haskell answered. "What's on your mind?"

"Sir, was the incident at Puerto Obaldia really an accident?" She calmly asked.

"As far as I know it was," He replied. "Did you know someone who was there?"

"Yes, sir, my older brother was stationed there with the Marine Security Force," she replied with tears in her eyes.

"Oh, I'm so sorry," Ambassador Haskell commented while he got up from his seat. He walked over to Jennifer Masterson and gave her a hug. "I didn't know; why don't you take some time off?"

"You need me here," she said while breaking their embrace. "Besides, I need to stay busy."

"I understand," Ambassador Haskell commented. He walked back to his seat and sat down. "If you change your mind about taking some time off just let me know; I'll understand."

"Thank you, Mr. Ambassador," Jennifer Masterson said. "Sir, I would like to keep what happened to my brother between us. I don't want everyone to know about it."

"I will tell no one," Ambassador Haskell assured her, "You have my word on it."

"Thank you, Mr. Ambassador," Jennifer Masterson said and then she left the ambassador's office.

Ambassador Haskell went to get up from his seat when the intercom on the telephone on his desk began to beep. He pushed the intercom button on the telephone. "Yes," he said as he returned to his seat.

"Mr. Ambassador, you have a call on the secure line," Jennifer Masterson reported. "Sir, it's the president calling."

"I am not to be disturbed while I take this call."

"Yes, Mr. Ambassador."

Ambassador Haskell pushed the intercom button to cancel the intercom call, and grabbed the telephone receiver from the telephone on his desk. He put the telephone receiver to his ear, and pushed the button on the telephone that was flashing. "This is Ambassador Haskell," he calmly said. "What can I do for you today Mr. President?"

"Robert, how's it going down there?"

"Everyone here is on edge since the incident at Puerto Obaldia."

"Yes, that was a tragic accident."

"So it was an accident?"

"I've not seen anything to suggest otherwise," President Elliot assured Ambassador Haskell. "We'll know more when the investigators complete their investigation. If there's anything you need to worry about, you'll be the first to know. However, as a precautionary measure, I've talked to President Roberto, and he has agreed to allow us to increase the Marine Security Force there. The Marines should be arriving there in a few hours."

"I appreciate that Mr. President."

"Robert, the main reason I called was to let you know that I'm sending you an important dispatch by special courier. When you receive it, you are to follow my instructions to the letter and discuss the contents of that message with no one. I will explain everything to you in due time."

"I understand Mr. President. You can count on me, sir."

"Take care Robert," President Elliot said, and then he ended the call.

That was odd; Ambassador Haskell thought as he returned the telephone receiver to the telephone on his desk. *I wonder what that was all about?* He continued to think while he leaned back in his chair.

* * * * *

Langley Air Force Base
Langley, Virginia

The Gulfstream G550 twin-engine jet aircraft that was carrying CIA officer, Michael Lawrence, along with CIA Deputy Director, Karen Hicks and CIA officer, Kate Livingston, touched down on the runway and taxied to where two black SUV's were waiting. The pilot powered down the aircraft's engines while the ground crew opened the exit door.

Michael Lawrence removed his seat restraints and began to collect his things. "You can leave your stuff here," Deputy Director Hicks commented. "The ground crew will take care of it for you."

"Yes Ma'am," Michael Lawrence acknowledged. "If you say so."

Deputy Director Hicks smiled and continued walking to the exit. Kate Livingston looked at Michael Lawrence and shook her head in disbelief. "You know Lawrence; your sarcasm towards the Deputy Director is going to come back and bite you on the ass someday," she commented, and then she hurried off to catch up with Deputy Director Hicks.

Michael Lawrence got up from his seat and hurried to the back of the aircraft. He followed Deputy Director Hicks and Kate Livingston down the exit ramp, and they walked toward the lead SUV.

When they arrived at the lead SUV, Deputy Director Hicks turned to face Michael Lawrence. "Kate and I will be riding in this car," she informed Michael Lawrence. "You'll be riding in the car behind us," she continued while she pointed to the other SUV.

"Yes Ma'am," Michael Lawrence acknowledged. "Whatever you say," he said sarcastically and walked over to the other SUV.

"What an asshole," Deputy Director Hicks commented as she opened the back door to the SUV. "He needs to learn some damn manners," she continued while she got into the back seat of the SUV.

"Yeah, maybe someday," Kate Livingston said while she joined Deputy Director Hicks in the back seat and closed the door.

Michael Lawrence walked over to the other SUV as directed by Deputy Director Hicks. He opened the door and climbed inside, and closed the door while the SUV that contained Deputy Director Hicks, and Kate Livingston drove off.

A few minutes later, Michael Lawrence felt the SUV begin to move. He stared out the window while the SUV exited Langley Air Force Base and got on the interstate. "This isn't the way to headquarters," he said when he noticed that they were traveling in the wrong direction.

"We're not going to headquarters," the driver pointed out.

"Then where in the hell are we going?"

"You will find out soon enough," the driver answered. "Just sit back and enjoy the ride sir. We'll be at our destination shortly."

Michael Lawrence got comfortable and looked out the side window of the SUV. A few minutes later, the SUV exited the interstate and continued down a two-lane road. *Where the fuck is this jackass taking me?* He thought as the SUV turned off the two-lane road onto a graveled driveway.

The SUV traveled a few miles down the graveled driveway and stopped in front of an old farmhouse where two men were standing outside. One of the men opened the back door to the SUV and motioned for Lawrence to get out.

Where the fuck am I? Michael Lawrence asked himself as he stepped out of the SUV. The man closed the door, and he followed the two men to the front door of the farmhouse. "The first doorway on your left," one of the men said while the other opened the front door. Lawrence stepped inside the farmhouse, and the man closed the door.

Eager to find out what was going on, he walked to the first doorway on his left and entered. He quickly scanned the room and found a man sitting on the sofa in the back of the room reading something that was on the coffee table in front of him. When the man was finished, he put the paper back into an opened briefcase that was on the table, and looked up at him. Lawrence was surprised to see that the man was none other than CIA Director, Robert Müller. "Director Müller, sir, I was under the impression that I was to meet with you at headquarters right after I took my polygraph."

"I thought it best if we meet here instead of in my office," Director Müller commented. "I use this place for special meetings such as this one."

"I don't understand, sir."

"There have been some new developments while you were on your way back here," Director Müller pointed out. "Have a seat," he continued while he motioned to the sitting chair across from him. "I have a few more things to go over with you concerning the incident at Puerto Obaldia."

"I've already told Deputy Director Hicks everything I know about what happened," Michael Lawrence said while he walked over to the sitting chair and sat down. "I don't understand. What could I possibly tell you that you don't already know?"

"As I said, there have been some new developments, Director Müller continued while he removed a paper enclosed in plastic. "This was found in Hastings' office," he said while holding up the paper in his hand. "Does this look familiar?"

"That's the message that I gave to Hastings. That clearly proves that I was telling the truth about the message that no one wants to admit sending."

"No one at Langley sent that message, and no one at Puerto Obaldia received it; it was a plant."

"Are you sure about that, sir?"

"Yes, I am. The paper that the message was printed on does not match the paper stock that we were using at Puerto Obaldia," Director Müller pointed out while he placed the paper back into his briefcase. "I believe that someone got into the com-center and planted that message."

"I don't see how anyone could have gotten around the security at the entrance to the com-center."

"Well, they did," Director Müller fired back. "There were three sets of fingerprints found on the message. Yours, Hastings, and an unknown, which doesn't match anyone in our files. It's now believed that the message was a diversion to get our operations in the area temporarily suspended, so we would be blinded to what they were going to do."

"So, when is the consulate going to reopen?" Michael Lawrence inquired.

"It's not," Director Müller answered. "The president has ordered the consulate closed, and all diplomatic functions are to be handled by the Embassy in Panama City. However, the president has agreed to allow us and the NSA, and the DEA to continue using the facility at Puerto Obaldia to gather intelligence and to run field operations when necessary. New security measures, along with a medium-size Marine Security Force are being set in place to prevent this from happening again. The facility should be operational soon."

"I don't understand, sir. What does any of this have to do with me? Surely you're not sending me back to Puerto Obaldia."

"No, I'm not sending you back to Puerto Obaldia," Director Müller assured Michael Lawrence. "How would you like to be involved in an operation to take down General Juarez?"

"I'd like to be the one to put a bullet in his head."

"So, I take that as a yes to my proposal?"

"Yes, sir. When do I leave?"

"Shortly," Director Müller said while he pulled a large brown envelope from the briefcase on the table in front of him. "I've put together a five-man assault team, and I want you to assume tactical command of this unit," he continued as he offered the large brown envelope to Michael Lawrence. "I've personally hand-picked each member of your team. They're good people, and trustworthy."

"Thank you, sir," was all Lawrence could manage to say as he reached over and took the large brown envelope from Director Müller. "Sir, who do I report to?"

"You will report directly to me and no one else. You will not discuss this operation with anyone outside of your unit. Everything you need to know is in that envelope."

"Yes, sir."

"The SUV that brought you here will take you back to Langley. You will fly out on the same jet that you flew in on from Panama City. The rest of your team should be on the aircraft by the time you arrive. You will open your mission brief while in flight. Questions?"

"No, sir," Michael Lawrence acknowledged as he got up from the sitting chair.

"Remember, tell no one what you're doing. Is that clear?"

"Crystal clear, sir."

With the large brown envelope in hand, Michael Lawrence hurried out of the room. He walked to the front door, and a man who was standing by the door opened it, and Michael Lawrence stepped outside. He rushed to the SUV that was waiting, and the man that was standing by the back door opened the door. He got into the back seat, and the man closed the door, and the SUV drove off.

$$* * * * *$$

Strike Force Delta Command
Tinker Air Force Base
Oklahoma City, Oklahoma

Colonel Wilson sat behind his desk going over the latest reports on the terrorist attack on the consulate at Puerto Obaldia when Operations Specialist First Lieutenant Kate Stanton, nicknamed Barbie entered his office.

"Wolverine, I'm sorry to bother you, but I may have a solution to the satellite problem in northern Columbia," Lieutenant Stanton reported while she closed the office door. "I've talked with Major Sullivan from the Army CID (Criminal Investigation Division). She says that there's a way to disable those satellite jammers, and the mobile command stations."

"Go on; I'm all ears," Colonel Wilson commented.

"During her investigation, she discovered that there was a failsafe built into these satellite jammers and mobile command stations, in case they ever fell into the wrong hands. She said that we could send a coded signal to the jammers and the mobile command stations, and rendered them inoperable."

"Do you have the codes?"

"Yes, I do."

"I don't like it. It sounds too easy. Are you sure about this?"

"That's what Major Sullivan said."

"Barbie, What if she's wrong?"

"I see your point Wolverine."

"Is there any way to verify these codes?"

"Yes, but it will take some time."

"Time, is one luxury we don't have. We need..." Colonel Wilson stopped in mid-sentence.

"What's wrong Wolverine?"

"I just thought of something. How are those jammers and command stations powered?"

"When deployed in the field, they're powered by diesel generators," Lieutenant Stanton answered, and then smiled. "That's it Wolverine, carbon-dioxide emissions. That's the key to finding them."

"Are you sure?"

"Without a doubt. They were never designed for stealth operations. I can task the satellites to look for large pockets of carbon-dioxide emissions."

"How long will this take?"

"Thirty minutes."

Colonel Wilson glanced at the clock on the wall. "Popeye and Crazy Horse are moving out in about an hour, so be quick about it."

"I'll be in the Command Center," Lieutenant Stanton said as she walked to the office door.

"Let me know the minute you get something," Colonel Wilson said while he removed the telephone receiver from the telephone on his desk. He dialed the number for General Richwood and put the telephone receiver to his ear while Lieutenant Stanton exited his office and closed the door.

Chapter 14

Tocumen International Airport
Panama City, Panama

Lieutenant McDonald stood in the doorway of the hangar and watched while the ground crew pulled the two UH-60L Black Hawk helicopters from the hangar next to him and began preparing them for their upcoming mission. Before the sun fully set on the horizon, the ground crew had the two Black Hawk helicopters ready.

Both Black Hawk helicopters were specially modified to be support gunships. They were each equipped with two M-230 thirty-millimeter automatic chain gun cannons with rocket pods mounted on each side of the helicopter and two M-134D mini guns.

"Sure is a pretty sunset," Lieutenant Milestone commented, who was standing next to Lieutenant McDonald.

"That it is," Lieutenant McDonald agreed.

"Excuse me Popeye, but Bulldog wants to see both of you," one of the Strike Force team members said, who was standing behind Lieutenant McDonald and Lieutenant Milestone. "He said it's urgent."

"We better go and find out what Bulldog wants," Lieutenant McDonald remarked as he stepped back into the hangar.

"Right behind you," Lieutenant Milestone said and followed Lieutenant McDonald to the back of the hangar where the mobile command center was located. They walked over to Captain Hale, who was standing in front of the plasma screen that displayed the satellite image of the area twenty kilometers from Puerto Obaldia Panama on the

Colombian side of the border. The screen was blank except for eight red dots and one blue dot.

"What's up?" Lieutenant McDonald asked.

"There has been a slight change in the mission," Captain Hale answered. "Wolverine believes that the satellite jammers and the mobile command stations have been located. The red dots on the screen indicate where we believe they are hiding the satellite jammers and the mobile command stations. The Navy is getting ready to hit the satellite jammers and the mobile command stations positions."

"What's the blue dot for?" Lieutenant Milestone asked.

"That's where we think General Juarez and A'zam al Shammari are hiding."

"What gives you the idea that General Juarez and A'zam al Shammari are in the blue dot area?" Lieutenant McDonald asked.

"Over the past twelve hours, two CIA field operatives and two NSA agents have gone missing in that area," Captain Hale answered. "No one has heard a peep from any of them. That's why it's believed that Juarez and Shammari are in the area.

"That's a hell of an assumption," Lieutenant Milestone was quick to point out.

"I got to agree with Crazy Horse on this one," Lieutenant McDonald added. "We could be going on a wild-goose chase or worse; we could be walking into an ambush."

"Prepare your teams for departure," Captain Hale fired back. " Popeye, you will assume tactical command of both teams. Crazy Horse you will assist Popeye. A CH-53, accompanied by two Black Hawk gunships will take you to the target area. You will be inserted ten clicks north of the target area and check in with me before proceeding south. Understood?"

"Affirmative," Lieutenant McDonald and Lieutenant Milestone acknowledged at the same time.

"There is no way of knowing what you might run into down there so keep a sharp lookout," Captain Hale pointed out. "Are there any questions?"

"What do we do if we find General Juarez and his army or Shammari and his companions?" Lieutenant McDonald asked.

"You are to observe and report their position back to me," Captain

Hale answered. "You are not to engage unless fired upon; any more questions?" Captain Hale paused for a moment before he continued. "You will move out in twenty. Good hunting; and watch your backs down there."

Lieutenant McDonald and Lieutenant Milestone walked back into the hangar. "Team One and two gear up and assemble on me and Crazy Horse at the hangar entrance," Lieutenant McDonald shouted while he and Lieutenant Milestone walked to the hangar entrance.

The Strike Force team members hurried to the hangar entrance and prepared for their departure. A few minutes later, the ground crew pulled the Sikorsky CH-53 Sea Stallion helicopter from its hangar and began preparing it for its upcoming mission.

"Alright people, grab your gear and get a move on it," Lieutenant McDonald ordered when he noticed that one of the ground crew was signaling him that it was time for them to board the helicopter. "It's time to get this show on the road."

The Strike Force team grabbed their weapons and equipment and followed Lieutenant McDonald and Lieutenant Milestone to the Sikorsky CH-53 Sea Stallion helicopter and climbed onboard. Not long Afterwards, the Sikorsky CH-53 Sea Stallion helicopter and both UH-60L Black Hawk helicopter gunships lifted off from the ground and headed south with both UH-60L Black Hawk helicopter gunships leading the way.

A few hours later, they arrived at the insertion point. The Sikorsky CH-53 Sea Stallion helicopter hovered a few inches from the treetops while the two UH-60L Black Hawk helicopter gunships remained airborne to provide air support if needed.

The Strike Force team quickly line repelled in groups of two from the back of the helicopter to the thick jungle below. When they were safely on the ground, the CH-53 Sea Stallion helicopter joined the two UH-60L Black Hawk helicopter gunships. They headed north toward the US consulate at Puerto Obaldia, Panama; where they would stand by until they were needed.

Terminator handed Lieutenant McDonald the satellite radiotelephone receiver, so he could check in with the Strike Force Mobile Command Center at the airport in Panama City.

"You read my mind," Lieutenant McDonald commented while he

took the satellite radiotelephone receiver from Terminator and put it to his ear. "Eagle Nest One this is Sandstorm, over."

"Sandstorm, this is Eagle Nest One, over."

" Eagle Nest One we are on the ground; mission status, over," Lieutenant McDonald reported.

"Roger Sandstorm; the mission is a go. I say again, the mission is a go. We now have eyes on the target. Target area is hot. Do you copy, over?"

"Eagle Nest One we copy; the mission is a go. We're heading to the target area, over and out."

"Roger Sandstorm; Eagle Nest One out."

"Alright people, let's move out," Lieutenant McDonald ordered while handing Terminator the satellite radiotelephone receiver. "Preacher, you and Cowboy take point. Snake, you bring up the rear."

The Strike Force team made their way through the jungle carefully and quietly. A few minutes before sunrise they arrived at their target area. Lieutenant McDonald and Lieutenant Milestone took out their binoculars and scanned the area while the rest of the strike force team took up defensive positions around the camp's perimeter.

"Looks like General Juarez and his band of idiots moved out in a hurry," Lieutenant McDonald said to Lieutenant Milestone, who was standing next to him. "Like they knew we were coming."

"Wait, I see some movement," Lieutenant Milestone pointed out. "Take a look at your two o'clock. Do you see what I see?"

Lieutenant McDonald turned his attention to his right and saw what Lieutenant Milestone was looking at. "Well hello there Shammari," he mumbled in excitement. "Your ass is mine this time." He looked closer and saw Shammari's travel companions not far away armed with AK-47 assault rifles and wearing M-42 gas masks. "Alright, listen up," he said over the radio headset while he put the binoculars back into its carrying case. "I want everyone to put on their gas masks. It looks like there might be some VX Nerve Gas in that camp."

Everyone did as Lieutenant McDonald had ordered and put their M-42 gas mask on over their headset. They readied their HK-416N assault rifles with silencers attached for action and waited for Lieutenant McDonald's next order.

Terminator, who was standing on the other side of Lieutenant

McDonald, handed Lieutenant McDonald the satellite radiotelephone receiver, and he put it to his ear. "Eagle Nest One this is Sandstorm, over."

"Sandstorm, this is Eagle Nest One, over."

"Eagle Nest One, we have arrived at target and have located The Scorpion and his travel companions. They have the bad stuff with them; request permission to move in, over."

"Negative Sandstorm; stand fast at your position. We have two Sparrows coming in. Light up the target and stand-by, over."

"Roger Eagle Nest One; Sandstorm standing-by." Lieutenant McDonald handed Terminator the satellite radiotelephone receiver. "Crazy Horse, light up the target," he said over the radio headset while he removed his binoculars from its carrying case and waited.

"Roger that," Lieutenant Milestone acknowledged and pulled out his laser guiding unit. He pointed it toward the camp and powered it up.

Lieutenant McDonald watched as two BGM-109D Tomahawk cruise missiles hit the target area a few seconds apart with devastating accuracy. When the dust cleared, he looked through his binoculars and saw that only a large tent and the tent next to it remained intact. "Got you this time you motherfucker," he remarked while he put his binoculars back into its carrying case.

"Eagle Nest wants to talk to you Popeye," Terminator, the unit's radio operator said while he handed Lieutenant McDonald the satellite radiotelephone receiver. "It's Wolverine."

Lieutenant McDonald put the satellite radiotelephone receiver to his ear, "Eagle Nest, this is Sandstorm, over."

"Sandstorm I want you and your people to check out what's left of that camp and report back to me ASAP. I need to know the status on The Scorpion, over."

"Roger Eagle Nest I copy, Sandstorm out." Lieutenant McDonald handed the satellite radiotelephone receiver back to Terminator. "Alright, listen up people," he said over the radio headset. "Wolverine wants us to check out what's left of that camp. Leave your gas masks on and proceed with caution. Anything moves down there with two legs you light it up. Let's move out."

The Strike Force team converged on the camp, keeping a sharp lookout for anything suspicious. Snake and Cowboy watched the road that led into the camp while the rest of the Strike Force team began sifting through the rubble. The M-42 gas mask blocked the stench of burning flesh, but the sight of scattered body parts was a horrible sight to see.

Lieutenant Milestone found what was left of A'zam al Shammari a few feet from the large tent. "We got the motherfucker this time," he reported over the radio headset. "We won't have to worry about this cocksucker anymore."

Lieutenant McDonald ran over to where Lieutenant Milestone was standing to take a look at what he had found. "Terminator, get Wolverine on the radio," Lieutenant McDonald said over the radio headset. "Tell him that The Scorpion has been neutralized, and we're checking the rest of the camp to see what they left behind."

"I'm on it," Terminator acknowledged.

"Crazy Horse, take Ice Man and check out the small tent," Lieutenant McDonald suggested. "Preacher and I will check out the large one."

"Ice Man, meet me over by the small tent," Lieutenant Milestone said over the radio headset.

"On my way," Ice Man acknowledged.

Lieutenant McDonald looked at Preacher, who was standing next to him. "Let's go."

"Right behind you," Preacher remarked.

Lieutenant McDonald and Preacher walked over to the large tent and carefully entered. They pulled out their biological, chemical and poisonous gas detection meter to check the air inside the tent. Even though, the air appeared to be safe inside the tent; they kept their M-42 gas masks on as a precautionary measure.

"This must have been their command tent," Preacher pointed out. "It looks as though they left in a hurry; as if they knew we were coming."

"It appears that way," Lieutenant McDonald commented. "But we still got Shammari's ass."

"Yeah, we did, but what if he was sacrificed for our benefit?" Preacher asked.

"What are you getting at?" Lieutenant McDonald fired back.

"I think we're being played," Preacher answered. "I mean finding

Shammari here long enough to take him out with a missile strike. Popeye, something just doesn't feel right."

"There's nothing in here," Lieutenant McDonald said to change the subject. "Let's get the fuck out of here."

Lieutenant McDonald and Preacher exited the tent. Lieutenant McDonald walked over to the other tent while Preacher rejoined the Strike force team. He entered and was stunned by what he saw. There were all kinds of laboratory equipment everywhere. He knew that he had just stepped into a working laboratory.

"This is where they were making the VX Nerve Gas," Lieutenant Milestone reported. "Those tanks in the corner are where they were storing the shit," he continued, pointing at two large tanks in the corner. "The tanks are empty, but the gas concentration in here is high. They must have put what gas they had made up into smaller containers and moved them out of here not long ago."

"You don't say," Lieutenant McDonald commented.

"We also found the formula, building blueprints, and a lot of other documents," Lieutenant Milestone pointed out.

This doesn't make any sense; Lieutenant McDonald thought. *What am I missing?* A cold chill ran up his spine when it came to him. "Bring as much of that shit with you as you can," he ordered. "I want this place rigged for demolition. We leave in five mikes (minutes)."

Lieutenant McDonald hurried out of the tent and stood at the tent's entrance. Snake, a member of Lieutenant Milestone's team, walked over to where he was standing. "I found something that you need to see."

"Let's see what you found," Lieutenant McDonald remarked. He followed Snake a few feet until Snake stopped in front of a body on the ground. "Well, I be damned," he commented when he saw the body of Bill Riley; the CIA Station Chief in Kabul Afghanistan who was reported killed by a car bomb. "I guess we know now how they got around the security at Puerto Obaldia. He must have been in on it from the beginning."

"Popeye, I went through his pockets and found nothing," Snake reported. "I did find this briefcase not far from the body," he continued, referring to the briefcase next to Bill Riley's body.

"Bring it with you. We can go through it on the way back to base,"

"What do you want me to do with Riley's body?"

"Nothing. He's already had one funeral. Leave the traitorous bastard where he is."

"Popeye, Bulldog, wants to talk to you," Terminator said as he approached. "He said that it's urgent."

"I want everyone ready to move out," Lieutenant McDonald said over the radio headset while Snake handed him the briefcase. He took the satellite radiotelephone receiver from Terminator, and he put it to his ear while Snake hurried back to join the other Strike Force team members. "Eagle Nest One this is Sandstorm, over."

"Sandstorm, this is Eagle Nest One. Stand-by for Bulldog, over."

"Roger that. Standing-by, over"

"Popeye, Looking-glass (satellite) has spotted a large number of unknowns heading your way from the south, over."

"How far out are they? Over."

"About twenty klicks, and closing fast, over."

"Roger that. We're Oscar-Mike (on the move). Advise Tiger Two and Ark Angel that this might be a hot extract, over and out."

Lieutenant Milestone and Ice Man emerged from the tent after they had finished placing the explosive charges, and hurried over to where Lieutenant McDonald and Terminator were standing. "What's up?" Lieutenant Milestone asked.

"There's a large number of unknowns coming up fast from the south," Lieutenant McDonald answered while he handed Terminator the satellite radiotelephone receiver. "Listen up," Lieutenant McDonald said over the radio headset. "We need to get the fuck out of here. Preacher take point, Cowboy and Snake, bring up the rear."

The Strike Force team headed north at a fast pace. When they were at a safe distance from the camp, they stopped. Lieutenant Milestone pulled the remote detonator from his Combat Tactical Vest. He extended the antenna and pushed the button. A few seconds later, the explosive charges that he and Ice Man had planted in the small tent went off. He closed the antenna and put the remote detonator back where he got it from.

"Let's keep moving," Lieutenant McDonald ordered, "We got a long walk ahead of us."

The Strike Force team continued to head north through the dense jungle toward the Panamanian border while Cowboy and Snake remained a hundred yards behind them as a safeguard. After hours of traveling through the thick jungle, the Strike Force team came to a grassy clearing.

"You know; this is a good place for an ambush," Lieutenant Milestone was quick to point out.

"Yep, that's just what I was thinking," Lieutenant McDonald remarked. "Terminator I need the radio," he said over the radio headset.

Terminator ran over to Lieutenant McDonald. He handed him the satellite radiotelephone receiver, and he put it to his ear. "Tiger Two, this is Sandstorm, over."

"Sandstorm, this is Tiger Two; we're about two klicks from your position. Ark Angel is standing by, over."

"Roger, standby." Lieutenant McDonald handed Terminator the satellite radiotelephone receiver. He removed one of his AN-M18 smoke grenades from his Combat Tactical Vest, pulled the pin, and threw it as far as he could. The smoke grenade hit the ground about thirty yards away, and green smoke began to spew from it.

Seconds later mortars, located a few yards north of the Strike Force team's location, began firing on the grassy area.

"Everyone keep your gas mask on," Lieutenant McDonald said over the radio headset. "Get ready to move out on my order."

An F/A-18F Super Hornet aircraft came out of nowhere and dropped several CBU-100 Cluster Bombs filled with tear gas on the area where the mortar fire was coming from. A few seconds later, the mortar fire stopped.

A Sikorsky CH-53 Sea Stallion helicopter, accompanied by two UH-60L Black Hawk helicopter gunships appeared over the horizon. The CH-53 helicopter landed in a clearing a few yards from where the Strike Force team was waiting while the Black Hawk helicopter gunships remained airborne to provide air support if needed.

"Let's move," Lieutenant McDonald ordered over the radio headset.

The Strike Force team hurried to the awaiting helicopter and climbed onboard. The Sikorsky CH-53 Sea Stallion helicopter lifted off and headed north with the two UH-60L Black Hawk helicopter gunships following close behind them.

Chapter 15

Tocumen International Airport
Panama City, Panama

The Sikorsky CH-53 Sea Stallion helicopter landed close to the hangar where their command center was located and shut down the rotor blades. The two UH-60L Black Hawk helicopter gunships landed a few feet away. The Strike Force team disembarked from the helicopter and walked over to the hangar where Captain Hale was standing.

"Mission accomplished," Lieutenant McDonald reported.

"Good job everyone," Captain Hale said. "Popeye, I need to talk to you. The rest of you go inside and relax, but don't get too comfortable; we're pulling out soon; we're going home."

What did I do now? Lieutenant McDonald thought.

"What's in the briefcase?" Captain Hale asked, referring to the briefcase that Lieutenant McDonald was carrying.

"Don't know. I hadn't gone through it yet."

"Was that Shammari's?"

"Not sure; it was found a few feet from the body of CIA Station Chief, Bill Riley."

"So, Riley wasn't killed in that car bombing in Kabul Afghanistan?"

"Not unless there's two of him," Lieutenant McDonald answered as he handed the briefcase to Captain Hale.

"I'll look through this when we get back to headquarters," Captain Hale pointed out. "Did you find anything else?"

"We found blueprints of several Colombian government buildings in Bogotá and our embassy in a tent that I suspect they were using as a command tent. My best guess is that Juarez is planning the same thing in Bogotá as he did at Puerto Obaldia."

"Just as Wolverine had suspected," Captain Hale commented. "Who have you told about this information?"

"No one."

"Good; let's keep it that way for now. We don't need..." Captain Hale stopped talking when a limousine pulled up and parked a few feet from where they were standing.

Lieutenant McDonald and Captain Hale walked towards the limousine. As they drew closer, two men, dressed in expensive suits got out of the front. Moments later, President Elliot stepped out of the back of the limousine.

"Mr. President, What an unexpected surprise sir," Captain Hale said as he and Lieutenant McDonald snapped to attention, and saluted the president.

"Is this the man who led the operation that took out A'zam al Shammari?" President Elliot asked while he saluted them back.

"Yes, Mr. President," Captain Hale answered. "Sir, this is our senior team leader Popeye."

"I need to borrow this man for a while," The president said. "I'll bring him back when I'm done."

"Yes Mr. President," Captain Hale said. He saluted President Elliot and then he did an about face and walked away.

"Where did you come up with the name Popeye?" President Elliot asked.

"Well, Mr. President, I do love me Spinach," Lieutenant McDonald answered.

President Elliot laughed at Lieutenant McDonald's answer. "Let's go for a ride Popeye; I need to know about everything you and your people found in that camp."

"Yes, Mr. President," Lieutenant McDonald acknowledged.

President Elliot and Lieutenant McDonald got into the back of the limousine. The two men got in the front, and the limousine drove off.

President Elliot listened while Lieutenant McDonald told him about what he and his team had found in the camp where A'zam al Shammari was killed. He no sooner completed his report when the limousine stopped a few feet away from a Sikorsky CH-53 Sea Stallion helicopter that was waiting for them with its rotor blades warming up for departure.

"I want you to come with me," President Elliot said as the two men in the front seat of the limousine got out. "I might need your assistance," the president continued when one of the men opened the back door.

"Yes, Mr. President," Lieutenant McDonald was quick to acknowledge. "You can count on me, sir."

President Elliot and Lieutenant McDonald got out of the limousine, and the man handed them a pair of ear protection to put on while the other man closed the door. The two men escorted them to the back of the helicopter, and President Elliot, and Lieutenant McDonald entered.

The flight crew helped President Elliot and Lieutenant McDonald to their seats, and assisted them in preparing for flight. Once the flight crew was satisfied that the helicopter was ready for flight, they informed the pilot and the pilot throttled up the Sikorsky CH-53 Sea Stallion helicopter, and the helicopter lifted off the ground.

* * * * *

US Embassy
Bogotá, Colombia

Jennifer Masterson sat at her desk in the reception area to Ambassador Haskell's office reading the latest news article about the incident at the consulate at Puerto Obaldia, Panama. The door to the reception area opened, and a man entered carrying a Diplomatic Pouch. "I have an urgent message from the president for the ambassador," the man said. "It's imperative that I see the ambassador."

"I can take it into the ambassador for you," Masterson offered.

"I am to deliver this to the ambassador myself," the man shot back.

Masterson pushed the intercom button on her telephone and waited for the ambassador to answer. "Mr. Ambassador, there's a messenger here with a Diplomatic Pouch from Washington," She informed him. "He says that he's carrying an urgent message for you from the

President."

"Send him in," the ambassador said.

"Yes, sir," Masterson acknowledged and then pushed the intercom button to cancel the call. "You can go on in," she said to the man and got up from her seat. She walked over to the door and opened it. The man entered the ambassador's office. Masterson closed the door and returned to her desk.

"Mr. Ambassador, the President instructed me to give you this pouch personally," the man said while he walked over to the ambassador's desk and handed the ambassador the Diplomatic Pouch.

"Is there anything else?" Ambassador Haskell asked and sat the Diplomatic Pouch down on the desk in front of him.

"No, sir, there is not," the man answered and then left the ambassador's office, closing the door behind him.

Ambassador Haskell opened the Diplomatic Pouch and removed its contents. He read each page twice before putting the contents back inside the Diplomatic Pouch. He then pushed the intercom button on his telephone and waited for Jennifer Masterson to answer.

"Yes, Mr. Ambassador."

"Jennifer, there's a helicopter coming here to pick me up. Let me know when it gets here."

"Yes, Mr. Ambassador; I'll let you know the minute it arrives." Jennifer Masterson no sooner canceled the intercom call when the door opened to the reception area, and CIA Station Chief John Marrow, along with NSA Operations Chief, Carmelita Martinez, entered. "We need to see the Ambassador," Marrow said while Martinez closed the door. "It's urgent that we see him."

Masterson picked up the telephone receiver from the telephone on her desk and put it to her ear. She pushed the intercom button and waited for the ambassador to pick up on the other end. "Mr. Ambassador, John Marrow and Carmelita Martinez are here to see you; they say it's urgent." She listened for a few moments before returning the telephone receiver to its normal resting place, canceling the intercom call. "You may go on in."

John Marrow opened the door to the ambassador's office and entered, with Carmelita Martinez following. They walked over to the ambassador's desk while Jennifer Masterson closed the door.

Have a seat," Ambassador Haskell said, motioning to the two chairs in front of his desk. "What can I do for you?"

"Mr. Ambassador, I'll get right to the point," John Marrow said while he and Carmelita Martinez sat in the chairs, in front of the ambassador's desk. "Carmelita and I think that what happened at the consulate at Puerto Obaldia, Panama could happen here. We also believe that what happened there was no accident."

"Do you realize what you're implying?" Ambassador Haskell fired back. "If the president says that what happened at the consulate at Puerto Obaldia, Panama was an accident, then that's what it was; an accident." Ambassador Haskell looked at John Marrow before continuing. "You better have proof to the contrary, before you call the president a liar."

"We're not calling the president a liar," Carmelita Martinez jumped in. "We just feel that there's more to this than what Washington is willing to admit." Martinez looked at John Marrow and then looked back at Ambassador Haskell. "Like John said, we both believe that the incident at Puerto Obaldia was no accident."

"Do you have any proof that it wasn't an accident?" Ambassador Haskell asked.

"We're working on it," John Marrow answered. "Carmelita and I have people in the field looking into this. We believe that General Juarez or A'zam al Shammari might be behind this so-called accident."

"I think that the two of you need to relay your concerns to your prospective directors," Ambassador Haskell pointed out. "If you have concerns about security here at the embassy; I suggest you get with the Marine Security Force. Do whatever you need to do to secure this embassy," Ambassador Haskell paused for a moment before continuing. "Is there anything else?"

Before Marrow or Martinez could answer, the door to the ambassador's office opened, and Jennifer Masterson entered. "I'm sorry for the intrusion Mr. Ambassador, but your ride is here."

"Thanks, Jennifer," Ambassador Haskell commented while he got up from his seat. He looked at Marrow and Martinez before continuing. "If you'll excuse me this meeting is over."

John Marrow and Carmelita Martinez got up from their seats and left the ambassador's office, with Ambassador Haskell following.

Jennifer Masterson closed the door to the ambassador's office and sat down behind her desk.

Ambassador Haskell walked over to the exit door of the reception area, opened it, and stepped into the hallway outside, with Marrow and Martinez following. Ambassador Haskell walked over to the elevator and pushed the button to call for the elevator while Martinez closed the door.

The elevator arrived, and Ambassador Haskell stepped inside. He pushed the button for the roof, and the door closed. The elevator stopped on the roof, and the door opened. Ambassador Haskell exited the elevator and walked over to the Marine Sikorsky CH-53 Sea Stallion helicopter that was waiting with its rotor blades whirling in the wind.

Ambassador Haskell entered the helicopter and sat down in the seat that he was instructed to sit in and strapped himself in. He put on the insulated headgear that he was provided to protect his ears from the noise.

Moments later, the pilot throttled up the helicopter's rotor blades and lifted off from the embassy's rooftop.

* * * * *

Bogotá, Colombia
President Manuel Roberto's Office

President Manuel Roberto had been president of Colombia for almost three years. At thirty-five, he was the youngest president to be elected to the office. He sat behind his desk trying to relax when the Ministry of National Defense Rafael Salazar, entered his office without knocking first.

"Rafael, what's the meaning of this?" President Roberto asked.

"The Americans have fired missiles at our people," Minister Salazar replied while he closed the door and walked over to President Roberto's desk. "They also sent aircraft into our airspace and dropped bombs; he continued while he sat down in the chair.

"I know."

"What!" Minister Salazar fired back. "You knew about this?"

"The Americans were after some terrorist named The Scorpion that they suspected was working with General Juarez," President Roberto answered. "I told the American President, he could do what he needed to do to take out this terrorist as long as no civilians got hurt."

"I don't believe this," Minister Salazar remarked in a rage.

"Calm down Rafael," President Roberto calmly said. "This American President is willing to help me get rid of General Juarez, and put an end to his bullshit once and for all. We need his help."

"We don't need their help. We can take care of our own problems."

"Look, I'm meeting with the American President in about an hour. Why don't you come with me, and you'll see that he's only trying to help us."

"You're meeting with the American President today?"

"That's right, why?"

"What about the banquet that you're supposed to attend tonight?"

"We'll be back in plenty of time for me to attend the banquet," President Roberto answered. "Come with me to this meeting, and you'll see that there's nothing for you to worry about. The Americans are our friends in this fight."

There was a knock on the door, and the door opened. President Roberto's personal secretary, Mrs. Gabriela Cruz, who was also President Roberto's niece, entered the office.

"Mr. President, the helicopter that you were expecting has arrived and is waiting for you on the helicopter pad."

"Let's go Rafael; we don't want to keep the American President waiting."

President Roberto left the office with Minister Salazar following. Mrs. Cruz closed the door and sat down behind her desk.

* * * * *

Strike Force Delta Command
Tinker Air Force Base
Oklahoma City, Oklahoma

Colonel Wilson left the Command Center and walked to his office. He entered his office and found his personal assistant, Lieutenant Cooltrain, nicknamed Giggles standing by the coffee pot pouring a cup of coffee.

"I'll have one too," he said as he walked over to his desk. "It has been a long night," he continued while he sat down in the chair behind his desk.

Lieutenant Cooltrain removed Colonel Wilson's coffee cup from the shelf by the coffee pot. "I put the latest Intel reports on your desk," she said while she filled Colonel Wilson's coffee cup. She walked over to Colonel Wilson's desk and sat the cup of coffee on the back corner of his desk. "I put the most important ones on top."

"Thanks, Giggles," Colonel Wilson remarked. "I don't know what I'd do without you."

"Oh, I'm sure you'd manage," Lieutenant Cooltrain commented and smiled. "Now if you'd excuse me, I have a few things that need my immediate attention."

"By all means; go do what you need to do. I'll page you if I should need you."

Lieutenant Cooltrain started to leave Colonel Wilson's office when Operations Specialist, Lieutenant Stanton, nicknamed Barbie entered. Lieutenant Cooltrain left Colonel Wilson's office while Lieutenant Stanton walked over to Colonel Wilson's desk.

"You look troubled Barbie," Colonel Wilson commented. "Is there something wrong?"

"I think I almost made a terrible mistake that could have had disastrous consequences."

"What the hell are you talking about?"

"Wolverine, I have been trying to get in touch with Major Sullivan from the Army CID (Criminal Investigation Division) at the number she gave me, but I kept getting no answer. However, after a few more attempts, a man answered her phone; he was a CID investigator."

"I hope you didn't tell him who you were," Colonel Wilson snapped.

"Of course not," Lieutenant Stanton fired back. "I told him that I was Major Sullivan's cousin; and that I have been trying to get a hold of her."

"Good," Colonel Wilson said. "We don't need this tracing back to us."

"It won't," Lieutenant Stanton assured Colonel Wilson.

"Did he tell you anything?"

"All he would tell me was that he was investigating the murder of Major Sullivan; and that she has been dead for almost a week."

"Then who the hell gave you those codes?"

"I know that it couldn't have been Major Sullivan, so I did some checking around and found that those codes I was given would have knocked out communications down there. Wolverine, for some reason someone was trying to blind us down there."

"I hope now you realize the importance of verifying things like that before you bring them to me."

"Yes, I do," Lieutenant Stanton said. "It will never happen again."

"I hope not," Colonel Wilson fired back. "Now leave before I say something that I'll regret later."

Asshole, Lieutenant Stanton thought as she stormed out of Colonel Wilson's office and closed the door.

Colonel Wilson finished his cup of coffee and got up from his seat. He walked over to the coffee pot and poured himself another cup of coffee. He returned to his seat behind his desk and sat his cup of coffee down on the corner of the desk, and then he began to read the intelligence reports Lieutenant Cooltrain had put on his desk.

Chapter 16

USS Ronald Reagan CVN-76
The Pacific Ocean
160 Nautical Miles Off The Cost Of Colombia.

The Sikorsky CH-53 Sea Stallion helicopter that was carrying Ambassador Haskell landed safely on the carrier's flight deck. The pilot shut down the rotor blades while the deck crew secured the helicopter to the carrier's flight deck. Ambassador Haskell removed his seat restraints and walked to the back of the helicopter; where a member of the flight deck crew was waiting.

Ambassador Haskell was escorted from the flight deck into the superstructure of the carrier. He followed his escort down several levels until they stopped in front of a door where two Marines, dressed in full combat dress with their M16-A4 assault rifles, were standing.

"Please wait inside," one of the Marines said while he opened the door. "Your party will meet you here."

Ambassador Haskell stepped inside, and the Marine closed the door. *Wow, what a setup,* he thought as he looked around before sitting down at the table in the room.

Ambassador Haskell jumped to his feet when the door suddenly opened, and President Elliot and Lieutenant McDonald entered. "Robert it's nice to see you again," President Elliot said while he walked over to the table. The Marine guard closed the door, and President Elliot sat down at the table across from Ambassador Haskell. Lieutenant

McDonald took a seat next to the president, and Ambassador Haskell returned to his seat.

"Robert this is Popeye," President Elliot began. "He'll be sitting in on this meeting."

"Nice to meet you Popeye."

"Same here Mr. Ambassador."

"Mr. President I heard that A'zam al Shammari was killed," Ambassador Haskell Inquired.

"Yes, he was," President Elliot answered.

President Elliot stopped talking when the door opened, and President Roberto and Minister Salazar entered the room. They walked over to the table and sat down next to Ambassador Haskell.

"Mr. President I wasn't informed that weapons would be present at this meeting," President Roberto said, referring to the HK-416N assault rifle that Lieutenant McDonald had on him. "Is this really necessary when you have two armed Marines standing outside?"

President Elliot looked at Lieutenant McDonald and nodded. Lieutenant McDonald removed the rifle from his person and removed the magazine. He then removed the round in the firing chamber and placed everything on the table.

"Now we can begin," President Roberto calmly said. "Mr. President I don't have much time. I have a benefit banquet that I must attend in a few hours."

"Yes, my wife and I are going to attend as well," Ambassador Haskell added.

"I'm aware of the benefit banquet that the two of you are talking about," President Elliot pointed out. "You all know about the accident at our consulate in Puerto Obaldia, Panama. Well, I'm here to say that it was no accident. It was an act of terrorism; the terrorist used a deadly poisonous gas. I'm certain that the purpose of this attack was to provoke an act of aggression between the United States and Colombia, so the terrorist could strike their primary target in Colombia and blame the United States."

"Are you sure about this?" President Roberto asked.

"Yes, I am," President Elliot answered. The terrorist A'zam al Shammari, known as The Scorpion, was the terrorist who made this poisonous gas."

"I was told that you had successfully neutralized this terrorist," President Roberto remarked.

"We have," President Elliot said. "We also took out the laboratory that was manufacturing this deadly poisonous gas."

"Then the threat no longer exists," Minister Salazar was quick to point out.

"Oh, but it does," President Elliot fired back. "When we took down Shammari, we discovered an operational laboratory and empty storage tanks. We believe that another attack with this deadly gas is in play."

"Do you have any substantial proof that another attack is coming?" President Roberto asked.

"Not yet," Lieutenant McDonald jumped in.

"This is a waste of time," Minister Salazar said while he got up from his seat.

"Sit down Rafael," President Roberto ordered. "I believe President Elliot has more to say on this subject."

Minister Salazar returned to his seat. The door opened, and one of the Marine guards entered. He walked over to President Elliot and handed him the paper he had in his hand. The Marine stood at attention while President Elliot read what was on the paper. When he was finished, he handed the paper to Lieutenant McDonald. Lieutenant McDonald read what was on the paper and handed it back to President Elliot.

"Thank you, Marine," President Elliot commented, "Return to your post."

"Yes, sir, Mr. President," The Marine acknowledged, and then he saluted President Elliot. The Marine left the room and closed the door.

"On a hunch I had the ventilation system at our embassy in Bogotá checked while we've been here on this ship," President Elliot began. "Several canisters of the deadly VX nerve gas were found. They were tied into the embassy's ventilation system and set to release the gas during the benefit banquet tonight."

"Mr. President," Ambassador Haskell started to say.

"Hang on John; this is where it gets interesting," President Elliot continued. "With President Roberto's permission, I had the ventilation system checked in all five of the Colombian government buildings in Bogotá. My people found the same type of deadly gas that was used in the attack on our consulate at Puerto Obaldia, Panama connected to the ventilation systems in these buildings.

"How did this terrorist gain access to your embassy's ventilation system and my government buildings?" President Roberto asked.

"I think that the person who done this was someone who was in these buildings frequently," President Elliot answered. "Someone who was well-known and I believe that this person is someone in this room; a trader to his people and his government," President Elliot concluded while looking at Minister Salazar.

President Roberto looked at Minister Salazar. "Did you do this?" After a moment of silence, he continued. "Rafael, please tell me that this isn't true?"

Minister Salazar jumped to his feet and pulled out the forty-five caliber pistol that he had hidden between his back and his belt. "Long live the revolution," he said in Spanish as he put the forty-five to his temple.

"Rafael, what are you doing?" President Roberto asked in Spanish, shocked at the fact that Minister Salazar had the forty-five against his temple. "You think killing yourself is going to prove something?"

Minister Salazar smiled and pulled the trigger, and he fell to the floor. Hearing the gunshot the Marine Guards stationed outside the room charged in with their M16-A4 assault rifles ready for action.

"Stand down Marines," President Elliot ordered.

The Marines stopped their charge and stood at attention.

President Roberto got up from his seat. He walked over to Minister Salazar's body and kicked him. "I treated you like a brother," he said in Spanish. "I trusted you with my life you traitorous dog." He kicked Minister Salazar's body again and looked at President Elliot. "Do me a favor and throw this piece of garbage overboard," he said in English.

"Marines, you heard the man," President Elliot snapped. "Throw this piece of garbage overboard."

"Yes, Sir, Mr. President," the Marines acknowledged.

The Marines slung their M16-A4 assault rifles over their shoulder and walked over to Minister Salazar's body. One Marine picked him up by the legs while the other Marine picked him up by his shoulders, and they carried him out of the room.

Lieutenant McDonald reloaded his HK-416N assault rifle and laid it back down on the table in front of him while President Roberto walked back to where he was sitting and sat back down.

"I guess I'll have to find me another Minister of National Defense," President Roberto jokingly remarked. "I'll have to be extra careful who I select this time."

"I might be able to help you with that Mr. President," Lieutenant McDonald commented.

"Go on; I'm listening," President Roberto said.

"When we took down Shammari, we found a lot of documents," Lieutenant McDonald continued. "I've had a chance to go through most of the documents, and I found a list of everyone that's been helping General Juarez."

"Do you have that list with you?" President Roberto asked.

Lieutenant McDonald pulled a piece of folded paper from his pants pocket and handed it to President Roberto. "I hope this list helps you put an end to your General Juarez problem."

President Roberto opened the folded paper and looked over the names on the paper. Afterwards, he folded the paper back up and put it in his suit jacket pocket. "The people of Colombia thank you for your assistance."

"Just doing my job sir," Lieutenant McDonald pointed out.

A Navy commander appeared in the doorway and stood at attention. "Excuse me Mr. President, but a helicopter is standing by to take President Roberto and Ambassador Haskell back to Bogotá."

President Roberto and President Elliot got up from their seats and shook hands while Lieutenant McDonald jumped to his feet and stood at attention.

"I will give you any assistance you need," President Elliot was quick to point out. "All you have to do is ask."

"Thank you, my friend," President Roberto commented.

"John it was nice to see you again," President Elliot said while he shook hands with Ambassador Haskell. "Tell Joan I wish her well."

"I sure will Mr. President."

Ambassador Haskell and President Roberto walked to the doorway and exited the room. The commander closed the door, and Lieutenant McDonald returned to his seat at the table.

"What happened here is not to leave this room," President Elliot said while he sat back down at the table. "You are not to tell anyone about this."

"I understand Mr. President," Lieutenant McDonald acknowledged.

A few minutes later, the door opened, and a sailor appeared in the doorway. "Excuse me Mr. President, but the commander sent me to get you, sir. Your helicopter is ready, sir. If the two of you would follow me, I'll show you the way."

"Lead the way sailor," President Elliot said as he got up from his seat.

Lieutenant McDonald grabbed his HK-416N assault rifle from the table and got up from his seat. He followed the sailor and President Elliot out of the room, and closed the door.

* * * * *

Tocumen International Airport
Panama City, Panama

The Sikorsky CH-53 Sea Stallion helicopter that was carrying Lieutenant McDonald and President Elliot landed a few feet away from the limousine that was waiting. President Elliot and Lieutenant McDonald exited the helicopter and walked to the limousine while the pilot throttled up the helicopter, and lifted off the ground.

As they approached, a man standing by the back door to the limousine opened the door. President Elliot was the first to get into the back seat of the limousine, with Lieutenant McDonald close behind him. The man closed the door and walked to the front passenger's side. He opened the door and got in, and they drove off.

When the limousine arrived at the hangar where the Strike Force Command Center was located, Lieutenant McDonald exited the limousine and hurried to the hangar while the limousine drove off.

He was greeted at the entrance by Lieutenant Milestone. "Who was that?"

"No one, in particular," Lieutenant McDonald commented. "So don't ask again."

"Well, excuse the hell out of me. I'm sorry I asked."

Lieutenant McDonald looked inside the hangar and saw that it was empty except for the Strike Force assault teams. "Where's Bulldog?" He asked as he looked back at Lieutenant Milestone.

"He's on his way back to Strike Force Command with the Strike Force Mobile Command Center. He and everyone else, except for our people, left about an hour ago. Bulldog said that we were to wait here until you returned."

"Is that our C-130 out there warming up?" Lieutenant McDonald asked, pointing to the C-130J Hercules aircraft that was a few feet away warming up its jet engines.

"Yes, it is. All our gear is loaded on board the aircraft. It shouldn't be too much longer before we can board, and head out of here. I..." Lieutenant Milestone abruptly stopped talking when one of the ground crew walked over to where he and Lieutenant McDonald were standing.

"The pilot said he wants everyone on board so he can take off," the ground crewman said.

"Thanks," Lieutenant McDonald said, and then he stepped into the hanger. "Let's go people. It's time to go back home."

Lieutenant McDonald and Lieutenant Milestone stood at the hangar entrance while the Strike Force assault teams walked out of the hangar. They followed their people to the C-130J Hercules aircraft, and everyone boarded the aircraft.

Once everyone was properly secured in their seats, the back cargo door closed. Minutes later, the aircraft taxied on to the runway. The pilot powered up the jet engines, and the aircraft began to move forward. Not long Afterwards, the aircraft lifted off the ground and climbed to its cruising altitude.

Chapter 17

CIA Headquarters
Langley, Virginia

CIA Deputy Director, Karen Hicks, arrived at her office early. She walked over to her desk and sat down in the chair that was behind her desk. She opened the bottom right side drawer and placed her purse inside. She was surprised when her office door opened, and her personal assistant, twenty-five-year-old Carla Garcia, entered with a stack of papers in one hand, and a cup of coffee in the other hand. "Carla, I didn't think you were here yet," Deputy Director Hicks commented while she closed the drawer.

"I brought you a fresh cup of coffee," Garcia commented. "I thought you might need some," she continued while she walked over to Deputy Director Hicks' desk and sat down in the chair in front of the desk.

"Thanks," Deputy Director Hicks said as she took the cup of coffee from Garcia. "I got a feeling that it's going to be a long day," she remarked and then she took a drink of her coffee. "Anything new?" She asked while she placed the cup of coffee down on her desk.

"Mostly routine," Garcia answered, and then she handed Deputy Director Hicks the stack of papers that she had in her hand. "I put the important ones on the top for you to read first."

"Thanks, Carla," Deputy Director Hicks said as she put the stack of papers down on her desk in front of her. She read the first page and learned about an operation that Director Müller had personally approved involving Michael Lawrence, and that he put Michael Lawrence in charge of a five-man assault team that he sent to Columbia. "This doesn't make any sense," she commented. "I don't..." Deputy Director Hicks stopped talking when the telephone on her desk began to ring. She picked up the telephone receiver and put it to her ear. "Yes."

"Karen, have you read your morning traffic yet?" Director Müller asked.

"I just started to, sir. Is there a problem?"

"I wanted you to know that I put Michael Lawrence in charge of an assault team that I sent to Columbia."

"Sir, I haven't concluded the Puerto Obaldia investigation."

"That investigation is concluded," Director Müller fired back. "Lawrence was just lucky he got out of there before the attack."

"Sir, I..."

"Drop it Karen; understood?"

"Yes, sir."

"Good day Karen," Director Müller said, and then the line went dead.

Dickhead, Deputy Director Hicks, thought while she returned the telephone receiver to the telephone on her desk.

"Is there something wrong?" Carla Garcia curiously asked.

"That was the director. He just ordered me to close my investigation into the involvement of Michael Lawrence in the attack at Puerto Obaldia."

"Do you really think that Michael Lawrence was involved in the attack?"

"It doesn't matter now what I think. The director said the case is closed. I'll have to get in touch with Kate Livingston, and let her know that the investigation is concluded."

"That might be hard to do right now," Carla Garcia was quick to point out. "Kate was transferred to the London office. She's probably somewhere over the Atlantic by now."

"Oh, that was quick," Deputy Director Hicks commented.

"Is it true that we're going to reopen the Puerto Obaldia facility?"

"Why do you want to know that?"

"A friend of mine was transferred to Puerto Obaldia with only an hour's notice," Carla Garcia answered. "I hope it's safer there now than it was before."

"I can't talk about that; it's classified. I shouldn't be talking about any of this with you."

"Deputy Director, I have been working side by side with you for the past three years. You know you can trust me with anything."

"Carla, believe me, the less you know about this, the better. "Don't worry, extra security measures have been put in place to assure that what happened at Puerto Obaldia doesn't happen again. That's all I'm going to say on this; understood?"

"Yes, ma'am. I understand."

"If you have nothing more for me, I'd like to read the rest of this pile."

"I'll be at my desk if you should need me," Carla Garcia said as she got up from her seat. She walked over to the entryway and exited Deputy Director Hicks' office. She closed the door and walked to her desk, and sat down in the chair behind her desk. She started to log onto her computer when the door to the reception area opened and thirty-two-year-old, CIA analyst, Joan Murray entered.

"Is the Deputy Director in?" Joan Murray asked while she closed the door.

"I'll let her know you're here," Garcia said as she picked up the telephone receiver from the telephone on her desk and put it to her ear. She pushed the intercom button and waited for Deputy Director Hicks to answer.

"Yes, Carla."

"Joan Murray is here to see you," Carla Garcia informed Deputy Director Hicks.

"Send her in," Deputy Director Hicks said, and then she ended the intercom call.

"You can go in," Garcia said as she returned the telephone receiver to the telephone on her desk.

Joan Murray walked over to the door to Deputy Director Hicks' office and opened it, and stepped inside. "Good morning, Deputy Director," she cheerfully said as she closed the office door.

"Good morning, Joan."

"I know it's early, but the director wanted me to stop by and give you an update on the situation in Columbia. That way you can brief the president on this at your security meeting later this afternoon," Joan Murray replied as she walked over to Deputy Director Hicks' desk. "Things down there are heating up," she continued while she sat in the chair in front of Deputy Director Hicks' desk.

"I thought the situation down there was under control," Deputy Director Hicks commented.

"It's contained, but far from being under control." Joan Murray was quick to point out. "Since we got back our satellite coverage of the area, we can see first-hand what's going on down there."

"How bad is it?"

"The Columbian Army is closing in on General Juarez and the rebels in the dense jungle a few kilometers west of Carepa. Casualties on both sides have been heavy. I doubt that Juarez's army can hold off the Columbian Army much longer."

"Any news from Michael Lawrence and his team?" Deputy Director Hicks asked.

"They checked in about an hour ago," Joan Murray answered. "They're on the ground, and proceeding with their mission."

"Exactly what is their mission?"

"I have no idea. Their mission came directly from the director. All I know is that the director informed me to let him know when Lawrence checks in."

"What else do you have for me?"

"There's a rumor that A'zam al Shammari is still alive; and that he's planning another gas attack."

"I thought he was taken out?"

"That's what was reported, but my sources say that Shammari has been seen in General Juarez's Headquarters near Carepa, Columbia and that he's very much alive."

"Can you confirm this?"

"I'm working on it."

"What's our satellites picking up?"

"Nothing out of the ordinary," Joan Murray answered. "I'm still going through the satellite feed of the area. I'm hoping to find some proof one way or the other and put an end to this rumor before it gets out of hand."

"Does the director know about any of this?"

"No, I haven't told him. I wanted to be sure that Shammari is alive before I brought this to his attention."

"Then why in the hell are you telling me about this?" Deputy Director Hicks curiously asked. "You know, keeping the director in the dark about this could come back and bite you on the ass. Especially, if he finds out from an outside source. You need to tell him a-sap."

"Yes, ma'am. I will go to the director's office when I leave here."

"Good, in the meantime, I want you to keep looking into this, and let me know the minute you have something. If Shammari is still out there, we need confirmation."

"I will let you know the moment I find out anything," Joan Murray said as she got up from her seat. "Good-day ma'am," she concluded and walked over to the office door. She opened the door and stepped into the reception area, and closed the door.

Deputy Director Hicks removed the telephone receiver from the telephone on her desk and put it to her ear. She dialed the phone number to the Chairman of the Joint Chiefs of Staff, General Thomas Richwood's Office, and then waited for her call to be answered.

After a few rings, thirty-three-year-old, Major Emily Harris answered."General Richwood's office."

"This is CIA Deputy Director Hicks. I need to talk to General Richwood."

"I'm sorry, Deputy Director but the general's not in yet. Would you like for him to call you back?"

"That won't be necessary. It's nothing of importance. I'll talk to him later."

"Good day Deputy Director," Major Harris said, and then she ended the call.

Deputy Director Hicks returned the telephone receiver to the telephone on her desk. Seconds later, there was a knock on her office door. The door opened, and Carla Garcia entered. "There's a car waiting to take you to the helo pad."

"Thanks, Carla," Deputy Director Hicks remarked as she got up from her seat behind her desk. "I should be back sometime this afternoon," she continued as she walked over to where Carla Garcia was standing. "If anyone should call, just get their number, and I'll call them back when I return," she concluded as she stepped into the reception area with Garcia close behind her.

Carla Garcia closed the door to Deputy Director Hicks' office while Deputy Director Hicks walked out of the reception area and closed the door. Garcia walked over to the chair behind her desk and sat down.

* * * * *

The White House Briefing Room
Washington, D. C.

White House Chief of Staff, Howard Gordon, was busy setting up the Briefing Room for the intelligence briefing with President Elliot about the situation in Columbia.

Secretary of State, George Maxwell and National-Security Adviser, John Haig was already seated at the conference table in the middle of the room. They were soon joined by Secretary of the Navy, John Forsythe and Secretary of Defense, Mark Roberts, along with NSA Analyst, Maria Carlos.

"Good morning, Howard," CIA Deputy Director Karen Hicks said when she entered the room.

"Good morning, Deputy Director," Gordon acknowledged.

Deputy Director Hicks walked over to the conference table and sat down. Vice President James Conrad, along with General Thomas Richwood, Chairman of the Joint Chiefs of Staff and Major General Larry McCoy, commanding general of the Joint Special Operations Command (JSOC) were the last to arrive. They walked over to the conference table and sat down.

A few minutes later, President Elliot entered the room, and everyone jumped to their feet. Howard Gordon left the room and closed the door while President Elliot walked over to the conference table and took a seat at the head of the table. "Let's get started," he said as he sat down at the conference table. He waited until everyone returned to their seats before he continued. "A few minutes ago, I talked to President Roberto in Bogotá. He's asking for our help with his General Juarez problem. He's asking us to provide air support for his ground forces."

"What's wrong with him using his own Air Force?" Vice President Conrad respectfully asked.

"The Columbian Air Force has been grounded. President Roberto has reason to believe that some of his high-ranking officers are loyal to General Juarez and his army. That's why the ground forces are commanded by low-ranking officers that are loyal to President Roberto, and they receive their orders directly from him in Bogotá."

"Surely, you don't want to get involved in this Columbian mess?" Vice President Conrad boldly asked. "I think we need to stay out of this, and let President Roberto handle his own problems."

"This is not open for debate," President Elliot fired back. "We need to end this Juarez problem once and for all."

"I agree with the president," Secretary of Defense, Mark Roberts jumped in. "Juarez needs to be stopped before he gets too powerful to do so. We can't afford to let his reign of terror continue any longer. We need to put this idiot down as quickly as possible. We have the necessary fire power already there to do this."

"Just what are you proposing?" Secretary of the Navy, John Forsythe asked. "Are you suggesting that we go in there and bomb the piss out of Juarez?"

"That would be a political nightmare," Secretary of State, George Maxwell pointed out. "The blow-back from such an attack could come back and bite us on the ass. I'm certain that our allies would condone such an attack."

"Mr. President, I may have a better solution to this problem," Major General Larry McCoy, commanding general of the Joint Special Operations Command (JSOC) jumped in. "Something that I'm sure our allied friends would accept as an appropriate measure."

"Go on general, I'm listening," President Elliot said. "What's on your mind?"

"Sir, we can send in some two or three man teams to the front area, and have them locate potential targets," General McCoy began. "They can paint the targets, and the Navy can send in cruise missiles to destroy these targets. This in turn will minimize collateral damage; and our involvement in this conflict."

"If I authorized this action, how soon can you get your people in place?" President Elliot asked.

"Three hours, sir," General McCoy responded. "I have fifteen Delta Force Operators at Camp Freedom in Panama doing some routine training."

"General Richwood, what's your opinion on General McCoy's proposal?" President Elliot asked.

"I think it's a good idea," General Richwood answered. "It would minimize collateral damage, and give the Columbian Army the upper hand against Juarez."

The room fell silent as everyone waited for the president to speak. President Elliot thought about the pros and cons of General McCoy's proposal before he rendered his decision. "I am authorizing General McCoy's operation," he informed everyone. "General McCoy, I want you and Secretary Forsythe to nail down the operating procedures for this mission," he continued. "George, I want you and your staff at state to be prepared for the blow-back on this," the president instructed Secretary of State Maxwell. "Jim, I want you to brief the Chairman of the Senate Armed Forces Committee about this operation," the president said to Vice President Conrad. "Are there any questions?" President Elliot waited for a few minutes, and then he got up from his seat. "Let's get to it."

Everyone at the table got up from their seats. President Elliot waited for them to depart the Briefing Room before he returned to his seat. A few minutes later, Howard Gordon stepped into the Briefing Room and was surprised to see that President Elliot hadn't left. "Is there something you need Mr. President?"

"No, Howard, I'm fine, thank you. Please close the door. I would like to be alone for a few minutes."

"Yes, Mr. President," Howard Gordon acknowledged, and then he left the Briefing Room and closed the door.

* * * * *

Ten kilometers West Of Carepa, Columbia

After several long backbreaking hours of traveling through the dense jungle, CIA officer Michael Lawrence and his five-man assault team reached a grassy clearing. The sound of gunfire filled the air and was drawing closer to their position. "Let's take a break here before we continue," Michael Lawrence suggested.

"Sounds like the Columbian Army is closing in on Juarez," one of the assault team members pointed out. "Maybe we ought to let the Columbians take care of Juarez."

"We stay on mission," Michael Lawrence fired back. "We have our orders."

"You're the boss," another team member commented.

Michael Lawrence took a couple of steps back from his team. *Sorry guys,* he thought as he removed his nine-millimeter Beretta M9-A1 sidearm from its holster. Without warning, he opened fire, killing his entire team. Satisfied that his team was no longer a threat, he put his Beretta back into its holster that was attached to his leg.

He stood there with his back to the jungle looking down at his dead teammates that lay dead on the ground in front of him. Suddenly, he heard a noise coming from the jungle behind him. He readied his M4-A1 assault rifle for action and turned to face the threat.

"Easy my friend," a familiar voice said in English. A few seconds later, A'zam al Shammari emerged from the jungle, followed by four other men of Middle-Eastern descent. Each man had a steel cylinder canister, similar to what firefighters used to hold oxygen while fighting fires, strapped to their backs.

"I was told that you were dead," Michael Lawrence remarked as he lowered his M4-A1 assault rifle. "I guess the reports were wrong."

"I left the camp with the remainder of the gas a few hours before it was attacked," Shammari said. "Sadly, my twin brother and Bill Riley were not so lucky."

"Their sacrifice won't be forgotten," Lawrence commented.

"They knew the risks," A'zam al Shammari said as he walked over to where Lawrence was standing. "They were true patriots to our cause."

"Yes, they were," Michael Lawrence agreed. "I take it that the canisters have the gas in them."

"That is correct," Shammari said. He turned to face the men that were with him. "We will rest here for a few minutes," he said in Arabic. "Mr. Lawrence and I need to have a talk."

The four men carefully removed the steel cylinder canisters that they had strapped to their backs. They laid the canisters gently on the ground and sat down next to them.

Shammari turned his attention back to Michael Lawrence. "You did an excellent job at Puerto Obaldia, " he said in English. "I could not have pulled it off without your help."

"It was easier than I thought it would be. I just had to make my story sound believable."

"I am glad that everything worked out to your advantage. I am curious though, as to why you are here?"

"I am looking for General Juarez's headquarters. Do you know where it's located?"

"The general's headquarters is a few kilometers east of here," Shammari answered, pointing in the direction to where General Juarez's headquarters was located. "Things are not going well for him and his people. I fear that his days are numbered."

"Juarez needs to be neutralized," Michael Lawrence was quick to point out. "He knows too much about us, and our mission."

"Is that why you are here?

"Yes."

"General Juarez has no idea what my next target is, or where I am going to from here," Shammari pointed out. "He is no threat to the mission."

"This doesn't make any sense," Michael Lawrence mumbled. "I was ordered to put him down."

"By whom?"

"My director; I assumed that he was part of this."

"Your boss knows nothing about my plans," Shammari was quick to point out. "If he wants General Juarez taken out it must be because the general knows something that your director does not want him to speak of."

"I knew there was more to this than what I was told."

"Tell me, why did you see the need to kill your friends?"

"They weren't my friends. I overheard two of them talking about taking me out after Juarez was put down. I just did to them what they were planning to do to me."

"You are a clever man Michael Lawrence. I can use a man with your cunning abilities. Come with me, and help me finish what we started. Let the Colombian Army take care of General Juarez."

"Okay, count me in."

"Good," Shammari commented, and then he turned to face his people. "We need to conceal these bodies," he said to them in Arabic while he pointed to the dead men on the ground. "Take them out into the jungle, and be quick about it."

One by one Michael Lawrence's team members were carried into the jungle. Afterwards, the four men picked up the steel cylinder canisters from the ground and secured them to their backs.

"Come, we need to get as far away from this area as quickly as possible," A'zam al Shammari said to Michael Lawrence in English. "We can use the jungle to conceal our whereabouts from the prying satellites overhead.

Michael Lawrence nodded his head to acknowledge that he understood and followed A'zam al Shammari back into the jungle, with Shammari's people following.

Chapter 18

Washington, D. C.
The White House

CIA Director, Robert Müller arrived at the White House and headed directly to the Oval Office. President Elliot's Personal Assistant, Mrs. Joan Wyatt, opened the door to the Oval Office and Director Müller entered, and she closed the door.

"I apologize if I kept you waiting Mr. President," Director Müller said when he noticed that the president was sitting on one of the sofas that was in the room. "I got here as quick as possible."

"Take a seat Robert," President Elliot instructed Director Müller, motioning to the sofa across from him.

"Yes, Mr. President," Director Müller acknowledged, and walked over to the sofa and sat down.

"Robert, I'm afraid I might have some bad news for you," President Elliot said as he picked up one of the folders that was on the sofa next to him. "These pictures were taken by the Colombian Army on their way to secure the area around what was left of General Juarez's camp that we took out." President Elliot continued while he handed Director Müller the folder. "I need to know if the men in those pictures are CIA."

Director Müller opened the folder and looked at each picture carefully. "Yes, Mr. President they're CIA. Their names are Diego Romero and Jose Martinez. We lost contact with them just before the attack on Puerto Obaldia." Director Müller closed the folder. "They were checking on a lead on General Juarez's whereabouts," he continued while he handed the folder back to President Elliot.

"Robert, do you have any of your people operating in Columbia near Carepa?" President Elliot asked while he placed the folder underneath another folder that was on the sofa next to him.

"Yes, Mr. President I do. I sent a six-man assault team down there to locate General Juarez."

"Have you heard from them recently?" President Elliot asked.

"Yes, sir. They checked in when they hit the ground."

"Have you heard from them since?"

"No, I haven't," Director Müller answered. "Why do you ask?"

President Elliot picked up another folder from the pile on the sofa next to him. "The Colombian Army took these pictures a few hours ago. Are these the men you sent down there?"

Director Müller opened the folder and looked at each picture. "Yes, Mr. President," Director Müller answered as he closed the folder. "However, I only see five of the six men I sent. I don't see the leader of the assault team. He must have been taken by the persons responsible for this."

"Or, he's working with these people, and we're to believe otherwise," President Elliot was quick to point out. "Find these people, and get me some answers."

"Yes, Mr. President. I'll look into this when I get back to Langley. Is there any chance that we'll be able to recover our people's remains?"

"President Roberto has informed me that the remains are being taken back to Bogotá. They will be released to our embassy shortly Afterwards. Notify your people at the embassy to make the necessary arrangements to have our people flown back here."

"Yes, Mr. President," Director Müller acknowledged. "I'll make the necessary arrangements. Is there anything else, sir?"

" Deputy Director Hicks told me that rumor has it that A'zam al Shammari might still be alive. Is this true?"

"Mr. President, there's no way anyone could have survived the attack on General Juarez's camp. Sir, I assure you, it's just a rumor."

"Then prove it," President Elliot snapped. "You need to put this rumor to rest and fast; before the media gets a hold of this."

"Sir, have you talked to General Richwood about this?"

"I've personally talked to the man that saw Shammari's mangled body after the air strike. He has no doubt that Shammari is dead. However, when the Colombian Army arrived at the camp, Shammari's remains were nowhere to be found. I want you to get some people down there and find Shammari's body."

"I'll get right on it, sir," Director Müller said as he got up from the sofa. "Is there anything else you need from me?"

"Not right now."

Director Müller walked over to the door and opened it, and stepped into the reception area. *God damn you Karen,* he thought as he closed the door. *What were you thinking?*

* * * * *

CIA Headquarters
Langley, Virginia

After a long day at the office, Carla Garcia, CIA Deputy Director, Karen Hicks' assistant, was preparing to leave for the day. She was startled when the door to the reception area opened, and CIA Director, Robert Müller, entered. " Director Müller, sir," Carla Garcia said as she got up from her seat.

"Is Karen in?" Director Müller asked as he closed the door.

"Yes, sir, she is."

Director Müller walked over to the door to Deputy Director Hicks' office and opened it, and entered. "Karen, what in the hell were you thinking when you told the president that A'zam al Shammari might still be alive?" He asked in a raised voice while he walked over to Deputy Director Hicks' desk. "That information hasn't been confirmed yet," he continued in a louder tone.

"Sir, I..."

"You've made me look like an ass in front of the president," Director Müller shouted. "Your job is to inform the president about situations that have been confirmed and wasn't in his morning brief; not rumors."

"Yes, sir," Deputy Director Hicks acknowledged. "I assure you it won't happen again, sir."

"See to it that it doesn't," the director snapped. "I don't want to have to have this conversation with you again."

Director Müller stormed out of Deputy Director Hicks' office into the reception area. He walked over to the door and opened the door. He exited the reception area and slammed the door shut.

Boy, he's pissed, Carla Garcia thought as she stood next to her desk, surprised by Director Müller's outburst towards Deputy Director Hicks.

"Go home Carla," Deputy Director Hicks said, who was standing in the doorway to her office. "I'll see you in the morning."

"Yes, ma'am. I'll..." Carla Garcia suddenly stopped talking when the door to the reception area suddenly opened, and CIA analyst, Joan Murray, entered.

"I'm glad I caught you before you left," Joan Murray said as she closed the door. "I have some satellite photos that somehow ended up on my desk," she continued, referring to the sealed folder she was holding in her hand. "It's marked urgent."

"If it's that important then why don't you take it to the director?" Deputy Director Hicks boldly asked.

"I ran into the director in the hallway on his way out. He told me that if it was too important to wait that I should bring this to you."

"Come on in Joan. Let's take a look at what you got," Deputy Director Hicks said as she stepped back into her office. She walked over to the chair behind her desk and sat down.

Joan Murray entered Deputy Director Hicks' office and closed the door. She walked over to Deputy Director Hicks' desk and sat down in the chair that was in front of the desk, and handed Deputy Director Hicks the sealed folder.

"Let's see what's so damn important," Deputy Director Hicks commented as she broke the security seal on the folder, and then she opened it. She quickly looked at the three satellite photographs inside and closed the folder. "Has anyone else besides me seen these photos?"

"Not to my knowledge," Joan Murray answered. "The folder was sealed when I got it from the satellite surveillance division."

"These photographs should have never landed on your desk," Deputy Director Hicks was quick to point out. "I'll have a talk with the head of the satellite surveillance division, and see to it that this doesn't happen again," she continued. "In the meantime, you are to mention this to no one. Is that clear?"

"Yes, ma'am, I understand."

"I will see to it that the director gets these photographs as soon as he returns from the White House," Deputy Director Hicks assured Joan Murray. "Is there anything else you need to talk to me about?"

"Nothing else," Joan Murray answered as she got up from her seat.

Deputy Director Hicks sat at her desk while Joan Murray walked over to the office door and opened it. She waited until Joan Murray stepped into the reception area and closed the office door before she opened the folder, and began to look at the photographs again.

She stared at the first photograph that showed a group of men who were apparently traveling in the jungle not far behind the CIA black ops team. She picked up a magnifying glass from her desk and looked at the photo again, but could not identify any of the men.

She looked at the second photograph with the magnifying glass and saw that the entire CIA black ops team had been killed except for CIA officer Michael Lawrence. "You motherfucker," she mumbled as she examined the last photograph with the magnifying glass which clearly showed Michael Lawrence shaking hands with A'zam al Shammari. "Holy shit," she said as she dropped the magnifying glass down on her desk.

Deputy Director Hicks removed the telephone receiver from the telephone on her desk and dialed Director Müller's cell phone number while she put the telephone receiver to her ear. "Damn it," she said when the director's voice mail picked up. She picked up the folder from her desk as she got up from her seat. She walked over to the office door and opened it, and left her office.

＊ ＊ ＊ ＊ ＊

Strike Force Delta Command
Tinker Air Force Base
Oklahoma City, Oklahoma

Captain Nathan Hale entered his office with the briefcase that Lieutenant McDonald had found near the body of the CIA Station Chief

Bill Riley. He sat down in the chair behind his desk and placed the briefcase in front of him. He opened the briefcase and discovered that the only thing inside was a photo album. He removed it and closed the briefcase, and then he placed the photo album down on top of it.

He opened the photo album and began to thumb through its contents. *Holy shit*, Captain Hale thought after he viewed the first couple of pages. He closed the photo album and got up from his seat, and hurried out of his office. He walked to Colonel Wilson's office and stood in the doorway. "Wolverine, do you have a minute?"

"Sure, come on in."

Captain Hale entered Colonel Wilson's office with the photo album in his hand and closed the door. "Wolverine, this was the only item in the briefcase that Popeye found on the ground next to the body of Bill Riley," Captain Hale said while he walked over to Colonel Wilson's desk. "I believe it belonged to Bill Riley," he continued as he placed the photo album down on the desk in front of Colonel Wilson. "You're going to shit when you see this," he said while he sat down in the chair in front of Colonel Wilson's desk, and handed Colonel Wilson the photo album.

Colonel Wilson opened the photo album. He stared at the photographs on the first page for a few seconds before he continued to look at the remaining photos in the album. "So Shammari has a twin brother," he remarked as he closed the photo album. "How in the hell did we miss this?"

"We're not the only ones that missed this," Captain Hale pointed out. "No one has ever mentioned that there was two of them, or that they knew Bill Riley and Michael Lawrence."

"It's no secret now as to how Shammari pulled off the attack at Puerto Obaldia," Colonel Wilson said. "I'm certain now that Michael Lawrence was the inside man. Those poor bastards at Puerto Obaldia didn't stand a chance."

"Do you really think that Michael Lawrence was involved in the Puerto Obaldia attack?"

"I have no doubt now," Colonel Wilson fired back. "This photo album is proof of Lawrence's association with Shammari."

"At least we got one of the Shammari brothers and Bill Riley," Captain Hale commented. "Now all we have to do is find the other one and Michael Lawrence. I'm sure if we find one; the other won't be far away."

"Yeah, but where do we start looking?" Colonel Wilson was quick to point out. "Hell, they could be anywhere by now."

"I guess we..." Captain Hale stopped talking when the door to Colonel Wilson's office suddenly opened, and twenty-four-year-old Language Expert, Second Lieutenant Susan Mallory, nicknamed Daisy, entered.

"I apologize for the interruption, but I have the translation of the papers that Popeye sent back with Bulldog," Lieutenant Mallory said as she closed the office door. "I was under the impression that you wanted this the minute I was done," she continued while she walked over to Colonel Wilson's desk. "You're going to want to see this," she concluded as she handed Colonel Wilson the folder that contained the translated documents.

"Is there anything else?" Colonel Wilson asked as he placed the folder down on his desk next to the photo album.

"No, that's it," Lieutenant Mallory answered. "Now if you'll excuse me, I have some work that I need to finish. I'll be in my office if you should need me."

Colonel Wilson picked up the folder from his desk and opened it. He began to read the documents inside while Lieutenant Mallory left his office and closed the door. When he was finished, he closed the folder. "You need to read this," he said as he handed Captain Hale the folder.

Captain Hale opened the folder and thumbed through the documents inside. "This is not good," he commented as he closed the folder, and then handed it back to Colonel Wilson. "According to those documents, Shammari still has around a hundred pounds of VX with him."

"Yeah, and you can bet your ass he's going to use it the first chance he gets," Colonel Wilson was quick to point out.

"How do you want to handle this?" Captain Hale inquired.

Before Colonel Wilson could answer Captain Hale, the door to his office suddenly opened, and Second Lieutenant, Samantha Cooltrain, nicknamed, Giggles, entered. "Wolverine, I have a message for you from General Richwood hot off the decoding machine," Lieutenant Cooltrain said as she walked over to Colonel Wilson's desk. "It's marked urgent," she continued while she handed Colonel Wilson the message.

"Thanks, Giggles. Let me know the minute anything else comes in."

"Roger that," Lieutenant Cooltrain acknowledged and then she left the office and closed the door.

"You're not going to believe this shit," Colonel Wilson commented after he had finished reading General Richwood's message. "The CIA director sent a black-ops team into Columbia to put down General Juarez, and he put Michael Lawrence in charge."

"What in the hell did he do that for?" Captain Hale asked.

"I don't have the answer to that one, but it gets better. A few hours ago, the Columbian Army found the bodies of the CIA black-ops team in the jungle ten kilometers west of Carepa. It would appear that Michael Lawrence was not among the dead, and he's now a person of interest in their deaths."

"Do you want me to have Barbie, (the Strike Force Delta Operations Specialist in charge of the satellite reconnaissance), do a quick sweep of the area around Carepa?" Captain Hale inquired. "We might get lucky, and find those assholes."

"Yes, have Barbie do an extensive sweep of the area and report her findings back to me a-sap. We need..." Colonel Wilson stopped talking when the telephone on his desk began to ring. He picked up the telephone receiver and put it to his ear. "Wilson," he calmly said.

"Wilson, what in the hell is going on?" General Richwood asked in a loud voice. "The CIA is telling the president that The Scorpion is still walking and breathing. Is this true?"

"General, I can explain. Sir, I..."

"You better have a damn good explanation for the president," General Richwood snapped. "I want you in Washington a-sap. I've already made a reservation for you at the Hay-Adams Hotel. Call me when you get there."

"Yes, sir," Colonel Wilson acknowledged. "I'll be in the air within the hour, sir."

"I'll see you when you get here," General Richwood fired back, and then the line went dead.

"Fuck," Colonel Wilson remarked as he returned the telephone receiver to its resting place.

"I take it that was General Richwood?"

"Yes, it was," Colonel Wilson calmly answered. "He's pissed because the CIA told the president that we misinformed him about Shammari's demise. I've been ordered to Washington to explain to the general and the president about how we dropped the ball on this."

"Wolverine, we had no idea that there were two of them until now," Captain Hale was quick to point out. "We're not the only ones that got caught with our pants down."

"True, but it still hurts our credibility with the general and the president," Colonel Wilson said. He picked up his briefcase from the floor next to his desk and sat it down in front of him. "There's a lot of powerful people out there that would love to see this unit flop," he continued as he opened his briefcase. He placed the photo album and the folder that contained the translated documents that Lieutenant Mallory had given him inside, and then continued. "If this unit is going to continue we need to keep the president on our side. If he can't rely on us to provide accurate intel, he'll shut us down in a heartbeat," he concluded while he closed his briefcase.

"I'll have Barbie get on the surveillance," Captain Hale said as he got up from his seat.

"Let me know the minute you find something. In the meantime, I want you to brief the strike teams on the new developments when they get back."

"I'm on it," Captain Hale acknowledged while he walked over to the office door. He opened the door and exited Colonel Wilson's office, and closed the door.

Colonel Wilson picked up the telephone receiver from the telephone on his desk. He dialed the extension number for the aircraft maintenance chief that was responsible for the maintenance on the Gulfstream G550 twin-engine jet aircraft he used to fly back and forth to Washington. He put the telephone receiver to his ear and waited for the maintenance chief to answer. "Chief, this is Wilson," he said when the maintenance chief answered his call. "I want the Gulfstream ready to go in thirty. Tell the pilot that he is to be ready to take off when I get there."

"It'll be ready when you get here," the maintenance chief acknowledged.

"Good," Colonel Wilson said, and then he returned the telephone receiver to the telephone on his desk, ending the call.

He pressed the intercom button on the telephone and waited for his personal assistant, Second Lieutenant Samantha Cooltrain, to answer.

"Yes, Wolverine," Lieutenant Cooltrain said when she answered the intercom call.

"Giggles, I'll be leaving for Washington in a few minutes," Colonel Wilson began. "If anyone should call just take a message, and I'll call them back when I return. I should be back sometime tomorrow."

"What if something should come up that can't wait?"

"Take it to Bulldog, and have him handle it."

"Roger that," Lieutenant Cooltrain acknowledged.

"I'll see you when I get back," Colonel Wilson said and canceled the intercom call. He grabbed his briefcase from his desk as he got up from his seat. He walked over to the office door and opened it, and left his office.

Chapter 19

The Hay-Adams Hotel
Washington, D. C.

Colonel Wilson was sitting at the table reading the documents that language expert, Second Lieutenant Mallory, had given him before he left Strike Force Delta Command when there was a knock on his door. He got up from his seat and walked over to the door, and looked through the peephole. He was surprised to see thirty-two-year-old, CIA analyst Joan Murray, whom he had dated a few times when he was in Washington, standing there on the other side of the door. *What the fuck does she want,* he thought as he opened the door.

"Hello John; do you have a minute?"

Colonel Wilson smiled. "I must say this is a pleasant surprise," he said as he motioned for Joan Murray to enter."

"I'm here on business, so you can wipe that smile off your face," Joan Murray said as she entered Colonel Wilson's room. "I have something that might interest you," she continued, referring to the folder that she was holding in her hand.

Colonel Wilson closed the door. *What a fine looking ass,* he thought while Joan Murray walked over to the table and sat down. He walked over to the table and sat down across from Joan Murray. "So, what's so important that brings you here?"

Joan Murray placed the folder she had brought with her on the table in front of Colonel Wilson. "I was hoping that you could pass the information in that folder to the president."

"If it's that important then why didn't you show it to Director Müller?''

"I tried to, but he blew me off. I got the impression that he knew what was in this folder and that he didn't want to see it."

"That doesn't make any sense," Colonel Wilson commented as he picked up the folder from the table. "Let's take a look," he continued while he opened the folder and looked at the photos inside. When he was finished, he closed the folder. "You're right. The president needs to see these photographs."

"Just don't tell anybody where you got those pictures from. Please, keep me out of this. I don't need this to come back and bite me on the ass."

"Who else knows about these pictures?" Colonel Wilson asked while he tapped on the folder laying on the table in front of him.

"I first took them to Deputy Director Hicks. I have no idea what she did with the copies I gave her."

"Does she know you're here?"

"No one knows I'm here, and I'd like to keep it that way," Joan Murray said as she got up from her seat.

"Leaving so soon?" Colonel Wilson asked as he too got up from his seat.

"I told you John; I'm here on business," Joan Murray was quick to point out while she walked over to the door. "Give me a call the next time you're in town. Maybe we can meet, and grab some dinner," she continued as she opened the door. "Don't wait too long," she said as she stepped into the hallway, and then closed the door.

Damn it, Colonel Wilson thought as he returned to his seat. He opened the folder on the table and stared at the photograph of Michael Lawrence shaking hand's with A'zam al Shammari. "You fuckin' trader," he mumbled. He closed the folder when there was a knock on his door. *She must of changed her mind,* he thought while he got up from his seat.

He hurried over to the door and looked out the peephole. *What the fuck is he doing here? He thought when he saw* General Richwood standing there on the other side of the door. He opened the door. "General Richwood, what a surprise, sir."

"We need to talk," General Richwood said as he stepped inside the room. "Are you alone?"

"Yes, sir, I am," Colonel Wilson answered while he closed the door. "I thought I was supposed to meet you at your office at the Pentagon in the morning."

"The situation has changed," General Richwood said while he removed his cell phone from the outside pocket of his dress uniform. He dialed a number and put the cell phone to his ear. "All clear," he said when his call was answered. He canceled the call and returned his cell phone to his jacket pocket.

What the fuck is going on? Colonel Wilson thought.

A few minutes later there was a knock on the door. General Richwood walked over to the door and looked through the peephole before he opened the door.

Colonel Wilson instantly recognized Secret Service Agent, John Haskell, when he entered the room. He was one of the Secret Service Agents assigned to President Elliot. *What's he doing here?* Colonel Wilson thought.

Seconds later, President Elliot entered, and General Richwood, along with Colonel Wilson, snapped to attention. Secret Service Agent, John Haskell left the room and closed the door. He joined another Secret Service Agent that was standing guard by the door to Colonel Wilson's room.

"Colonel Wilson, the general told me that you have some vital information for me," President Elliot said while he walked over to the table. "So, let's hear what you have found out," he continued as he sat down in the chair at the table.

"Mr. President, I have reason to believe that the VX Nerve Gas is still a threat," Colonel Wilson said while he walked over to the opened briefcase on his bed.

"Do you have proof of this?" General Richwood asked while he walked over to the table. "The big question is, is A'zam al Shammari alive?" The general asked as he sat down in the chair next to President Elliot at the table.

"I'm sure that what I have to show you will answer your questions," Colonel Wilson said while he removed the documents that language expert, Lieutenant Mallory, had given him. Next he removed the photo album that Captain Hale brought to him before he left Strike Force

Delta Command. "The most devastating info is the documents that were recovered from General Juarez's camp that we raided," He continued while he walked over to the table.

"What kind of documents?" President Elliot inquired.

"I'll have to show you," Colonel Wilson answered as he sat down in the chair across from President Elliot and General Richwood.

"Get to the point Wilson," General Richwood snapped. "Is A'zam al Shammari alive?"

"Yes, and no," Colonel Wilson answered while he removed a picture from the photo album.

"What the hell kind of answer is that?" General Richwood fired back.

"This picture will explain everything," Colonel Wilson said as he placed the photograph of the Shammari brothers with Michael Lawrence and Bill Riley on the table for them to see.

"Identical twins," President Elliot remarked as he picked up the photograph from the table."Why haven't I heard about this?"

"No one had a clue that there was two of them," Colonel Wilson answered. "If they did, they kept it to themselves for reasons of their own."

"Who's the other two men in this photograph?" General Richwood inquired.

"They have been identified as CIA operative Michael Lawrence, and former Station Chief Bill Riley," Colonel Wilson replied. "The good news is, we did get one of the Shammari brothers and Bill Riley."

"Yeah, but the other Shammari brother is still out there somewhere," President Elliot was quick to point out. "Any news on his whereabouts?"

"My people are frantically working to locate the other Shammari brother."

"Find him Colonel," President Elliot ordered.

"Yes, Mr. President," Colonel Wilson acknowledged.

"Who else knows about this picture?" General Richwood asked in an attempt to change the subject.

"A hand full of my people, and the two of you."

"Keep it that way," General Richwood fired back.

"What else do you have for me?" President Elliot asked.

Colonel Wilson pulled out the folder that CIA analyst Joan Murray had given him from the bottom of the pile in front of him. "I got this from a friend at Langley," he said while he handed the folder to President Elliot. "The satellite photos in that folder clearly show that Michael Lawrence is in bed with Shammari."

"You don't say?" President Elliot remarked as he opened the folder. He looked at the satellite photos and closed the folder. "I see that Director Müller has a big problem on his hands," President Elliot commented as he handed the folder to General Richwood. "Do you have anything else for me?"

"There is one more thing I need to show you Mr. President," Colonel Wilson answered. He removed the folder underneath the photo album which contained the documents that language expert, Lieutenant Mallory, had given him. "The contents in this folder are the translation of the documents that was retrieved from General Juarez's camp," Colonel Wilson said as he handed President Elliot the folder.

President Elliot opened the folder and scanned the documents inside. *Holy shit,* he thought when he read the last document in the folder. "I don't believe this," he remarked as he closed the folder. "You mean to tell me that Shammari has about a hundred pounds of VX Nerve Gas with him?" he asked while he handed the folder to General Richwood.

"Yes Mr. President, I'm afraid it looks that way," Colonel Wilson sadly answered.

"What do you think general?" President Elliot asked, noticing that General Richwood had finished viewing the documents in the folder.

"I would recommend that we find this Shammari brother before he strikes somewhere." General Richwood handed the folder to Colonel Wilson. "It's time to put an end to the Shammari brothers."

"I agree," President Elliot said as he got up from his seat. "Colonel, I don't care what it takes, or what you have to do to find this Shammari brother."

"Yes Mr. President," Colonel Wilson said as he and General Richwood jumped to their feet.

President Elliot walked over to the door and opened it. He stepped into the hallway and was joined by the two Secret Service agents that were waiting, and closed the door.

"You have your orders from the president," General Richwood pointed out. "Pack your gear and get your ass downstairs," he continued while he walked to the door. "I'll call Andrews and have them ready the jet, and send a car to pick you up."

"Roger that, sir," Colonel Wilson acknowledged. "I'll be ready when they get here."

"Keep me updated on your progress," General Richwood said as he opened the door. He stepped into the hallway and closed the door.

"Fuck" Colonel Wilson mumbled. He removed his cell phone from his shirt pocket and dialed the phone number for Captain Hale, and put the cell phone to his ear. "Bulldog," he said when Captain Hale answered his call. "I'll be leaving here shortly. I want all team leaders in the conference room at zero seven-thirty. Also, have Hammer report to my office at zero seven-hundred."

"Roger that," Captain Hale acknowledged. "Anything else?"

"Nope; that's all. I'll see you when I get there."

Colonel Wilson ended the call and put the cell phone back into his pocket. He collected everything from the table and walked over to the bed. He threw the items from the table into his opened briefcase and closed it.

He quickly packed his personal belongings into his carry bag and slung it over his shoulder. He grabbed the briefcase from the bed and walked to the door. He opened the door and exited the room, and closed the door.

Colonel Wilson walked to the elevator and pushed the call button. The elevator door opened, and he stepped inside. He pushed the button for the first floor where the lobby was located. The elevator door closed and began to move downwards.

When the elevator reached the first floor, the door opened, and Colonel Wilson emerged from the elevator. He walked to the lobby and sat down where he could see the cars that pulled up out front.

A few minutes later, a car pulled up in front of the hotel. The driver, dressed in an Air Force dress uniform, got out of the vehicle and walked to the back of the vehicle.

Colonel Wilson got up from his seat and walked to the main entrance of the hotel. He exited the hotel and walked towards the vehicle while the driver opened the trunk.

He placed his carry bag and briefcase in the trunk, and the driver closed the trunk lid. The driver hurried around to the passenger side rear door and opened it. Colonel Wilson got in, and the driver closed the door.

The driver walked around to the front driver side door and opened it. He jumped in behind the wheel and started up the vehicle. A few seconds later, he put it in gear, and they drove away.

Two hours later, they arrived at the main gate to Andrews. The sentry at the main gate looked at the driver's and Colonel Wilson's identification before allowing them to proceed.

They continued on to the runway where Colonel Wilson's Gulfstream G-550 jet aircraft was waiting and stopped a few yards from the entrance walkway.

The driver got out of the vehicle and walked around to the back passenger's side door. He opened the door, and Colonel Wilson got out of the vehicle.

The driver walked back to the driver's side front door and got back into the vehicle, and drove off.

Colonel Wilson entered the Gulfstream G-550 jet aircraft. *What the fuck,* he thought when he noticed a young red-haired woman sitting in a seat a few feet away.

The young woman stood up as Colonel Wilson approached. "General Richwood sent me here to brief you on new developments in Colombia that you should know about before you leave here."

Colonel Wilson walked over and sat down in the seat across from the young woman.

"So, you're not going with me?"

"No, I'm afraid not, " the young woman replied as she returned to her seat.

"What a shame. I could use the company for the trip back."

"I'm not here for your amusement, or your goddamn play toy," the young woman said in a sarcastic tone. "I'm here on business only."

"Well, excuse the hell out of me," Colonel Wilson shot back. "Let's try this again. "What do you have for me?"

"As I'm sure you've probably heard by now that three hours ago, General Juarez and his army were defeated by the Colombian army. All that's left now is for the military to mop things up."

"Yes, I heard about it on the news. It looked to me like President Roberto has the situation under control."

"The general still wants you to keep a sharp eye on what's going on down there."

"Okay, any news about Shammari and Michael Lawrence?" Colonel Wilson inquired. "Anything new on their whereabouts?"

"According to the latest reports from your people, Shammari and Michael Lawrence have been spotted a few kilometers north of Carepa. It's believed that they are heading to Turbo on the coast."

"Anything else? I need to get back to my command."

"I believe I'm done here," the young woman said as she got up from her seat. "Keep the general informed of any progress," she continued while she walk to the exit. "Have a nice day whoever you are," she added as she exited the aircraft.

The ground crew removed the entrance walkway while the aircraft attendant inside the aircraft closed the exit door and secured it properly, and walked to the front of the aircraft while Colonel Wilson fastened his seat restraint.

When the pilot received clearance from the tower to take off, he throttled up the jet engines, and the aircraft began to move, and taxi to the runway. Seconds later, the aircraft picked up speed as it traveled down the runway and lifted off the ground, and climbed to its assigned cruising altitude.

$$* * * * *$$

Turbo, Colombia

A'zam al Shammari and his four travel companions, with Michael Lawrence leading the way, carefully approached a farmhouse on the outskirts of town.

They concealed themselves in the tall brush while Michael Lawrence walked up the steps onto the front porch and knocked on the door.

The door opened. "Don't move," a woman said in Spanish while pointing an MP-5 assault rifle at Michael Lawrence. "What do you want?"

"Easy there," Michael Lawrence said to the woman in Spanish.

"It's okay; let him in," a man's voice said in Spanish.

The woman lowered the AK-47 assault rifle and stepped aside. Michael Lawrence entered the farmhouse, and she closed the door.

"Michael, it is good to see you again, my friend," the man said in English as he walked up to Michael Lawrence. "I was worried that I would not see you again," the man continued as he shook hands with Michael Lawrence. "I was worried that you met the same demise as General Juarez?"

"What about General Juarez?"

"You mean you haven't heard about what happened to General Juarez?"

"What happened?"

"A few hours ago, General Juarez was killed when the Colombian army overran his position and defeated his army."

"Do you have any other information that I need to know about?"

"All I know is that the CIA has offered a reward for information about your whereabouts."

"What else do you have for me?"

"That's all I can think of for now."

"I need a favor."

"What do you need Michael?"

"I need for you to make arrangements for me and five of my friends to get out of the country."

"It's going to take me a couple of days. Meanwhile, you and your friends can stay in my basement if you like. It has its own entrance."

"Sounds like a good idea. Show me the basement."

"This way," the man said and walked into the kitchen, with Michael Lawrence following close behind him.

The man walked over to the door that lead to the basement and opened it. He flipped on the light switch and Michael Lawrence followed him down the steps.

"What do you think? He asked when they reached the bottom of the steps.

Michael Lawrence glanced around the basement. He walked over to the stairway that led to the outside and walked up the steps. He opened the door and looked around. He closed the door and walked back down the steps to join his friend.

"I know it's not much, but it's the best I can do under such short notice."

"It'll work," Michael Lawrence commented. out. "Just make sure that we're not disturbed. My friends don't want anyone knowing that they're here."

"You will not be disturbed. I will let you know when the arrangements have been made for your departure. Until then, just make yourself at home and relax."

Michael Lawrence watched his friend walk up the stairs into the kitchen and close the door. He hurried over to the stairs that lead to the outside. He ran up the stairs and opened the door, and stepped outside.

He walked over to where Shammari and the others were waiting. "We can hold up here while my friend makes arrangements for our departure," Michael Lawrence informed Shammari.

"Can we trust this man?" Shammari asked.

"He is trustworthy," Michael Lawrence assured Shammari.

Shammari and the others followed Michael Lawrence to the entrance to the basement and entered. The four men carefully placed the tanks that they had strapped on their backs in a corner of the basement while Michael Lawrence walked over to the table in the kitchenette and sat down.

Shammari opened a duffle bag that they had brought with them and removed several wireless cameras from inside the duffle bag. He handed each man a camera, and they hurried back outside to install the cameras around the perimeter of the farmhouse. A few minutes later, the four men returned to the basement.

Shammari walked over to the table. "My people have placed the wireless cameras on the perimeter of the house," he informed Michael Lawrence as he sat down at the table next to him.

"Good," Lawrence commented as he removed his backpack and placed it on the table. "If anyone tries to sneak up on us, the cameras should lock in on their helmet cams." He continued while he removed a laptop computer from the backpack and sat it down in front of him.

"Do you think your government is looking for us?" Shammari inquired.

"There's always that possibility," Lawrence pointed out as he opened the laptop. "Either way, it doesn't hurt to be prepared," he continued while he powered up his laptop.

"Who do you think they are going to send after us?"

"Probably another CIA assault team," Michael Lawrence replied while he entered the password to gain access to his laptop. "Don't worry, there's no way they can sneak up on us without us knowing it."

Shammari watched while Michael Lawrence connected to the wireless cameras using the Bluetooth on his laptop.

"Everything appears to be working," Michael Lawrence commented, satisfied that the cameras were working properly.

One of the men walked over to the table with another duffle bag and sat it down. He opened the double bag and began to remove several pieces of radio surveillance equipment.

Michael Lawrence got up from his seat and walked over to the radio surveillance equipment and started to set it up. When he was done, he turned to Shammari. "Now we can listen in on the radio traffic and get a heads up if they locate us, and we'll know if they decide to come after us before we get out of here." He walked back to his seat and sat down. "Relax... sit back... and listen."

A'zam al Shammari looked at Michael Lawrence and smiled, acknowledging his approval.

Chapter 20

Strike Force Delta Command
Tinker Air Force Base
Oklahoma City, Oklahoma

Colonel Wilson arrived at his office early. When he entered, he found his Training Officer, Second Lieutenant Daniel Shea, nicknamed Hammer, sitting in the chair in front of his desk. He was surprised to see Operations Specialist, First Lieutenant Kate Stanton, nickname Barbie, sitting in the chair next to Lieutenant Shea.

"Barbie, what a pleasant surprise," Colonel Wilson said while he closed the office door. He walked over to his desk and sat down in the chair behind his desk. "I was only expecting Hammer to be here."

"I have something that you need to see," Lieutenant Stanton said as she pulled out a thumb drive from her shirt pocket and offered it to Colonel Wilson.

Colonel Wilson took the thumb drive from Lieutenant Stanton. "Hammer, please step outside while I have a talk with Barbie."

"I'll be waiting outside when you're ready for me," Lieutenant Shea said as he got up from his seat. He walked over to the door and opened it. Lieutenant Shea stepped into the hallway and closed the door.

Colonel Wilson plugged the thumb drive into the USB port on his computer on his desk. A few seconds later, the folder on the thumb drive loaded into the computer. Using his pointer mouse, Colonel

Wilson opened the folder and several satellite pictures displayed on his computer monitor.

One by one, he silently viewed each photograph in the file. When he was finished, he closed the file. "How old are these photographs?"

"They were taken a couple hours ago around Turbo, Columbia," Lieutenant Stanton answered. "The photographs clearly show that Michael Lawrence, along with A'zam al Shammari and four other men are taking refuge at a farmhouse just outside of town."

"Who else knows about these photographs?"

"Myself, and a few others in my office."

"Make sure it stays that way. I don't want anyone else knowing about these photographs."

"Roger that," Lieutenant Stanton acknowledged.

"I want you to keep a constant surveillance on that farmhouse. I need to know how many people are living there. Report your findings directly to me."

"I'll get right on it," Lieutenant Stanton said as she got up from her seat. "Shall I tell Hammer to come back in?" She continued while she headed for the door.

"Yes, please do."

Lieutenant Stanton opened the door and stepped out into the hallway. Moments later, Lieutenants Shea entered Colonel Wilson's office. He walked over to Colonel Wilson's desk and sat down in one of the chairs in front of the desk.

"Hammer, the reason I wanted to see you is I need to talk to you about the status of Condor's training," Colonel Wilson began. "Is Condor ready to take command of an assault team?"

"Yeah, he's ready."

"Good: send me the final paperwork by the end of today."

"Is there anything else you need?" Lieutenant Shea asked as he got up from the seat.

"No, that'll be all. Please close the door on your way out."

"Roger that," Lieutenant Shea commented and walked out of Colonel Wilson's office, and close the door.

Colonel Wilson opened his email program and typed in General Richwood's email address, and then he attached the satellite photographs that Lieutenant Stanton had brought to him.

Using the special decryption code that he and General Richwood used when communicating using email, he typed his message and then sent the email message. When he received confirmation that his email to General Richwood was received, he closed his email program.

Colonel Wilson removed the thumb drive from his computer and put it in his pants pocket. He got up from his seat and walked over to the door, and opened it. He stepped into the hallway and closed the door.

He walked to the conference room where Captain Hale and the assault team leaders were waiting, and entered.

Everyone in the room jumped to their feet and stood at attention.

"As you were gentleman," Colonel Wilson said as he closed the door. "I'm sure by now everyone has heard about the General Juarez takedown," he continued as he walked over to the plasma screen on the wall.

"Is it true that Shammari has an identical twin brother?" Second Lieutenant Roger Milestone, nickname, Crazy Horse, asked.

"Yes, it was a surprise to everyone," Colonel Wilson answered while he removed the thumb drive from his pants pocket. "No one had any idea that there were two of them," he continued as he plugged the thumb drive into the side of the plasma screen. "If Popeye hadn't found that briefcase, we may not of found out about the Shammari brothers or their connection with Bill Riley and Michael Lawrence," Colonel Wilson pointed out. "However, there's been some new developments," he continued while he walked over to the conference table. "We now know, without any doubt, where they're hiding." He said as he picked up the remote control for the plasma screen from the table and took a seat at the head of the table.

"So, we're going after them?" First Lieutenant Mathew McDonald, nickname Popeye, anxiously asked.

"That's the president's call, not mine," Colonel Wilson answered. "We'll have to wait and see what he decides to do about this. Until then, we can familiarize ourselves with what's going on down there, and be ready to move when and if the order is issued. Any more questions?"

Colonel Wilson waited for a few seconds before he pushed a button on the remote control, and the first satellite photograph appeared on the screen. "This photograph was taken a few hours ago. It clearly shows that Michael Lawrence is traveling with the remaining Shammari brother and four other individuals."

"So, Lawrence did kill the CIA black ops assault team," Second Lieutenant, Jackson Lakewood, nickname Wild Man remarked.

"It looks that way," Colonel Wilson pointed out. "He was probably the one that helped Shammari get around the security at Puerto Obaldia."

"Fuckin' traitor," Second Lieutenant Roger Milestone, nickname Crazy Horse, mumbled.

Colonel Wilson smiled as he pushed the button on the remote control again, and the next picture displayed on the plasma screen. One by one, he displayed the remainder of the satellite photographs on the plasma screen. Everyone in the room remained silent as they viewed each photograph.

"Well, that's the end of the photos," Colonel Wilson said when the last photograph was displayed on the plasma screen. "Does anybody have any suggestions?"

"I say let's go down there and put those no-good son-of-a-bitches down before they get away, and strike again," Captain Hale suggested.

"That'll be up to the president to decide," Colonel Wilson said.

The door to the conference room suddenly opened, and Lieutenant Cooltrain entered. She walked over to Colonel Wilson and whispered in his ear, and hurried out of the conference room.

"I want everyone here to study those photos and come up with a workable operational plan that we can use when the president authorizes the mission," Colonel Wilson said while he got up from his seat. "I want it on my desk within the hour." He walked out of the conference room and closed the door.

Colonel Wilson hurried back to his office. He entered his office and closed the door. He rushed over to the chair behind his desk and sat down.

A few minutes later, Lieutenant Cooltrain knocked on the office door, and then entered. "The president is standing by on video call."

"Thanks, Giggles."

Lieutenant Cooltrain left Colonel Wilson's office and closed the door while he powered up his computer monitor. *That was quick*, he thought as he typed in his password and waited to be connected to his video call.

Seconds later, President Elliot appeared on the monitor. "Colonel Wilson, I've seen the photographs and your message that you sent to General Richwood," the president began. "I have to admit the photographs were very compelling. What is your recommendation for dealing with this new development?"

"I would recommend that we go down there and eliminate this problem once and for all," Colonel Wilson was quick to point out. "I would also suggest that we take action as quickly as possible before they disappear again."

"Do you have a plan?" President Elliot asked.

"My people are working on a plan. All we'll need is your approval to strike."

"What is the probability that you can take down the target without collateral damage?"

"If we strike now the probability of minimizing collateral damage is good. However, the longer we wait the situation could change."

"I will inform General Richwood of my decision shortly. Take no action until you hear from the general."

"Yes, Mr. President. I will await your decision."

"Good day Colonel," President Elliott said, and then the screen went blank.

"Fuckin' wait," Colonel Wilson mumbled while he turned off his monitor.

The door to Colonel Wilson's office open, and Captain Hale entered. "I have an operational plan for you to review," he said, referring to the thumb drive he had in his hand.

"That was quick," Colonel Wilson commented.

"I got the impression that you wanted us to put a rush on this," Captain Hale said as he closed the office door.

"I just want to be ready, so we can move when we get the go ahead."

"Any word yet?" Captain Hale asked while he walked over to Colonel Wilson's desk.

The president hasn't made a decision yet, "Colonel Wilson replied. "He's still thinking it over."

"I hope he doesn't take too long to decide what he's going to do,"

Captain Hale commented as he handed Colonel Wilson the thumb drive. "Everyone's ready to go," He continued while he sat down in the chair in front of Colonel Wilson's desk.

"We can't do a damn thing about it until the president authorizes us to do so, Colonel Wilson fired back." For now, we'll just have to wait. I'll let you know the minute I hear something from the president."

"Roger that," Captain Hale acknowledged and got up from his seat. He walked over to the door and opened it. He stepped out of the office and closed the door.

Colonel Wilson powered up the computer monitor and attached the thumb drive to his computer. The documents on the thumb drive displayed on a monitor. He downloaded the documents to his computer and then removed the thumb drive.

He carefully viewed each document. "That'll work for me," he said as he opened his email program. He typed up a message to General Richwood and sent the message to the general, and then closed his email program.

He removed the telephone receiver from the telephone on his desk. He dialed the extension number for Operations Specialist, First Lieutenant Kate Stanton while he put the telephone receiver to his ear.

"Operations," Lieutenant Stanton said when she answered the call.

"Barbie, has there been any changes in the target area?" Colonel Wilson inquired.

"Nothing has changed. The subjects are still at the farmhouse."

"Keep a sharp eye on that farmhouse and let me know the minute anything changes."

"Roger that," Lieutenant Stanton acknowledged. "I'll let you know the minute the situation down there changes."

Colonel Wilson returned the telephone receiver to the telephone on his desk. He started to get up from his seat when the door of his office opened. He returned to his seat while Captain Hale entered his office and closed the door.

"Bulldog, I haven't heard from the general yet." Colonel Wilson was quick to point out.

Captain Hale smiled. "I was leaving my office when I ran into Raven (Encryption Specialist, Second Lieutenant Williams)," he said while he walked over to Colonel Wilson's desk. "She wanted me to give you this message," he continued, referring to the envelope he had in his hand. "I think this is what you've been waiting for," he concluded as he handed Colonel Wilson the envelope.

Colonel Wilson opened the envelope and removed the message. He read the message twice before he put it back into the envelope. "This is not what I was expecting," he remarked as he tossed the envelope down on his desk. "Sometimes I wonder why the fuck we do this job."

"What's up?" Captain Hale inquired.

"The president has decided not to authorize the operation at this time," Colonel Wilson answered. "He said he needs more time to think this over."

"Time is one luxury we don't have," Captain Hale was quick to point out. "I don't understand why the president is so hesitant about authorizing this mission."

"It's probably some political bullshit," Colonel Wilson remarked. "However, the president didn't say no. He just said he needed more time to think this over."

"Wolverine, what are you thinking?"

"We've been told to wait, so we'll have to wait. In the meantime, our assault teams will remain on tactical alert, and our aircrafts will be fueled and ready to go at a moment's notice."

"Isn't that jumping the gun a little bit?" Captain Hale inquired.

"What the hell do you mean by that?"

"There's still a chance that the President may decide not to use us for this operation. He may choose to give the mission to JSOC (Joint Special Operations Command)."

"Now that would piss me off, and it would be a slap in the face," Colonel Wilson said in an outrage. "Especially, since everyone here has worked so hard to come up with this plan."

"I'm sure the president will make the right decision," Captain Hale assured Colonel Wilson.

"Still, I want everything to be ready in case we get the go order."

"I'll get right on it," Captain Hale said while he got up from his seat. He walked over to the office door and opened it. He exited the office and closed the door.

What a day, Colonel Wilson thought while he leaned back in his chair, and then propped his feet up on his desk.

* * * * *

US Embassy
Bogotá, Colombia

Ambassador Haskell was sitting behind his desk finishing up some last minute paperwork when the intercom on his desk beeped. He stopped what he was doing and pushed the intercom button on the telephone on his desk. 'Yes."

"Sir, I know it's late, but President Roberto is here, and he wishes to see you."

"Please show him in," Ambassador Haskell said. He pushed the intercom button to cancel the intercom call, and got up from his seat.

The door to the ambassador's office suddenly opened and President Roberto entered, and Jennifer Masterson closed the door.

"Mr. President, what a pleasant surprise," Ambassador Haskell said while the president walked over to the ambassador's desk. "What can I do for you today?"

"Mr. Ambassador, I am here on a pressing matter that cannot wait," President Roberto said while he sat down in the chair in front of the ambassador's desk. "I thought it best that we talk here rather than in my office."

"Yes, of course, Mr. President," Ambassador Haskell said while he returned to his seat. "What can I do for you, sir?"

"I understand that your government has located a missing CIA agent here in Colombia; and that he is being held hostage by terrorist."

"I have heard that a CIA agent was missing, but that's all I know. I'm afraid that you have me at a disadvantage Mr. President."

"Mr. Ambassador, I am here because I need your help in getting a message to your president without anybody here knowing."

"How fast do you need it to get there Mr. President?"

"The sooner, the better. It is very important that your president gets my message as soon as he possibly can."

"Why wait; I can call the president right now, and the two of you can talk in private, and no one will ever know." Ambassador Haskell picked up the telephone receiver from the telephone on the desk. He dialed the extension number for the Embassy's Communication Center. "This is Ambassador Haskell. I need a secure line to the president," he said when his call was answered. "Priority alpha-delta."

"Yes, Mr. Ambassador," the Communications operator said. "Please remain on the line while I connect you."

Ambassador Haskell patiently waited for his call to be connected. After a series of clicks, he was connected to President Elliott's private line in the presidential residence at the White House.

Mr. President, I apologize for the interruption this late at night, but President Roberto is in my office and needs to talk to you about a delicate matter that can't wait."

"By all means put him on, Robert," President Elliott anxiously said. "I would like to talk to the president in private, so please leave the room until we are done talking."

"Yes, Mr. President, Ambassador Haskell said, and then handed President Roberto the telephone receiver. "I will wait outside in the reception area so you may have some privacy," he continued while he got up from his seat.

President Roberto watched Ambassador Haskell walk over to the door and open it. The ambassador stepped into the reception area and closed the door.

"Is there something wrong Mr. Ambassador?" Jennifer Masterson asked while she got up from her seat. "Do you need something, sir?"

"No, I need nothing," Ambassador Haskell said as he sat down in the chair next to Jennifer Masterson's desk. "President Elliot wanted to talk to President Roberto in private. I shall wait here until they're done talking."

"Are you going to need me to stay over until President Roberto is finished talking with President Elliot?"

"No, I think I can handle it from here. Go on home Jennifer."

"Thank you, Mr. Ambassador," Jennifer Masterson said as she got up from her seat. "I'll see you tomorrow morning Mr. Ambassador," she remarked while she walked over to the door and opened it. She left the office and closed the door.

Ambassador Haskell got up from his seat when the door of his office suddenly opened and President Roberto emerged from his office and closed the door.

"I thank you for the use of your office."

"It was my pleasure Mr. President. Is there anything else I could do for you?"

"I am having a banquet tomorrow night to celebrate our victory over General Juarez. I invited your president to attend, but, unfortunately, he had to decline because of his busy schedule. He did recommend that perhaps you and your wife would like to attend."

"Mr. President, my wife and I would be honored to attend the banquet."

"Excellent!" President Roberto exclaimed. "I look forward to seeing you and your lovely wife tomorrow night at six o'clock."

"Yes, Mr. President."

"Good-day Mr. Ambassador.

"Good-day Mr. President."

President Roberto walked towards the door with Ambassador Haskell leading the way. Ambassador Haskell opened the door, and the president exited his office. Ambassador Haskell stepped out of his office and into the hallway and closed the door.

Chapter 21

Washington, D.C.
The White House Briefing Room

CIA Director, Robert Müller and NSA Director, Jack Parkinson were seated at the table in the middle of the room waiting for the president's arrival. They were joined by Secretary of Defense, Mark Roberts and Secretary of Navy, John Forsythe. Major General Larry McCoy, commanding officer of the Joint Special Operations Command (JSOC) and General Thomas Richwood, Chairman of the Joint Chiefs of Staff, was also seated at the table next to Vice President James Conrad.

Everyone in the room jumped to their feet when President Elliot entered. "Be seated gentleman," President Elliot said while he walked over to the table and sat down. He waited for everyone to return to their seats before he continued. "I've talked with President Roberto in Colombia. He has reluctantly authorized us to use lethal force to capture or kill the remaining Shammari brother and his traveling companions who are hiding in Colombia."

"Mr. President, the latest satellite surveillance shows that the targets are still holding up at the farmhouse near Turbo," NSA Director Jack Parkinson reported. "I strongly recommend that we hit them at the farmhouse to minimize collateral damage."

"I agree with Director Parkinson," CIA Director Müller jumped in. "I can have an assault team ready to go in about forty-eight hours and on the ground twenty-four hours after that."

"That's the best you can do?" President Elliot inquired. "I don't understand why it's going to take you that long. Don't you have any people already down there?"

"We have the assets already down there. However, the biggest problem is getting our logistics in place," Director Müller replied. "It would be suicide to proceed with this operation without our logistics properly in place."

"Is that the best you can come up with?" Vice President Conrad sarcastically asked.

"Calm down Jim," President Elliott jumped in. "We need to do this right the first time. We can't go in there half-cocked and unprepared."

"I apologize Mr. President," Vice President Conrad calmly said. "I meant no disrespect."

"Okay, let's move on," President Elliot commented. "General McCoy, how soon can JSOC (Joint Special Operations Command) put something together?"

"Forty-eight hours," General McCoy answered.

"Very well," President Eliot remarked. "You and Director Müller are to proceed with your planning and keep me informed of your progress. You are to take no action without my authorization. The rest of you are to keep me informed of any changes in the target area. Are there any questions?" The president waited for a few seconds before he continued. "Good. Director Müller, I want you and General McCoy to sit down and come up with a workable plan."

"Yes, Mr. President," Director Müller acknowledged. The general and I will get started on this right away."

"Keep me informed every step of the way. Time is of the essence gentleman; we don't have time to waste." President Elliott paused for a moment. "We're done here. I need Secretary Forsythe and General Richwood to remain. The rest of you can get back to work."

Secretary Forsythe and General Richwood remained in their seats while everybody else got up from their seats and left the room. Vice President Conrad was the last to leave the room and close the door.

"General, how long will it take Strike Force to deploy, and carry out the operation?"

"I talked to Colonel Wilson a few minutes ago. He informed me that he has his assault units on tactical alert. He said that they can be deployed within the hour and arrive at the target eight hours later. However, the extraction part of the operation may present a problem."

"What kind of problems?"

"He only has two stealth extraction helicopters and the mission calls for four."

"I can have two stealth helicopters from the Ronald Reagan meet your two at Camp Freedom," Secretary Forsythe suggested.

"That's an excellent idea," President Elliot commented. "Let's do it. General, send Colonel Wilson the go order and get the ball rolling."

"Mr. President, shouldn't we inform Director Müller and General McCoy about this?" Secretary Forsythe suggested.

"Tell no one outside this room about this," President Elliott fired back. "I'll notify Director Müller and General McCoy in due time."

"Yes, Mr. President," Secretary Forsythe acknowledged. "Is there anything else you need, sir?"

"General, is it possible to send a live satellite feed of the target area to the Oval Office?"

"Yes, Mr. President that will not be a problem. I can set it up for you if you wish?"

"Yes, set it up for me," President Elliott answered as he got up from his seat.

"I'll get right on it Mr. President," General Richwood said while he and Secretary Forsythe jumped to their feet.

President Elliott walked over to the door and opened it. He exited the Briefing Room with General Richwood and Secretary Forsythe a few steps behind him. Secretary Forsythe was the last to leave the Briefing Room and closed the door.

$$* * * * *$$

Turbo, Colombia

Michael Lawrence looked at his wrist watch and noticed that it had been several hours since his friend had gone into town. *Damn, what's taking him so long,* he thought. *I hope he gets back here soon;* he continued to think as he stared at the screen on his laptop that was on the table in front of him.

"Is something wrong?" A'zam al Shammari asked, who was sitting at the table across from Michael Lawrence.

"No, why do you ask?"

"You look like you have something weighing heavily on your mind."

"Just thinking about how nice it's going to be to be gone from this country."

"Speaking of which, your friend has been gone for quite a while. Are you certain that we can trust him?"

"Don't worry. We can trust him."

"For our sake, I hope you're right."

"I've known Jose for over thirty years. He and I grew up together; we're like brothers. He would never sell me out. He..." Michael Lawrence stopped talking when he heard the sound of a car pulling up to the farmhouse.

"Someone is here," A'zam al Shammari pointed out.

"I'll check it out," Michael Lawrence said as he got up from his seat at the table.

Everyone grabbed their weapons and readied them for action while Michael Lawrence hurried up the stairway that led to the kitchen on the ground floor of the farmhouse.

Michael Lawrence removed the forty-five pistol that he kept tucked in the small of his back and opened the door. He readied the forty-five and stepped into the kitchen, and closed the door.

He hurried over to the nearest window in the kitchen and looked out to see who had pulled up out front. He was relieved to see his friend Jose Morales and his wife Rosetta get out of their car and walk to the front door. Lawrence set the safety on the forty-five and returned the pistol to the small of his back while he walked to the front door.

Jose and Rosetta entered the house and closed the door. Rosetta walked into the living room while Jose and Michael Lawrence walked into the kitchen.

"Michael, what in the hell have you gotten yourself into?"Jose inquired.

"What are you talking about?"

"I found out that the CIA has put out a reward for information leading to your location. Also, your government is offering a large reward for the whereabouts of your friends that are down in my basement."

"What's up with all these damn questions?"

"Michael, I don't need any of this to come back on me."

"It won't, but I need your help. My friends and I need a way out of this country undetected."

"Don't worry Michael, I've secured passage for you and your friends on a freighter that's bound for San Juan, Puerto Rico and then Baltimore, Maryland. The freighter leaves port in three days."

"Great. "What's it going to cost?"

"The captain wants twelve-thousand dollars cash. Payable when you and your friends board the freighter."

"Thank you. How can I ever repay you for helping me?"

"Don't ever come back," Jose sadly said. "I will get you and your friends to the freighter, and from that day forward, we're done," he said as he walked out of the kitchen."

Fuckin' asshole, Michael Lawrence thought while he walked over to the door that led to the basement. He knocked on the door. "Everything's okay," he said before he opened the door. He stepped onto the landing at the top of the stairs and closed the door.

He walked down the stairs with a smile on his face. "We'll be out of here in three days," he announced as he walked toward the table where A'zam al Shammari was sitting. "My friend has secured our passage on a freighter that's bound for San Juan, Puerto Rico and then Baltimore, Maryland," he continued as he sat down at the table across from Shammari.

"Allah has blessed us my friend," A'zam al Shammari said, excited by what he had just heard. "We will be able to strike at the infidels in their own back yard and bring them down to their knees."

Michael Lawrence looked at Shammari and smiled. "Don't get too excited; we have to get there first."

"If Allah wills it, we will. First, we have to get out of this godforsaken country without being detected."

"I'm not worried about that," Michael Lawrence commented. "What worries me more is not knowing whether or not the Americans know where we're hiding."

"What do you mean by that?" Shammari curiously asked.

"I don't know why, but I got a feeling that something isn't right. We've been listening in on the radio traffic, and there's been no mention of them looking for us. It's as if they don't give a shit where we're at."

"Maybe, they are too busy with something else."

"That's possible," Michael Lawrence admitted. "Still, it would be nice to know what they're doing."

"I think you are worrying about nothing, my friend" Shammari pointed out. "Perhaps, they think the threat is over. It could be that the takedown of General Juarez has them believing that their work here in Colombia is finished."

"You could be right, but still, I'll feel better once we're out of here."

A'zam al Shammari smiled. "Things will work out for us," he said as he got up from his seat. "Allah will show us the way."

Yeah, right, Michael Lawrence thought while Shammari walked over to the others. *You keep right on believing that shit.*

* * * * *

Washington, D.C.
The Oval Office

President Elliot was sitting at his desk and viewed the live satellite feed of the farmhouse near Turbo, Colombia on his laptop when the intercom on the telephone beeped. He reached over and push the intercom button on the telephone. "Yes."

"Mr. President, Director Müller and General McCoy are here to see you," President Elliot's Personal Assistant, Mrs. Joan Wyatt, announced. "They say it's important, sir."

"Very well, show them in," President Elliot said, and then pushed the intercom button on his telephone to cancel the intercom call.

The door to the Oval Office opened, and Director Müller and General McCoy entered, and Mrs. Wyatt closed the door.

"Take a seat gentleman," President Elliott suggested as he motioned to the two chairs in front of his desk.

"Mr. President, General McCoy and I have come up with a plan that we feel would minimize collateral damage when we take down

Shammari," Director Müller said when he and General McCoy sat down in the chairs in front of President Elliot's desk.

"Go on; I'm listening."

"I did a quick check on what freighters are leaving Turbo within the next three or four days. I found that one of Michael Lawrence's old friends, Jose Morales, has arranged passage for them on a freighter that leaves port in three days."

"So, this Michael Lawrence of yours is in cahoots with Shammari?"

"It appears so," Director Müller reluctantly answered.

"Mr. President, Director Müller and I have devised a plan that we feel will work," General McCoy was quick to point out.

"What kind of plan do you have in mind?"

"I suggest that we allow Lawrence and Shammari to board this freighter, and leave Columbia," Director Müller answered.

"You want to let them leave Columbia with the VX nerve gas?" President Elliott fired back. "That's unacceptable."

"Sir, once the freighter is at sea, I can put a Seal Team on board and neutralize the threat." General McCoy was quick to point out.

"I'm not crazy about any of this," President Elliott remarked. "If they get off that freighter before you send in a Seal Team we're screwed."

"Mr. President, we can have a submarine follow the freighter to ensure that doesn't happen," Director Müller suggested.

"What's the freighter's destination?"

"San Juan, Puerto Rico and then on to Baltimore, Maryland," Director Müller replied.

"I don't like this plan of yours," President Elliott said. "There has to be a better way."

"Sir, we can contain the situation easier on the freighter than we can on land," General McCoy assured President Elliott.

"So, you're telling me that this is the best the two of you can come up with?"

"Sir, what we're saying is that this plan is the only plan that we can implement in such a short time," Director Müller pointed out.

"I will give you my answer sometime tomorrow," President Elliott said as he got up from his seat. "Until then, have your people prepare for the mission."

Director Müller and General McCoy jumped to their feet. "Yes, Mr. President," General McCoy said while he saluted President Elliott.

President Elliott returned to his seat while Director Müller walked over to the door, with General McCoy following. He opened the door, and they exited the Oval Office.

"Is there anything you need Mr. President?" Mrs. Wyatt asked, who was standing in the doorway.

"Is General Richwood still here?"

"I believe so, Mr. President."

"Tell the general, I need to see him."

"Yes, Mr. President," Mrs. Wyatt said and closed the door.

President Elliot returned to viewing the live satellite feed of the farmhouse near Turbo, Colombia on his laptop.

A few minutes later, there was a knock on the door. The door open and General Richwood entered. "You wanted to see me, Mr. President?" The general asked while he closed the door.

"Yes, I did, general. Please have a seat."

General Richwood walked over to the chairs in front of President Elliott's desk. "I've sent the go ahead order to Colonel Wilson," he said as he sat down in one of the chairs.

"What's the chances of his people pulling it off?"

"Wilson is confident that his people will succeed in taking down Shammari," General Richwood boldly answered.

"I hope you're right; because the backup plan that was proposed to me is not to my liking."

"Mr. President, I didn't know that there was a backup plan."

"Director Müller and General McCoy proposed that I allow Shammari and his cohorts to board a freighter with the VX nerve gas in hand. They want to put a Seal Team onboard the freighter while it's at sea."

"That's the best they can come up with?" General Richwood remarked, shocked by what he just heard. "There's a lot that can go wrong with their plan. It could come back and bite us."

"I'm not too thrilled about it either. I'm putting a lot of faith in Colonel Wilson and his people."

"Mr. President, Colonel Wilson, and his people, are good at what they do. I can assure you that they will get the job done."

"General, if you're wrong, this could become a political nightmare." President Elliott paused for a moment before he continued. "Let Colonel Wilson know that if I don't like the outcome of this, I will pull the plug on Strike Force."

"Yes, Mr. President," General Richwood acknowledged as he got up from his seat and saluted President Elliot.

President Elliott watched as General Richwood walked over to the door and opened it. The general stepped into the reception area and closed the door.

What a mess, President Elliot thought as he turned his attention back to the laptop on his desk and continued to view the live satellite feed of the farmhouse near Turbo, Colombia.

Chapter 22

Strike Force Delta Command
Tinker Air Force Base
Oklahoma City, Oklahoma

Colonel Wilson stood in the Operation Center staring at the plasma screen that displayed the live satellite feed of the farm house just outside of Turbo, Colombia.

Encryption Specialist, Second Lieutenant Betty Williams, nicknamed Raven entered the Operations Center and walked over to Colonel Wilson. "Wolverine, this just came in from Washington," she said as she handed him the message.

"Thanks, Raven," Colonel Wilson said while he read the message. "I'll be in the Briefing Room. If you get any more messages please bring them to me immediately."

"Roger that," Lieutenant Williams acknowledged, and left the Operation Center.

Colonel Wilson removed his cell phone from his shirt pocket. He flipped it open and pressed the speed dial button for Captain Hale, and put the cell phone to his ear.

"Hale," Captain Hale said when he answered Colonel Wilson's call.

"Bulldog, assemble all team leaders in the Briefing Room immediately."

"I'll get right on it," Captain Hale assured Colonel Wilson.

Colonel Wilson ended the call and closed his cell phone. He

returned it to his shirt pocket and walked over to Operations Specialist, First Lieutenant Kate Stanton. "Barbie, I want the latest satellite picture of the target area sent to the plasma screen in the Briefing Room."

"No problem," Lieutenant Stanton acknowledged. "I'll get right on it."

Colonel Wilson walked out of the Operation Center. He walked to the Briefing Room and was about to open the door when Lieutenant Williams came running up to him.

"Wolverine, I have something you might want to see." Lieutenant Williams handed Colonel Wilson the paper that she was holding in her hand.

Colonel Wilson looked at the paper. "Where did you get this?"

"It came from the CIA Station Chief at Puerto Obaldia, Panama. The message was sent to the CIA Director at Langley, Virginia."

"This changes everything," Colonel Wilson remarked as he handed the paper back to Lieutenant Williams. He opened the door and entered the Briefing Room. Everyone in the room jumped to their feet."As you were," he said while he closed the door. He walked over to the table and picked up the remote control for the wall-size plasma screen.

Colonel Wilson sat down at the table. He pointed the remote control at the plasma screen and pushed the power button. The plasma screen came to life and displayed a detailed map of the area around the farmhouse just outside of Turbo, Columbia. "The president has authorized the mission," he began. "I'm sending everyone on this mission. Bulldog, you're going with them and assume tactical command."

"When do we leave?" Captain Hale asked.

"As soon as we're done here."

"We've been over the operational plan several times," Captain Hale was quick to point out. "Everyone is ready to go."

"There's been some new developments; and a few changes." Colonel Wilson pushed another button on the remote control, and the farmhouse appeared on the plasma screen. "Does anyone see anything out of the ordinary around this farmhouse?"

"Holy shit; they have a sat-com antenna on the farmhouse," Lieutenant Milestone said in dismay. "As well as surveillance cameras covering the entire perimeter."

"How the hell did we miss this?" Captain Hale demanded to know. "Someone screwed the pooch this time. If we hadn't of picked up on this, it would have been disastrous for us when we went in there."

"Calm down Bulldog," Colonel Wilson said. "Our satellites just picked this up ten minutes ago; no one screwed up."

"One thing's for certain, we can kiss the element of surprise goodbye," Captain Hale pointed out. "They'll know we're coming before we even get there."

"Not necessarily, Lieutenant Nash jumped in. "There is another way."

"What do you have in mind?" Colonel Wilson inquired.

"It's no secret now that they have the technology to detect us. Why don't we use technology against them," Lieutenant Nash suggested.

"What are you proposing?" Captain Hale asked.

"We can do it the old fashion way. Let's use technology against them," Lieutenant Nash replied.

"What do you have in mind, Condor," Colonel Wilson curiously asked.

"I suggest that we go in using VHF radios to communicate with the other assault teams as we set up a perimeter to trap these assholes in the farmhouse."

"That might just work," Captain Hale commented. "We can take them down before they even know what hit them."

"Bulldog, I leave it up to you to make Condor's plan work," Colonel Wilson said. "Now, let's move on to the next piece of business. The CIA still believes that Michael Lawrence is being held hostage by Shammari. Until you have proof to the contrary, he is to be treated as a friendly."

"What if the CIA is wrong about Lawrence?" Captain Hale asked. "What then?

"It's simple, you put him down with the rest of those assholes." Colonel Wilson fired back. "The president wants results no matter who's involved."

"Roger that," Captain Hale acknowledged.

"Good hunting gentleman," Colonel Wilson said as he got up from his seat. Everyone jumped to their feet. "Give em hell," Colonel Wilson continued. "Let's put an end to Shammari once and for all." He walked over to the door and opened it, and left the Briefing Room, closing the door behind him.

Thirty Minutes Later

Two M-35 two and a half ton trucks carrying the Strike Force assault teams pulled up next to one of the two C-130J Hercules aircrafts that were waiting on the runway.

The first C-130J that was carrying two stealth UH-60L Black Hawk helicopters powered up its jet engines and began to move down the runway. Seconds later, the aircraft lifted off the ground and climbed to its cruising altitude.

Dressed in full combat dress, the Strike Force assault teams disembarked from the trucks, and the trucks drove away.

"Popeye, see to it that everyone gets on board and prepared for takeoff," Captain Hale ordered as he noticed a Humvee approaching.

"Roger that," Lieutenant McDonald acknowledged. "Okay, people, let's get our asses moving and get on board. We don't have all day."

The Humvee pulled up a few feet from where Captain Hale was standing. Colonel Wilson jumped out of the Humvee on the driver's side. He picked up a folder that was on the front seat, and walked over to Captain Hale.

Meanwhile, the Strike Force assault teams boarded the C-130J aircraft. They sat down in the seats that were available, and secured their seat restraints.

"Wolverine, I wasn't expecting you to come and see us off," Captain Hale said. "We're still a go aren't we?"

"Don't worry bulldog, the operation is still a go," Colonel Wilson assured Captain Hale. "I have some last minute changes that you need to go over with your people," Colonel Wilson said as he handed Captain Hale the folder that he had in his hand.

"Wolverine, don't take this the wrong way, but this is a stupid time to make changes."

"Relax Bulldog. There's no major changes to the operational plan. There's just been a few things added that might come in handy."

Captain Hale looked at his wrist watch. "We best be going if we're going to meet our target time."

"Good hunting," Colonel Wilson said as he shook hands with Captain Hale. "I'll see you when you get back."

"Roger that," Captain Hale acknowledged. He walked over to the cargo ramp at the back of the aircraft and entered. He hurried over to the seat next to Lieutenant McDonald and sat down.

"What you got there?" Lieutenant McDonald asked, referring to the folder that Captain Hale was holding in his hand.

"Wolverine, gave it to me," Captain Hale replied while he fastened his seat restraints. "I'll take a look at it once we're airborne."

The back cargo door on the C-130J aircraft closed. The aircraft personnel secured the cargo door for takeoff, and the aircraft taxied onto the runway. The pilot powered up the aircraft jet engines and began to move down the runway. The aircraft rapidly picked up speed and lifted off the ground, and climbed upward in the sky.

When the C-130J aircraft reached its cruising altitude, Captain Hale removed his seat restraints. He opened the folder that Colonel Wilson had given him and scanned through its contents.

"Anything new we need to know about?" Lieutenant McDonald curiously asked while he removed his seat restraints.

"Nothing you need to worry about," Captain Hale pointed out. "We should be at Camp Freedom in a few hours."

"I'll get right on it," Lieutenant McDonald acknowledged as he got up from his seat. He walked over to the Strike Force assault teams that were busy preparing their equipment for the upcoming mission.

"What's up with, bulldog?" Second Lieutenant Rick Johnson, nicknamed Maverick, asked Lieutenant McDonald.

"Nothing that I know of," Lieutenant McDonald answered. "He's probably pissed off because Wolverine made him come with us."

"Yeah, he's..."

"Listen up," Captain Hale said in a raised voice as he got up from his seat. "Once again, I want to reiterate that we will not be using helmet cams or satellite radios on this mission. It is suspected that our targets may have access to satellite surveillance. For this reason, we will be using the old VHS handheld radios to communicate with each other. Finally, make sure that your gas mask is one-hundred percent operational. Carry on."

Captain Hale returned to his seat, and the Strike Force team members continued to check their equipment. He removed the contents from the folder and folded each paper to a size that he desired, and put them in one of the pockets of the black jumpsuit that he was wearing. *Might as well get some shut-eye*, he thought as he closed his eyes and drifted off to sleep.

Six Hours Later

Captain Hale opened his eyes when he felt the aircraft begin to descend. One of the aircraft's crew members walked over to him. "Excuse me, sir, we'll be landing at Camp Freedom shortly."

"Very well, thank you," Captain Hale said. He looked around and noticed the Strike Force assault teams were secured in their seats. *Time to rockin' roll*, he thought while he double checked his seat restraint.

The aircraft personnel prepared the aircraft for landing. A few minutes later, the C-130J safely touched down and reduced speed as it traveled down the runway. When the aircraft came to a complete stop, the back cargo door opened, and the pilot powered down the aircraft's jet engines.

Captain Hale removed his seat restraint and jumped to his feet. He walked over to the Strike Force team leaders that were standing at the opened back cargo door of the aircraft. The rest of the Strike Force personnel got up from their seats and prepared to exit the aircraft.

"Bulldog, which teams are going in first?" Second Lieutenant, Rick Johnson, nicknamed Maverick, asked.

"We are all going in at the same time," Captain Hale answered. "The Navy has provided two stealth choppers for us to use on this mission."

"How the hell did Wolverine pull that off?" First Lieutenant, Jonathan Nash, nicknamed Condor, curiously asked.

"He didn't," Captain Hale fired back. "The order came from the White House. Any more questions?" He waited a few seconds before continuing. "Good. We move out in five."

"Roger that," Lieutenant McDonald acknowledged.

Captain Hale walked to the bottom of the ramp while Lieutenant McDonald and the other Strike Force team leaders walked back to their assault teams.

$* * * * *$

Strike Force Delta Command
Tinker Air Force Base
Oklahoma City, Oklahoma

Colonel Wilson entered the Operations Center and walked over to Operations Specialist, Lieutenant Stanton. "Has Bulldog and the Strike Force assault teams arrived at Camp Freedom?"

"They arrived a few minutes ago," Lieutenant Stanton reported. "Everything is on schedule. They should be departing Camp Freedom shortly."

"I take it by the look on your face; there's something bothering you?"

"My gut tells me that we've overlooked something. Something just doesn't feel right."

"Like what, for instance?"

"By the way the CIA is reacting to this, I don't think that Michael Lawrence is a hostage. I think he's working with Shammari. That would explain how Shammari has managed to keep one step ahead of us."

"You got any proof of this?"

"No, I don't. Still, I think the CIA is hiding something."

"You're probably right about that, but what? Why would they..." Colonel Wilson abruptly stopped talking and stared at the plasma screen on the wall that was displaying the satellite coverage of the target area. "Holy shit," he suddenly said.

"What is it, Wolverine?"

Colonel Wilson turned his attention back to Lieutenant Stanton. "What if they have the ability to not only tap into our satellite radio transmissions but also our satellite video transmissions as well?"

"If that was so, they would know when and where our Strike Force assault teams landed," Lieutenant Stanton commented. "They would be able to watch as they approached the farmhouse."

"Exactly. The assault force would be walking right into a trap." Barbie, is there any way to shut down the CIA and NSA satellites that are covering the target area?"

"It's possible to briefly cause a blackout," Lieutenant Stanton answered. "Do you really think this is necessary?"

"Yes, I do," Colonel Wilson fired back. "Now, how long will they're satellites be blacked-out?"

"Eight to ten hours."

"Good; how long will it take you to get this done?"

"Twenty minutes."

"I suggest you get started. I want this done in fifteen."

"Wolverine, If we do this, it's going to piss a lot of people off at the CIA and NSA, and bring a lot of heat down on you."

"Just do what I told you to do," Colonel Wilson snapped. "I want their coverage of the area terminated immediately."

"I'll get right on it," Lieutenant Stanton acknowledged.

Colonel Wilson turned his attention back to the plasma screen while Lieutenant Stanton hurried off to do what he had ordered her to do.

Chapter 23

Turbo, Columbia
The Farmhouse

Michael Lawrence was sitting at the table in the basement watching the live satellite feed of the area as it displayed on his laptop. "What the fuck," he said when the screen in front of him went blank.

"What's wrong?" A'zam al Shammari asked, who was sitting across from Michael Lawrence.

"The live satellite feed just went offline," Michael Lawrence answered as he looked up from the laptop.

"What does that mean?"

"It means that we have no eyes outside. We have no idea what's out there, or what's coming our way."

"You think this could be a prelude to an attack on us?"

"It's hard to say. I've not seen, nor heard anything that would indicate that they know where we are. It could be a coincidence, or that the satellites are doing a routine maintenance."

"Is there any way for you to find out why the satellites went dark?"

Michael Lawrence turned his attention back to the laptop just as a message displayed on the screen. "Well, that explains everything," he commented after reading the message that was displayed on the screen in front of him. "It seems that the CIA satellite covering this area will be down for several hours for routine maintenance."

"So, we have no idea of what's out there?" Shammari inquired.

"Not right now we don't."

"Easal, take Raul and check outside," Shammari ordered, speaking in Arabic. "Make sure you double check everything. Especially the Claymore mines that we placed on the perimeter."

Easal and Raul picked up their AK-47 assault rifles next to them and hung them over their shoulder, and then they exited the basement through the door that led to the outside.

"Relax, we still have the outside surveillance cameras, and they appear to be working properly," Michael Lawrence was quick to point out. "Stop worrying, we'll be out of here tomorrow."

"I will stop worrying when we are out of here," Shammari fired back as he got up from his seat. "Until then, we need to keep on our toes. This operation has already cost us my brother and several good friends. we need to complete this operation for their sake."

"I'll keep watching the perimeter cameras," Michael Lawrence said while he pulled up the outside surveillance cameras. "Trust me, no one is gonna just sneak up on us."

Shammari walked over to the two men while Michael Lawrence sat at the table and watched the live feed from the surveillance cameras as it displayed on his laptop.

* * * * *

Camp Freedom, Panama

Captain Hale and Lieutenant McDonald stood at the bottom of the cargo ramp of the C-130J aircraft and watched as the sun began to set. They were joined a few minutes later by Lieutenant Johnson and Lieutenant Milestone while the sun disappeared behind the mountains, bringing an end to another beautiful day and the start of a moonless night.

"No matter how many sunsets I see they just get more beautiful every time," Lieutenant Milestone commented.

"Let's just hope it's not our last," Lieutenant Johnson pointed out.

"Enough of that kinda talk," Captain Hale snapped. "We need to keep our focus on the mission at hand. I don't want to hear that kind of talk from any of you again. Is that clear?"

"Roger that," Lieutenant Johnson acknowledged.

"Bulldog, Wolverine, is on the sat-phone," Lieutenant Lakewood said as he and Lieutenant Nash walked down the ramp to join the others.

Captain Hale took the sat-phone from Lieutenant Nash and put it to his ear. "Bulldog here."

"Bulldog, I just wanted to let you know that the looking-glass (satellite) coverage of the target area has been temporarily terminated," Colonel Wilson informed Captain Hale. "The only type of communication in the target area that will work is the VHF radios you have with you."

"Roger that," Captain Hale acknowledged. "Will we have any type of surveillance in the area?"

"The Navy will have a Hawkeye in the area, code-name Watchdog. The Hawkeye will have complete surveillance coverage of the entire area. They will keep you informed of any threats that might be in the target area."

"Is there anything else I need to know?" Captain Hale inquired.

"That's all I have for you right now, Colonel Wilson replied. "Watch your six down there bulldog."

"Roger that," Captain Hale commented. "I'll see you when I get back." He ended the call and handed the sat-phone back to Lieutenant Nash.

"Are we still on?" Lieutenant McDonald curiously asked.

"Yes, Popeye, were still on," Captain Hale replied. "However, there has been some changes. Wolverine has informed me that the looking-glass (satellite) surveillance of the target area has been temporarily suspended. The only type of communication that will work in the area is the VHF radios we have brought with us."

"What about surveillance coverage?" Lieutenant Johnson was quick to ask. "We can't just go in there blind."

"We won't be going in there blind," Captain Hale fired back. "A Navy Hawkeye, code-name Watchdog, will have complete surveillance coverage of the entire area. They will keep us informed of any threats."

"Roger that," Lieutenant Johnson acknowledged.

"Heads up bulldog," Lieutenant McDonald said when a Humvee pulled up a few feet away from them. "We have company heading our way," he continued when a man got out of the Humvee and started to walk towards them.

"Wait here," Captain Hale said, and then walked down to the end of the ramp to greet the approaching man.

"Are you Bulldog?" The man asked when he reached where Captain Hale was standing.

"Yes, I am."

"The pilots report that they are ready," the man said. "You and your people can load up when you're ready."

"Thanks," Captain Hale said. "I'll get my people moving." He walked back up the ramp to rejoin the others while the man hurried back to the Humvee. "Listen up people," Captain Hale said in a raised voice as the man climbed into the Humvee, and then drove off. "Gear up."

Everyone grabbed their equipment and followed Captain Hale down the cargo ramp, and exited the C-130J aircraft. The Strike Force assault teams hurried over to the four Blackhawk stealth helicopters that sat on the runway warming up their rotors, and climbed on board.

With the Strike Force assault teams safely on board, the Blackhawk helicopters lifted off the runway and headed south.

Once across the border, one Blackhawk helicopter veered off from the formation and headed east; while another Blackhawk helicopter veered off and headed west. The remaining two Blackhawk helicopters continued on to their predetermined insertion point.

A few minutes later, the first Blackhawk helicopter carrying First Lieutenant Jonathan Nash's Strike Force assault team, reached its insertion point a few kilometers north of the target farmhouse. Not long Afterwards, the second Blackhawk helicopter carrying Second Lieutenant Jackson Lakewood's Strike Force assault team, reached its insertion point a few kilometers south of the target farmhouse. Both assault teams safely repelled to the ground from their helicopters as they hovered several feet from the ground.

Lieutenant Nash and Lieutenant Lakewood's Strike Force assault teams quickly set up a defensive position alongside the road while the Blackhawk helicopters headed back to Camp Freedom.

Ten minutes later, the other two Blackhawk helicopters carrying the remainder of the Strike Force assault teams and Captain Hale reached their insertion point. Once the Strike Force assault units and Captain Hale were on the ground, the Blackhawk helicopters headed back to Camp Freedom. Everyone double checked their equipment and weapons while the team leaders assembled with Captain Hale.

"Iceman, bring me the radio," Captain Hale ordered.

Iceman hurried over to Captain Hale and handed him the radio telephone receiver. He put the radio telephone receiver to his ear. "Watchdog, Watchdog, This is Bulldog, over."

"Bulldog, this is Watchdog, over."

"Watchdog, we are on the ground and proceeding to the target, over."

"Roger Bulldog. Be advised that the road watch teams are in position, over."

"Roger that. Do you have eyes on the target area, over?"

"The target area is quiet. Be advised that we count eight tangos at the target location. Six inside the farmhouse, and two outside, over."

"Copy that. Bulldog out." Captain Hale handed Iceman the radio telephone receiver. "Keep in constant contact with Watchdog," he ordered. "I want to know the minute Watchdog reports any changes in the situation at the target area."

"I'll let you know the minute I hear something over the radio," Iceman assured Captain Hale.

"Get your people ready to move out," Captain Hale said to the team leaders. "We go in five."

The Strike Force team leaders hurried back to their assault teams, and they prepared for their upcoming mission while Captain Hale pulled out a map from his combat vest. He unfolded the map and carefully examined it. When he was finished, he folded the map back up and returned it to the pocket on his combat vest. He double checked his equipment and walked over to where the assault teams were assembled.

"We're ready to move out Bulldog," Lieutenant McDonald reported.

"Good," Captain Hale acknowledged. "Popeye, take your team and go left. Wild Man, take your team and go right. Crazy Horse and I will take the remaining team and go up the middle. Any questions?" He waited for a few moments, and then continued. "Good. Remember, no headset chatter unless it's necessary. Let's put on our gas masks and move out."

Everyone put on their M-42 gas mask over their headset and attached their night-vision equipment to their battle helmet. They positioned their night-vision equipment into place and then activated it. They proceeded cautiously toward the farmhouse at a slow pace; careful not to trip any booby-traps that may have been placed in the jungle.

When the farmhouse was in sight, they stopped their advance just short of the clearing. Captain Hale removed his night-vision binoculars from its case. He scanned the area in front of them and noticed two men standing by the side entrance that led to the basement smoking a cigarette. He looked closer at the farmhouse and saw surveillance cameras on each corner of the house. *Fuck,* he thought while he returned his binoculars to its carrying case.

"Bulldog, someone just turned on a light upstairs," Lieutenant Milestone, who was a few feet away from Captain Hale, whispered. "By the silhouette in the window I'd say it looks to be a man and a woman."

Captain Hale looked back at the farmhouse. "That leaves four in the basement," he was quick to point out. He motioned for Lieutenant Lakewood and Lieutenant McDonald to join them and waited for them to arrive.

"What's up,?" Lieutenant McDonald asked in a whisper when he and Lieutenant Lakewood arrived.

"Popeye, I want you and your team to make your way to the back of the house, and wait for my order to breach, and keep your gas mask on at all times." He pointed to the window with the light on inside. "There's a man and a woman in that room, so watch your ass when you go in there. They will probably put up some resistance to your entrance. Do what you need to do to neutralize them. Let me know over the headset when you're in position, and be quiet about it."

"Roger that," Lieutenant McDonald acknowledged and hurried back to his assault team.

"Wild Man, take your team and position yourself so you can take out the two tangos at the side entrance and assault the basement, and..."

"I know," Lieutenant Lakewood interrupted. "We'll keep our gas masks on at all times, and I'll let you know over the headset when we're in position, and don't worry, we'll be quiet about it."

"Then get to it," Captain Hale snapped.

"Roger that," Lieutenant Lakewood acknowledged.

Fuckin' smart-ass, Captain Hale thought while Lieutenant Lakewood returned to his assault team.

"You know Bulldog, Wild Man wasn't being disrespectful," Lieutenant Milestone pointed out.

"I know. It's just fuckin' irritating when he does that shit."

Captain Hale and Lieutenant Milestone, along with their assault team waited while Lieutenant McDonald and Lieutenant Lakewood's assault teams moved into their assigned positions.

"Bulldog, Popeye, We're in position," Lieutenant McDonald said over the radio headset.

"Roger that, Popeye," Captain Hale acknowledged. "Stand by."

"Popeye, Standing by."

"Bulldog, Wild Man, We're also in position," Lieutenant Lakewood reported over the radio headset. "We're ready to take out the two tangos that are standing in front of the basement entrance on your command."

"Stand ready everyone," Captain Hale said over the radio headset. He turned his attention back to the room with the light on. A few minutes later, the lights went out. "Wild Man, you are go on neutralizing the two tangos in front of the basement entrance."

"Roger that," Lieutenant Lakewood acknowledged. He hand signaled the two snipers who had the two men that were standing in front of the basement entrance in their sights. Seconds later, the snipers fired one shot each, and the two men fell to the ground. "Tangos down," Lieutenant Lakewood reported over the radio headset.

"All teams move in," Captain Hale ordered over the radio headset.

Lieutenant Lakewood and his assault team jumped into action and hurried to the entrance to the basement, and entered. They rushed down the steps and entered the basement just as the two men with Shammari and Lawrence grabbed their AK-47 assault rifles. Before the two men could fire off a shot, the Strike Force assault team opened fire, and they fell to the floor.

Michael Lawrence, who was sitting at the table, threw his hands up in the air. "My name is Michael Lawrence; I'm with the CIA. Don't shoot."

Shammari, who was sitting at the table across from Michael

Lawrence, grabbed the AK-47 assault rifle that was on the table. He pointed it at Michael Lawrence and shot him in the chest four times. Lieutenant Lakewood was quick to react and fired a three round burst into Shammari's chest, and he fell to the floor.

Meanwhile, Lieutenant McDonald and his assault team rushed to the back entrance to the farmhouse and kicked in the door. Captain Hale, along with Lieutenant Lakewood and his assault team, stormed the front entrance to the farmhouse. Lieutenant McDonald led his assault team upstairs. Lieutenant Lakewood's assault team secured the first floor while Captain Hale went into the kitchen.

Startled by the sound of the front and back door being kicked in, and the sound of gunfire from the basement, Jose Morales, and his wife, Rosetta, jumped out of bed. They grabbed their AK-47 assault rifles next to their nightstands and readied them for action. When they heard, noises coming from the other side of the door, they opened fire with several round bursts and waited. Suddenly, the door was flung open, and Lieutenant McDonald entered the room firing two, three round bursts at Jose Morales, and his wife, Rosetta, and they fell to the floor dead.

"Upstairs cleared," Lieutenant McDonald reported over the radio headset.

"Downstairs cleared," Lieutenant Lakewood reported.

"Roger that," Captain Hale acknowledged. "Search every room for anything that might be of use to us. Wild Man, sit-rep."

"Basement secured," Lieutenant Lakewood reported. "All tangos have been neutralized, and we have retrieved the VX intact."

"Keep your gas masks on," Captain Hale said over the radio headset while he walked over to the door in the kitchen that led to the basement. He opened it, "I'm coming down," he said as he stepped onto the landing. "Hold your fire," he continued as he walked down the steps. When he reached the basement, he did a quick look around and smiled. "So the Scorpion has finally been put down," he commented.

"We won't have to worry about this asshole any longer," Lieutenant Lakewood pointed out. "The world is rid of one more terrorist."

"What happened to Lawrence?" Captain Hale inquired.

"Shammari killed him. I had no choice but take him out before he had a chance to take one of us out."

"Where's the VX?"

"The gas is safely contained in those tanks in the corner," Lieutenant Lakewood replied while he pointed to the small tanks. "My gas meter shows no VX in the air, so can we take off these gas masks?"

"Listen up everyone," Captain Hale said over the radio headset. "The VX is contained. It's now safe to remove your gas masks, but keep your mask close and monitor your gas meter." He took off his gas mask and placed it on his combat tactical vest. "Wild Man, grab everything of intelligence value and rig the gas canisters with the incendiary devices, and then assemble with the rest of us outside."

"Roger that, Bulldog. I'll get right on it. It won't take long." Lieutenant Lakewood assured Captain Hale.

Captain Hale walked back up the stairs to the kitchen and closed the door. "I want everyone to finish up their sweep and assemble outside," he ordered over the radio headset.

He walked out of the kitchen into the entryway and stepped onto the porch. He hurried down the steps and made his way over to a pickup truck parked in the driveway, and waited.

Not long Afterwards, the Strike Force assault teams exited the farmhouse and joined Captain Hale by the pickup truck.

"Bulldog, everything is ready," Lieutenant Lakewood reported. "We should be far enough away to be safe from the blast," he continued while he removed a remote detonator from his combat tactical vest and handed it to Captain Hale.

"Ice Man, radio."

Iceman, who was standing next to Captain Hale, handed him the radio telephone receiver, and he put it to his ear. "Watchdog, Bulldog, do you copy?"

"Bulldog, Watchdog, go ahead."

"Watchdog, advise command that the target is secured, and all tangos have been neutralized."

"Roger Bulldog, command will be notified."

"Is there anything in the area?" Captain Hale inquired.

"Negative Bulldog. The area is clear."

"Roger that, Watchdog. Advise road watch teams to proceed to rendezvous point alpha Mike. Our ETA is thirty mikes (minutes), over."

"Will do, Bulldog. Watchdog out."

Captain Hale handed Iceman the radio telephone receiver. He

looked at the remote detonator in his hand and smiled. "Time to end this fuckin' nightmare," he remarked and pushed the detonator button.

Seconds later, the farmhouse erupted into a massive fireball. Captain Hale and the Strike Force assault teams watched the farmhouse burn.

"Okay people, we're Oscar Mike (on the move)," Captain Hale ordered.

The Strike Force assault teams followed Captain Hale down the driveway. When they reached the main road, they headed west toward the rendezvous point.

Chapter 24

President Elliot walked into the room, and the Marine that was standing by the entryway closed the double doors. Everyone in the room jumped to their feet. "Have a seat," he said while he walked over to the table in the middle of the room and sat down. "I'm sure by now that everyone has heard about the successful operation in Columbia."

"Mr. President, Director Müller and I were both under the impression that the op we were working on was the one we were going to use." Major General Larry McCoy, the commander of the Joint Special Operations Command (JSOC), commented. "No one said anything about another plan."

"Speaking of Director Müller, where is he?" President Elliot asked.

"Director Müller is visiting his sick mother at the hospital," CIA Deputy Director, Karen Hicks, replied. "Doctors say she won't be with us much longer."

"I'm saddened to hear that," President Elliot sadly remarked. "General McCoy, I wasn't crazy about the plan you and Director Müller proposed, so I had General Richwood come up with a new plan. I wasn't crazy about letting these terrorists leave Columbia with the VX gas in their possession."

"Mr. President, the operation in Columbia has the Columbians in an uproar," Secretary of State, George Maxwell said. "They're not happy about us conducting a military operation on their soil without them knowing."

"I'll place a call to President Roberto. I'm sure he'll understand once he knows all the facts," President Elliot assured everyone. "The Shammari brothers have been eliminated and the VX gas destroyed. It's time to move on from this and put this matter behind us. John, I want the Navy to stand-down. The Columbian issue is settled."

"Yes, Mr. President," Secretary Forsythe acknowledged. "I'll issue the necessary orders immediately."

"Does anyone have anything else that wasn't in my morning intelligence briefing?" President Elliot asked. He waited for a few seconds before continuing. "Okay then, let's get back to work."

Thank god this Shammari mess is over with, President Elliot thought while everyone got up from their seats and collected their things from the table. *Maybe now things will go back to normal for a while;* he continued to think while everyone exited the briefing room, and the Marine outside closed the double-doors.

President Elliot started to reach for the telephone when there was a knock on the briefing room door. "Enter, he said in a strong voice."

One of the double doors opened and White House Chief of Staff, Howard Gordon entered. "Excuse me Mr. President," he said as he walked over to the conference table. "Columbian Ambassador Cruz is waiting for you in the Diplomat Room. He said it's important that he talks to you."

"Well, I guess I won't have to call President Roberto," President Elliot remarked as he got up from his seat. "Lead the way Howard," he said and he followed Howard Gordon out of the briefing room. The Marine standing by the doorway snapped to attention. "As you were Marine," President Elliot said, and he continued to follow Howard Gordon.

* * * * *

Strike Force Delta Command

Colonel Wilson sat at his desk going over the after-action report on the operation in Columbia. *Another group of terrorists neutralized,* he thought when he was finished reading the report. *Our first op...* His thoughts were interrupted when the door to his office opened, and Captain Hale entered.

"Excuse me, Wolverine," Captain Hale said while he closed the door. "Giggles, said you wanted to see me," he continued while he walked over to Colonel Wilson's desk.

"Take a seat, Bulldog," Colonel Wilson suggested while he motioned to the chair in front of his desk. "I have a few questions about your after-action report."

"Everything that happened down there is in my report," Captain Hale said as he sat down in the chair. "I'm positive that I left nothing out of my report."

"There's just one item I have a question about."

"Like what?"

"Did you find anything interesting on the laptop that you recovered?"

"I gave it to Raven, (Encryption Specialist, Second Lieutenant Betty Williams). She said it would be a couple of days before she had everything on the laptop decrypted."

"Tell her to hurry. I want that report on my desk ASAP."

"I'll pass it on. Is there anything else?"

"Yes, I want you to give the strike units a few days off to wind down; they've earned it."

"Roger that," Captain Hale acknowledged, and got up from his seat.

"Carry on, Bulldog."

Captain Hale walked over to the door and opened it. He exited Colonel Wilson's office and closed the door.

* * * * *

Washington, D. C.
The White House

President Elliot sat at his desk in the Oval Office going back over the report that he had received from Colonel Wilson about the latest mission in Columbia. He was interrupted when the intercom on the telephone on his desk beeped. He reached over and pushed the intercom button on the telephone. "Yes, Mrs. Wyatt."

"Sir, General Richwood is on line one."

"Thank you, Mrs. Wyatt," President Elliot said, and then he pushed the intercom button on the telephone to cancel the intercom call. He removed the telephone receiver and put it to his ear, and pushed the button that was flashing. "What do you have for me General?"

"Mr. President, have you had time to read Colonel Wilson's report on Columbia?"

"Yes, I have. Is there any news on the laptop they recovered?"

"I'm afraid the laptop will bear no fruit."

"So, we have nothing that would indicate who Michael Lawrence was working with?"

"No, sir, we don't. It appears that Michael Lawrence had a security protocol on the laptop that required him to log on every four hours. When he failed to do so, the hard drive was wiped clean."

"Well, at least they were stopped before they could use the VX gas again," President Elliot was quick to point out. "Not to mention that the Shammari brothers and their cohorts were eliminated. Overall, I'd say that the Columbian operation was a complete success."

"Yes, sir, it was," General Richwood agreed. "Colonel Wilson's people did a fine job."

"That they did, general. Tell Colonel Wilson and his people that I am pleased with their performance."

"Yes, Mr. President. I'll pass it on."

"General, is there anything else you have for me?"

"Not at this time, sir."

"Carry on, general," President Elliot said, and then he returned the telephone receiver to the telephone on his desk. "Enter," he said when there was a knock on the door.

The door to the Oval Office opened, and Mrs. Wyatt entered. "Excuse me Mr. President. I was getting ready to leave for the day. Do you need anything before I go."

President Elliot looked at his watch. "I didn't realize it was getting so late. Of course, go on home; I'm fine."

"Good-night Mr. President."

"See you in the morning Mrs. Wyatt."

Mrs. Wyatt left the Oval Office and closed the door while President Elliot leaned back in his chair.

www.ingramcontent.com/pod-product-compliance
Lightning Source LLC
Chambersburg PA
CBHW030137180626
46812CB00002B/725